*A grip of steel on her wrist
was her only warning.*

Within the space of a heartbeat, she was flipped onto her back, her arms stretched above her head.

Ramos loomed over her, his body covering hers, holding her immobile. His eyes glittered, reflecting the glow of the fire.

"Mairi?" Ramos whispered. "What the bloody hell do you think you're doing in here?"

How had he moved so quickly?

"I needed to . . ." The words stuck in her throat as he released one wrist, his hand slowly skimming down her arm.

"To talk to you." Once freed, the words came out in a breathless rush, one tumbling over the other.

"Talk?" A lazy smile curved his full lips.

Such a fascinating mouth, such mesmerizing lips. She sucked in her breath and he dipped his head, so close their lips almost touched.

"About?" With the one whispered word, his breath trickled over her face, an inviting tendril of air beckoning her closer.

She couldn't resist its call.

ALSO BY MELISSA MAYHUE

Thirty Nights with a Highland Husband

Highland Guardian

Available from Pocket Books

Soul of a
Highlander

MELISSA MAYHUE

POCKET BOOKS
New York London Toronto Sydney

Pocket Books
A Division of Simon & Schuster, Inc.
1230 Avenue of the Americas
New York, NY 10020

This book is a work of fiction. Names, characters, places, and incidents either are products of the author's imagination or are used fictitiously. Any resemblance to actual events or locales or persons, living or dead, is entirely coincidental.

First Pocket Books paperback edition June 2008

POCKET and colophon are registered trademarks of Simon & Schuster, Inc.

For information about special discounts for bulk purchases, please contact Simon & Schuster Special Sales at 1-800-456-6798 or business@simonandschuster.com.

Cover design by Min Choi
Front and back cover by Jaime DeJesus

Manufactured in the United States of America

10 9 8 7 6 5 4 3 2 1

ISBN-13: 978-1-4767-1104-1

My deepest appreciation to my family,
for their continued support and for all the
Every Man for Himself dinner nights
they put up with when I'm consumed with
finishing a book on time!

Acknowledgments

A very special thank-you goes out to the following people:

To the SoapBox Divas—Rena Marks and Kirsten Richard—for holding my feet to the fire when I try to slide. Writing would be so much less fun without you guys!

To my Monday Night Valentines for all their support—talented ladies all—Micole, Laura, Sherry, and Pat

To Nick and Chandra for the engraved, framed book cover I will treasure forever

To my agent, Elaine Spencer, for all her wonderful enthusiasm and all the amazing knowledge she shares so freely

To Marty for his help on our visit to the bookstore—pointing out my books to all the ladies there!

and as always

To my wonderful editor, Megan McKeever, for encouraging me to bigger, better, more!

Soul of a
Highlander

Prologue

$\mathcal{A}$re you sure you don't want to reconsider?" Ramos Servans looked into the eyes of the man who offered to champion his cause. The man from whom he'd very nearly stolen everything. "After all, you better than most know what I really am."

"Aye, that I do. And for that reason alone I stand as yer sponsor." Ian McCullough shrugged. "Besides, my Sarah vouches for yer character. That should be enough for anyone."

They stood deep in the forest, in the same clearing where only a short time ago they had faced one another as enemies. Now this man, this Guardian, had forgiven him. If only he could forgive himself.

"It's certainly enough for me." Dallyn nodded his head in agreement. The High General of the Faerie Realm stood with them. He had come to hear Ramos's decision. "Well, young man, what will it be?"

"You offer me an avenue to offset some small portion of the damage I have done. I am eternally grateful. And wholly unworthy. I will do my best to serve you in any way I can." Ramos bowed his head, guilt eating at his soul. He would never be able to right all his wrongs. The wrongs of his father.

Dallyn arched an eyebrow, trading a look with Ian before answering. "Eternity is a very long time, my young friend. A *very* long time. Welcome to our ranks."

Ian grasped his wrist and shook his hand. "You've made a good choice, Ramos. I'm sure you'll do well."

"I don't know how I can repay your kindness." Ramos stopped. What could he say to this man? "But know that I consider myself in your debt."

"There's no need for that. You've showed yer true colors. Now go on. You've work to do." Ian clapped him on the back before turning and striding away down the path.

"You're ready, then?" Dallyn held out a hand, inviting him forward toward the large rocky embankment in the dense trees.

"I am."

He was ready to leave this place.

Being here brought it all back, the pain and humiliation stark and fresh as if it had been yesterday. The physical wounds might have healed, but it would take more than time to heal the emotional wounds.

He had entered the clearing that day, his arm around Ian's throat, holding a knife there. The first thing he'd seen was the rage distorting Reynard's features, revealing a side of his father he'd only rarely experienced.

"You think to defy me? We'll see about that," Reynard had threatened Sarah. "Ramos, bring him."

Surprisingly Ian hadn't struggled as they'd moved forward.

"It's very simple, *ma petite*," his father had said to Sarah. "Take me to the Portal now, or Ramos kills him. You can watch the mighty Guardian, sworn Protector of the pitiful Mortals, die, his lifeblood spilled out on the ground. Here. In front of your very eyes. Is that what you want?"

What had his father said? "Sworn Protector of the Mortals? Is that true? You never told me that." He couldn't believe his ears. It flew in the face of everything he'd ever been taught.

"There are many things I've not told you. Many things you've no need to know," his father had dismissed.

"Is it the truth?" he had demanded.

"Aye, it's true." Ian had answered. "I've spent the last six centuries protecting them from the ravages of yer people. Those who murder Mortals at random for nothing more than the energy released when their soul is forced from its host before its time. Thousands upon thousands of lives lost to those monsters. Those same monsters who would capture the Fountain of Souls for their own purpose, throwing the cycle of life out of balance again, risking what's left of humanity in both worlds."

"Father?" He'd wanted desperately to have his father deny the horrendous accusations.

"You doubt me, son? You'd listen to the words of a Guardian? A creature who's no more than a lapdog to the enemies of our people?"

But that was no denial.

Instead Sarah had confirmed his fears. "Ian doesn't lie to you, Ramos. What he tells you is the truth. I attest to that. It's as I told you before."

"Father? Is what the Guardian says true?" He had to know. Had to hear the words from his father's own mouth.

A cruel smile curled Reynard's lip. "In a manner of speaking."

"*We're* responsible for all those deaths?" This couldn't be happening.

"Deaths that were of no consequence. Mortal deaths. Once we retake the Faerie Realm, once you taste the power of the Fountain, then you'll understand why all of this has been necessary." His father had turned his attention back to Sarah then, demanding again she take him to the Portal.

"Of no consequence?" How could Reynard say that? "Father, have you forgotten that I am as much Mortal as I am Fae? That those lives you so easily dismiss are my people, too?"

When Reynard had answered, he hadn't even bothered to look at his son. His words, the words that cut Ramos to the quick, were delivered with no more care for his son than for a complete stranger.

"No. I haven't forgotten what you are. Nicole, kill one of the men. I don't care which. Perhaps that will help our little Sarah to understand how serious we are."

"You can't mean that. He's your son." Sarah had sounded incredulous.

As incredulous as Ramos had felt.

Reynard shrugged carelessly. "He's also a Mortal."

His father had lied to him, used him his whole life. And at that moment, as he had looked into his father's eyes, he had seen nothing. No compassion, no care, no love.

Ramos had done the only thing he could think of at the time. He had taken the bullet meant for Ian.

All those years of training to fight the Fae because they were the monsters who threatened the World of Mortals. And they weren't the monsters at all. It was his people.

That betrayal had nearly driven him mad until he had been offered this opportunity.

Yes, he was ready. Ready for a new life. One he didn't deserve, but one he would spend in attempting to atone for the atrocities his people had caused.

Dallyn placed his hand on Ramos's shoulder and urged him forward, directly into the solid rock face tucked between two large, gnarled trees. One moment he thought he'd slam up against the boulder, the next he stood in a sylvan glen, a place more beautiful than any he had ever seen. The clarity of the colors stole his breath away. He glanced back the direction from which he had come and stopped in amazement at the sight of a huge carved rock door.

"Where did that . . . ?" He hadn't seen it before.

Dallyn smiled. "You will always be able to find this Portal now. That's how it works. Once you have been through a Portal, you will always be able to see it. Come now, you have much work to do before you're fully prepared."

They walked side by side on a wide stone path toward a massive building just ahead of them. Sunlight glinted off the doors and roof of the structure as if it were coated in gold. Ramos stared about in awe at the spectacular beauty. No wonder his people missed it so much.

"Here we are. Our quarters are inside." Dallyn

swept an arm toward the door, which slowly swung open ahead of them. "Let me be the first to officially welcome you to the Hall of the High Council in the Realm of Faerie and to the next chapter in your life."

Ramos nodded his head respectfully and then squared his shoulders. With a deep breath he readied himself for that next chapter. For the work and the training that would be required of him to prepare him for his new position.

As a Guardian, Protector of the Mortals and of the Fountain of the Souls.

One

So you'll do nothing to save her? You'll just sit here and allow her to die?" Mairi MacKiernan clasped her hands tightly in her lap, controlling the urge to strike out at the people sitting across from her.

"It's no a matter of us allowing anything to happen. She's already dead." Connor MacKiernan glanced sideways at his wife, Cate, before adding, "Long dead."

"You know it's forbidden for us to change history." Cate leaned across the empty space from her chair to Mairi's, laying a cool hand on her sister-in-law's forearm. "You can't torture yourself with what's past."

Mairi jerked her arm away and rose. They were being so unreasonable, she wanted to scream. Instead she spoke softly, barely more than a whisper. "That's yer final word on the matter?"

"Aye, it is, little sister." Connor wore the stubborn look she knew so well. "I warned you when you first set out to hunt our family's history this could happen. 'Oh no,' you said. 'I'm only curious.' Now you've worked yerself into a fine lather."

Mairi grated her teeth. She might love her older brother, but sometimes he could be the biggest pain in the ass she'd ever dealt with. Especially when he lectured her, as he always assumed he had the right to do.

"Verra well." She turned her back on her family and headed to the door.

"And where do you think yer going, lass?" Connor stood, but didn't follow, held back by his wife's gentle touch to his hand.

"I need to ride." Mairi strode purposefully from the room.

"Let her go, Connor. This is terribly hard for her. Give her some time." Cate's voice floated after her.

Damn the woman. Kindness was the hardest response to guard against.

Tears threatened, but Mairi refused to let them flow. Not yet. Not where anyone could see. She never cried in front of people. Not anymore.

Hasty steps took her down the hall and through the yard. Out across the back to the stables, her long legs covered the ground rapidly, carrying her to the one measure of freedom still left her. She grabbed her riding tack off the wall as she entered.

In very short order, her favorite horse was ready and she was mounted and outside, quickly bringing the animal to a full gallop across the open meadow. The wind whipped fine, blond hair loose from her long braid and stung her face, drying her tears almost as quickly as they fell.

This was what she needed.

Reaching the back side of the meadow, she slowed her mount to a walk. Patting his neck, she urged him onto the trail leading up the mountain, to the little forested stream she loved. There she could almost imagine herself home.

When she reached her favorite spot, she dismounted and tied her horse to a tree. He could munch the green grass and still reach the water while she brooded. Kicking off her shoes, she stretched out at the stream's edge, her arms behind her head, and allowed the sound of water rushing over the rocks to calm her, lull her back to normalcy.

They were right, of course, her brother and sister-in-law. She knew that, had known it even before she came up here to ask their help. Though Cate had the power to aid her, Mairi had known even before getting into her car for the drive up the mountain that she wouldn't.

Cate and Connor both had turned into the epitome of responsible adult behavior. Well, in fairness, her brother always had been, but the woman who had become her dear friend as well as her brother's wife had been more impetuous at one time.

Mairi sighed. The old Cate would have sent her to save Marsali Rose. The old Cate would have joined her in the quest.

Marsali Rose. Her beloved aunt Rosalyn's only daughter. The last of the MacKiernan women with the gift of Fae magic. The blessing of their line had died out with her.

Almost seven hundred years ago.

"It's wrong. It's so unfair." Mairi sat up and stared at the water as it rushed past. Though what few remaining records she had found said nothing of her aunt, Mairi knew that Rosalyn would have been devastated by the loss of her only daughter. The thought of the woman who had been like a mother to her suffering such a horrible twist of fate was almost more than Mairi could bear. After all Rosalyn had done for her, she desperately wanted her aunt to be happy.

It was more than that. To the very core of her, from the moment she had discovered the documents relating to her cousin's death, she'd felt consumed by the knowledge, as if this were where her destiny lay. Though, for the life of her, she could see no way to change what had happened.

Perhaps if she had remained in her own time she could have done something to change the outcome for her cousin.

"If I'd stayed, I would have been of no use, dead long before the lass was born." That was, after all, why her sister-in-law had pulled her out, forward to Cate's time. History showed that the Mairi MacKiernan who lived in 1272 had died, apparently murdered by the man she was to marry, MacPherson the Red.

Mairi shuddered. She knew it for a fact. She'd looked it up. She'd almost lived it.

"Thank the Fates," she whispered, more than grateful she'd been spared the horror of wedding that awful man. And yet, she sometimes wondered if the alternative wasn't worse than the original fate would have been.

For a MacKiernan woman, a descendant of the Fae

House of Pol, there was no higher purpose in life than to seek out her own true love, her other half, the one who would complete her. But Mairi was sure that for her this coupling of the souls could never be.

She was fated to have died in 1272 so there would have been no one for her in that time. And while she had made a new life for herself in this century, it was not where fate had intended her to be, so there would be no Soulmate for her here.

Thanks to Cate's having saved her from certain death, she would spend her life alone, a woman who didn't belong anywhere.

No wonder the Fae had that rule about time travel. *You cannot change the outcome of history, only alter the circumstances.*

Picking· up a handful of small stones, she tossed them one at a time into the burbling stream while she tried to untangle her thoughts.

Cate had justified bringing Mairi, Connor, and Connor's friend, Robert MacQuarrie, to the future because they were all to have died that day. Bringing them forward didn't change the outcome of history, so they had abided by the Fae rule.

Why couldn't she do the same for Marsali Rose?

"Because I dinna have the power." Reaching her last pebble, she tossed it and, without conscious thought, picked up more, rolling them back and forth between her hands.

Like Cate—and Marsali Rose, for that matter—Mairi descended from the Fae. She, however, claimed her ancestry through her father's family, Cate and Marsali Rose through their mothers'. Therein, she knew, lay the difference. The family blessing, and the powers, had been granted by an ancient Faerie prince, Pol, their ancestor. He had bestowed it on his daughters and all their daughters, throughout time. As the daughter of a *son*, Mairi had no power, the Fae blood in her veins her only tie to the race so long disappeared from the world of man.

But what if she did have the power? Would she honestly do things differently if it were up to her?

She didn't know.

Didn't know if she could find the courage to go back to the place where she had been betrayed by family she trusted. Back to the place where she had thought she was going to die. To the place where she would have died if not for Cate.

The thought of confronting her past terrified her and she hated herself for being afraid. Hated the nightmares that plagued her. Hated the idea that she'd become a weak, conforming, frightened woman.

The realization that given the opportunity to help her aunt she might lack the courage to do so gnawed at her almost as much as the knowledge of her aunt's loss.

Her life had turned out so very different from what she'd planned.

She drew up her knees and rested her forehead there. "Damned unfair if you ask me," she mumbled to herself.

"I knew I'd find you here. What are you pissin' and moanin' about now?"

Mairi groaned. Just what she needed to complete her day. Another overprotective he-man telling her what to do.

"Jesse." She peered up over her knees.

He leaned against the tree where he'd tied his horse, hands in his pockets, looking deceptively unconcerned and supremely handsome in his jeans and T-shirt.

"When did you get back?"

"Last night." He sauntered over to her spot, staring down at her with his unusual brown-green eyes. "I stopped by your apartment on the way in from the airport, but you were gone."

Checking on her again. He didn't say the words, but she knew.

"I left directly for here after my last class."

"Yeah. I know."

She was certain he did. One of Cate's other brothers, her landlady, or some other 'spy' Connor had in place would have told him.

"We've talked about that before, haven't we? You knew I was due back last night." He lowered his six-foot-plus frame to the ground beside her, stretching out his long legs. "Driving up the mountains in the dark, *alone*"—he emphasized the word with an arch of his eyebrow that reminded her of Connor—"isn't such a smart thing for you to be doing. Especially since you haven't been driving all that long."

She rolled her eyes, the only fitting comment on his annoying bossiness. Sometimes he made it hard to remember that he was Cate's brother, not her own.

All of Cate's brothers behaved the same way. They treated her like she was their little sister; they had from the first moment they had met. As if Connor weren't bad enough. No wonder she had no desire to find a man of her own and settle down. Not that they gave her any opportunity. To think, she'd once considered life in the thirteenth century restrictive. One thing was for certain—if she ever could have found a man she wanted to spend the rest of her life with, he wouldn't have been like the ones she was surrounded by now. No domineering, chauvinistic, staggeringly overconfident alpha male for her.

Of course, she would never have to worry about that.

"I'm no a child; dinna treat me like one. Besides, it's nearly all major highway. And I'm an excellent driver." She dropped her head back on her knees. "Now go away. I'm depressed and yer ruining my wallowing in it."

Jesse reached over and tugged on her braid. "That's right, Mairi-Mairi, Quite Contrary. I keep forgetting. You're all growed up and legal."

She peeked an eye out at him. "I'm twenty-six. In my day, that would have made me practically one of the old crones. Women my age had a pack of children hanging on their skirts."

"Yeah, well, the only rug rats around here belong to Cate, and I don't care how old you are, you're still new to this stuff in my book, kiddo." His grin lit up his face as he slapped her on the back. "So tell me, what's got you up here pouting on a glorious day like this, anyway?"

"Nothing I can do anything about." She sat up and rolled her shoulders. "So let's drop it. What about you? Did you enjoy your side trip, delivery boy?"

"Actually, I did. Other than the suitcase from hell Cate had me take to her friends." He turned and looked at her, incredulity etched on his face. "Do you realize my sister stuffed that damned huge thing full of books?"

"That she did." Now it was her turn to grin as she imagined his face when the suitcase was opened. "And baby girl clothes and those cute blankets she made for her friend."

"You knew?"

"Your mouth is hanging open. You'll catch bugs." She leaned back on her forearms. "I knew. What did you think she was so anxious to have delivered she'd no want to wait for the mails to get there?"

He shrugged. "I don't know. Didn't really think about it until I'd carted it around for a while. Then I panicked, thinking of what Cate would do if it ended up in lost luggage."

Mairi laughed at the images of both her sister-in-law's ire and Jesse's concern. "But you enjoyed yourself in spite of yer fears?" Like Jesse had ever in his life been afraid of anything.

"Yeah. I can see why Cate and Connor are so fond of the McCulloughs. They really made me feel welcome." He laughed. "Man, that Sarah is one huge preggo. Ian has to haul her up out of chairs."

"Well, Cate did say the poor thing's having twins, so it's no wonder."

"I'd planned on dropping the case and then heading back to Edinburgh, but they wouldn't hear of it. Insisted I stay the night. Sarah went off to bed early, so Ian and I spent the evening getting to know one another. It was quite educational." He nodded his head contentedly.

"Sports or drink?"

"Both." He grinned again. "I told you I enjoyed myself. We shared a bottle of some really fine Scots whisky and Ian invited me to come back in September to attend a rugby match with him." Jesse lay back on the ground, his arms behind his head.

"Hmm." *Really, what kind of proper response was there to a man's reminiscing about talk of sports and drink?*

"Yeah, Ian and I had quite the visit. Hey, did you know that both Ian and Sarah are Fae descendants?"

"Aye. Like Connor and Cate." Her sister-in-law had mentioned something to that effect. Little wonder they all got on so well.

"Not exactly." He turned on his side, propping his head on one arm.

"How's that?"

"I learned some really interesting things from him. Like, did you know that our great-great-great—however many times it is—granddaddy Pol wasn't the only Faerie finding female companionship in the land of mankind?"

"No, I dinna." But it did make sense. Why hadn't she ever considered that?

"Ian and Sarah both descend from completely different lines. And you know what else?"

Mairi shook her head. *Different lines?*

"They both have powers. Apparently *all* Fae descendants have powers of some sort."

"Every single one?"

"Yep. That's what Ian said." Jesse sat up and stretched his arms above his head before wrapping them around his knees.

For Mairi the idea was staggering. "How can that be? Why is it no that way with us?"

"My guess is that it has something to do with Pol's blessing. Apparently his words channeled all the power as he directed in the case of his descendants rather than letting Nature take her course. Although the daughters have powers, of course, and I suppose that even the sons have received a gift of sorts. You know, skills at warfare, healing quickly, things like that to enable us to better protect our females. Bizarre, huh?"

Not bizarre. Unfair. Wrong. Mairi's cheeks burned with her indignation. Jesse was forgetting one little piece. One very important piece to her.

"The daughters of *daughters* have powers," she quietly corrected. "The power passes from mother to daughter. Pol's female descendants like me, however, dinna fall into that category. I am the daughter of a son. I have no powers of any kind."

"That's not true. You're gifted, Mairi." Jesse smiled as he stood and brushed the pine needles off the seat of his jeans. "You're brilliant. You have an IQ way beyond the norm. I'm sure it's why you were able to step into life here so easily."

"That's no the same thing by any stretch of the imagination."

"It's close enough. Besides, having one witchy woman in the family is about all I could stand. Cate can handle the weird stuff, you do the brainiac routine, and I'll just stand around and look good." He held out a hand and, once she took it, pulled her to her feet. "Come on, genius, let's get back to the house before dinner's all gone."

Mairi dusted herself off as she walked over to her mount. She was sure Jesse's new information held the solution to her dilemma. She only needed to figure out how to use it. Ideas raced through her mind and were quickly discarded or filed under "has potential."

Unfortunately every single one of them pointed to her having to do the one thing she'd promised herself she never would.

Return to Scotland.

Two

I don't understand. What is this?" Sarah Douglas McCullough leaned awkwardly against the door frame of the guest bedroom, staring down at the large brown envelope in her hands.

"My insurance policy, so to speak." Mairi laughed. "It's the research I've done—information I've gathered, things like that. I dinna want to take a chance on losing it." She knew Sarah would assume it was research related to the doctoral dissertation she was preparing. No sense in correcting the woman. "I'm driving up to Sithean Fardach tomorrow. I only intend to be gone for a short while, but it's my first time back to the castle and I'm a little concerned about how I'm going to handle it."

She wasn't lying to her hostess. Exactly. She was

going up to the family castle. Right after a short side trip through the Faerie Glen on her way there. Then, if things worked out as she hoped in the Glen, one quick, well-planned detour and she should still be back to the castle in time to call Sarah tomorrow night.

After all, Cate had told her that when *she* had gone to the thirteenth century, she had returned within the space of a few minutes. There was no reason to expect her experience to be any different.

"You can leave this in your room, if you like. I assure you, no one will bother any of your things while you're gone." Sarah's confusion was evident in her voice as she looked up from the package she held.

"Oh no, it's no that. It's just . . ." Mairi paused. She'd need to be cautious with what she said or risk exposing her plan too soon. "There's a note inside for Cate. They dinna know I've come here." She paused again, allowing time for the shock to pass across the other woman's face.

"I see." Sarah looked down at the package again. "Cate told me you hadn't wanted to come back since . . . well, since your arrival."

"No. It was too painful to see the changes, to be reminded of what was gone, lost." Her family, everyone she'd cared about, her whole life. "But it's time now. Time for me to face things and deal with them. On my own." Deal with more than just the memories.

"I still don't understand this." Sarah nodded toward the envelope.

"I know this will sound silly, perhaps melodramatic even, but I'm no sure how things will work out for me here." She shrugged, stalling to find her footing on the delicate path she wove between the actual truth and the perception she wanted Sarah to accept as truth. "I'm no sure I'll be able to handle seeing the place. I'd hate to lose all that work because I panic and leave there in a rush. If for any reason you dinna hear from me by tomorrow night, I'd verra much appreciate yer opening that envelope and calling Cate. She'll know how to get those things back to me.

"Please understand. This is something I need to do. My brother is, has always been, and I'm sure will always be, the most overprotective man on the face of the planet. He loves me, but he treats me like a child. He's no likely to accept my doing this on my own."

"I certainly understand overprotective men. Believe me." Sarah smiled.

"On top of that, I dinna want to bother them right now. Between the children and Connor's accident, Cate has her hands full."

"No, I don't see him as the model, quiet patient. How long did the doctor say he'd be laid up?"

"At least six weeks before he can put any weight on the ankle, though it'll likely be a few less with the way we heal. When it first happened, they thought it might require surgery, but finally decided on the cast and keeping him off his feet."

"All right, Mairi. I'll hold on to your package if it makes you feel better."

"Thank you." Mairi leaned forward and awkwardly hugged the other woman, stretching around her stomach. "You'd best get off your feet as you promised Ian you would. I think he might have been serious about coming up to make sure you lie down for a while."

"Oh, he was completely serious. How do you think

I know so much about overprotective men?" She laughed and put her free hand at the small of her back as she turned and headed down the hall. "I can hardly wait for these babies to make their appearance. Thank goodness it's any day now."

"Good night, Sarah, and thank you. For everything."

Mairi stepped into her room and closed the door. That had gone even better than she had hoped, with far fewer questions than she had imagined there might be.

Ian and Sarah had been remarkably gracious when she had shown up at their door, inviting her in and treating her like family. Dinner was quite an interesting affair, with one of Ian's friends dropping by, an attractive but unusual man named Dallyn, who had stared at her throughout the entire meal.

She kicked off her shoes and looked around the room. Everything was falling into place. Now that she had her safety net arranged, she could proceed. Tomorrow she'd rise early and head for the Highlands, where she would put Part Two of her plan into action.

"Yer supposed to be in bed asleep, no sitting in a chair, staring out into the night. What's wrong?" Ian stood at the doorway of his darkened bedroom.

"I'm just a bit worried," Sarah said.

"I know. I felt it. That's why I sent Dallyn off to home so I could come see after you. What are you fretting over, luv?" He walked to her chair, reaching down to stroke the golden curls he so loved.

"I'm not exactly sure. There's just something not quite right with our guest." Sarah reached up for his hand, pulling it down to rest against her cheek. "A sense about her of purpose and frustration, a banked anger of some sort."

"Aye. That's what Dallyn said as well."

"Really? What else did he say?"

"Just that she seemed awfully tense, like a bowstring set to fire."

"There's more to it than that. She wasn't being dishonest with me, but she wasn't telling the whole truth either. She asked the oddest favor."

Ian reached down and pulled Sarah from the chair. She was exhausted, he could tell from the dark circles visible to him even in the pale moonlight shining through the window. "You need yer rest. Come on to bed, luv. You can tell me all about it there." While he held her close.

Tomorrow he would speak of it to Dallyn.

Mairi awoke in a panic. The unfamiliar bedroom was dark, the shadows in the corners large and threatening. She sat upright in bed, her hand clamped over her mouth to prevent the scream she felt building.

It had only been a dream, but it was the same as always. Not just some random nightmare, but the nightmare she had actually lived through. The one that had changed who she was.

Though sweat covered her brow, she shivered.

Even now, nine years later, she could taste the fear and desperation, a slick, putrid coating on her tongue; she who had never experienced fear before that night.

She could still feel her arms wrenched back tightly behind her, held helpless as Lyall's hot breath spidered across her cheek.

"What a fine gift you'll make to ensure my new ally, wee Mairi."

"How could you betray me like this?" How bitter that betrayal felt coming in the form of her cousin, the man she loved like a brother, the man she thought had cared for her. The cousin she had trusted with her life.

"Betray you?" His maddened eyes sparkled as he laughed at her. "I canna betray a fool. And you, my trusting little cousin, are indeed a fool. Foolish to trust in stories of Faeries and magic; foolish to believe I could ever care for you so much that I'd risk my own future for the likes of you."

She had tried to lash out at him, kick him, but Lyall had jumped back, laughing at her feeble attempts. The man who held her arms pinned behind her tightened his hold, joining in the derisive laughter, his stale breath curdling in her nostrils.

Lyall stepped forward and removed the binding from her braid, fanning her hair out loose. Then he tugged at the neck of her shift, lowering the material to expose her shoulders and more of her than she would ever have shown.

"There. A much better display of our wares." His laughter was that of a madman.

She had screamed as the hot breath of the man who held her flowed across her bared skin when he lowered his head, tracing the line of her neck with his tongue.

"No, Malcolm, I'm afraid I must deny you this. She's no for the likes of you. We must turn her over unharmed and pure." Lyall rubbed a strand of her hair between his fingers.

Robbed of any way to fight back, she had called him names then, spit at him before he had silenced her with a harsh backhanded blow.

"Take her to Dun Ard. Lock her in a storage room to wait for her bridegroom. He'll beat some respect into her, I fancy."

Mairi shivered again, the emotions fresh and raw, as if she could still feel Malcolm's touch when he threw her across the saddle of his horse, his hands moving over her body on the ride back to Dun Ard.

Lying back down, she consciously slowed her panicked breathing, waiting for her racing heart to slow as well. She wiped at the tears silently tracking down her face and renewed her determination.

Rosalyn had been like a mother to her and deserved better than to lose her only daughter. Mairi would not allow the fear to prevent her from going back to help her aunt. It was time to face the fear, to move beyond it.

Tomorrow she would take the first step by claiming her right to the magic.

Tomorrow she would go to the Faerie Glen and confront Pol.

Three

The strap of Mairi's small backpack slipped off her shoulder again and she stopped, dropping the bag as she sat down on an old log beside the trail.

Her hands shook as she fumbled with the strapping. She couldn't allow herself time to think about what she was getting ready to do. She'd done all her thinking, all her planning before she left home.

Home.

Had she left home or come back to it?

No more of that. There was no room for doubt.

She was very close now. She was sure of it. Not that she had ever been in the Faerie Glen before. There had never been a reason for her to be here.

Until now.

Still, she recognized it from the stories she'd heard.

Cate and Jesse both had described Cate's visit to this place. It certainly lived up to their descriptions. It was cool, quiet and lush with growth brought about by a wet climate. After almost a decade away, she'd nearly forgotten the odor of a moist woodlands, the smell of green, and the spongy feel of the ground beneath her feet.

She stood and hoisted the pack to her shoulder. Breathing deeply, she inhaled the scents of this forest. Memories beat at the door she kept so tightly shut, each one demanding its release. She refused them their exit. Just her olfactory system in hyperdrive. She'd read the studies about odor triggering memories. Their conclusions were much more convincing now that she experienced it for herself.

The stream widened as she moved deeper into the forest. She heard the waterfall up ahead, could visualize how it would look as the water rushed over the rocks, falling into the deep emerald pool.

His pool.

What if he refused to see her? The flurry of panic assaulted her again, but, as before, she brushed it away. She wouldn't allow him to ignore her. She would . . .

What?

For once she wished she were a bit more like her brother. Wished she had done more planning and less barging in. Wished she were less impetuous. Wished she were less afraid.

Pushing through the branches and forest growth, she entered a clearing. Ahead of her a waterfall tumbled down into a deep emerald pool ringed with trees whose branches were covered in bits of cloth.

The heart of the Faerie Glen. Pol's home.

She walked to the edge of the pool and squatted

down, shrugging her backpack off her shoulders. Unzipping the bag, she rummaged inside and pulled out a water bottle.

The Glen stilled for a moment, silent, as if holding its breath, waiting for her to make the next move.

But Mairi wasn't ready yet. As a woman surrounded all her life by warriors, she had learned a few useful things about battle. One of those was the importance of mental preparation. She needed her mind focused on the task at hand.

After a quick sip of the water, she unlaced her Merrell switchbacks and pulled them off, followed by her socks, stuffing them inside the hiking boots. She sat, her knees drawn up with her feet flat against the ground, and took a long, slow drink of the water. She concentrated on the feel of it in her mouth, the cool of it running down her throat, the damp grass beneath her feet as she wiggled her toes against the earth. It made her feel grounded, connected to the physical properties of this place.

Closing her eyes, she listened to the sounds of the forest, loud now to her ears, sensitive after the momentary silence that had greeted her. Chirping birds, irritated at her presence, rustled the leaves as they darted from tree to tree.

As she opened her eyes, a stray sunbeam filtered through the branches heavy with their cloth adornments and glinted off the emerald band on her toe. The ring Cate had given her so very long ago.

Cate. Her sister-in-law had been here, in this very place, and had done this very thing, had challenged their ancestor and demanded the right to save the man she loved. If Cate could do it, so could she, though her quest wasn't for the sake of a man. She'd long ago accepted that any hope for a true love intended for her by the Fates had been left behind in time along with the family whose loss she mourned.

Shaking her head against the unwanted memories, Mairi stood and brushed the damp grass and leaves from the seat of her walking shorts. She was happy in this time, had advantages and opportunities she could never have imagined had she not come here. Even so, she often felt as if she had one foot in each world, in each time, yet truly belonged to neither.

Since she'd learned of the others, of what she might have been, should have been, she couldn't help but wonder. If only she'd been allowed the power of her birthright, the whole of her history, and that of her family, might have been very different.

No matter. Now she intended to claim that birthright and make a difference for Rosalyn and Marsali Rose.

She faced the water and held her head high, tossing her braid over her shoulder. She had no reason to cower, no need to feel apprehension at being here. After all, this Fae owed her. Her and the multitude of women in her family, both before and after her, who had been abandoned by him.

"My name is Mairi MacKiernan. I seek an audience with Pol, Prince of the Fae," she called, her voice echoing off the rocks, bouncing back at her from the water.

Nothing happened.

Not surprising. The old legends spoke of the temperamental nature of the Fae.

She spread her feet, placed her hands on her hips

and tried again, more forcefully. "I demand my right to speak with Pol. Now."

A gentle breeze fluttered through the Glen, lifting little hairs that had escaped from her braid, causing them to tickle her face and neck. The wind grew, blowing across the pond, raising ripples, slapping them against the bank near her feet.

"By what right do you make this demand?"

The words drifted as if carried on the wind, a multitude of voices speaking in harmony echoing in her mind. She wasn't sure if she actually heard them or only imagined them. She chose to answer anyway.

"By right of birth. I am one of Pol's daughters."

The wind calmed, swirled about her, stroking her face, her shoulders, her body. She had the fleeting vision of tiny hands sliding over her skin, caressing her.

"That is not possible. Go from this place. Leave us now." The multitude of voices united in their command. The water calmed as the breeze withdrew.

"I won't leave this place until I see my ancestor."

"You do not belong here. You do not carry the mark of our Prince." Fewer voices now, still in unison, neither masculine nor feminine.

"I carry no mark because it was stolen from me along with my birthright."

"*Impossible!*"

The word echoed loudly, joined by a multitude of discordant denials. Mairi longed to cover her ears with her hands in an attempt to block the sound, but she remained still, holding her ground. Individual shouts, repeated, echoed, bounced around the Glen in a cacophony of indignation until one single command rose above the clamor.

"*Silence!*"

The sound seemed to come from everywhere at once. As the word rang out, everything stilled—the shouts, the birds, even the breeze ceased.

"Who would have dared such treachery?" A single low voice, distinctly masculine in nature, came from behind her.

She turned slowly, knowing who the speaker had to be.

He looked exactly as Cate had described him. Tall, taller than she, with long blond hair framing his face, sweeping his broad shoulders, and tilted eyes the brilliant green of the forest, though they sparked with anger at this moment.

Pol.

"You dared."

She spoke the words quietly, pleased by the startled expression that passed swiftly over his face. At least he didn't simply disappear. The arrogant arch of his eyebrow that followed reminded her of her brother.

"Explain yourself, Mairi MacKiernan." He crossed his arms and waited.

"You acknowledge that I am yer descendant?" It was important to her to know where she stood before she went any further. Everything she sought depended on this man. She was prepared to say or do whatever it took to convince him of her need.

Dropping his arms, and his frown, he approached her, reaching out to run a finger down her cheek. His touch felt exactly like the breeze that had caressed her before.

"I recognize the set of your jaw, the color of your eyes, the beauty of your face." His hand dropped

away. "You are my daughter, though I don't understand why you carry no mark. I specifically set it on
all my daughters to insure your protection."

"No all yer daughters. Only a chosen few. And
those of us without it were even cheated out of
whatever gifts we would have had if you'd no inter-
vened."

His eyes narrowed. "Again, I must insist that you
explain yourself."

"The legend of yer blessing has been carefully
passed from one generation to the next in my family.
'My blessing on my daughters, and thus my accompanying curse, will carry forward for all time, passed from
mother to daughter.' Sound familiar?" She watched as
his eyes clouded with memory.

"Yes." His answer so quiet, she barely heard the
first, but his voice strengthened. "My exact words.
Spoken in anger and sorrow, but spoken to guarantee
the safety of all my daughters from that day forward."

"No. No all, no by any stretch. Those words guarantee the safety of the daughters of yer *daughters*.
'Passed from mother to daughter,' you said. But what
about the daughters of yer sons? Did you never think
of us? Did you never care that we were excluded from
the blessing? Left without even the gifts our Fae blood
would have given us were it no for yer interference?"

Pol looked confused. "I never considered . . ."

She cut him off. "Obviously you never considered.
Never cared. Do you have any idea how many of yer
daughters you abandoned, how many of us have stood
by watching our families suffer, yet have no way of
helping, no more power than a mere Mortal. Women
who were forced into marriages they dinna want.

Beaten. Murdered." As she would have been had she stayed in her own time.

"What proof do you have of these things?"

"I am one of those forgotten daughters. I know this firsthand."

Pol's hand went to his heart. "I never intended . . . my words were meant to . . ." He stepped backward, sinking to sit on the boulder behind him. "I had no idea."

"Words are powerful, especially when spoken by one such as yerself. Action taken in haste, in the heat of emotion, rarely yields the desired result." Connor had lectured her with those very words a million times. She never thought she'd be turning them on someone else.

"I only wanted to protect my daughters from the pain their mother had suffered."

"Yet I'm yer daughter as much as any other. Yer blood flows in my body as surely as in those who received yer mark, does it no?"

He looked up, a sad little smile on his face as he rose and glided to her. "It does indeed. My blood and that of my beloved Rose." Reaching out, he again stroked her face. "You look so very like her. You are a daughter of my heart."

The wistfulness in his voice struck at her, preventing her from continuing to rage against the man.

"What would you have of me, Mairi? Where do I begin to make amends?"

"I want what's mine by rights. I want the gifts of my Fae blood denied me by yer blessing. I want my rightful powers restored to me and to all those other women like me."

He stepped back, arms crossed, one hand lifted to his chin, his forefinger tapping against his bottom lip thoughtfully, as if he were assessing her request. His eyes narrowed, watching her as he paced.

"Where are the men of your family, daughter? The ones who should be guarding you even now? Your father, your brothers, your husband?"

"My father is long dead. My brother is protecting his own wife and children. I have no husband." *Will never have one.* Since there could be no true love for her, she would never marry. "I live in a time when women take care of themselves."

Pol watched her silently, his brow wrinkling before he finally spoke again. "There are dangers to you as my daughter that other women of your time don't face. You need a man to protect you. A Guardian."

"I dinna require a guardian or a bodyguard or anything else. I can take care of myself." Saying the words out loud, she momentarily felt like her old self, like the Mairi she had been nine years ago, before her cousin's betrayal stripped away every shred of her confidence.

For the first time since she'd met him, Pol smiled. A genuine smile of amusement. One that quickly vented itself in lilting musical laughter that filled the Glen, echoing off the rocks and the water. "You certainly have the arrogance to be my child. I sense you are a woman who follows the rule of her heart rather than her head. But what of your heart? Why do you believe there is no true love for you?"

How did he know that? How could she explain?

"Because my life is no my own. I dinna belong anywhere. I live between two times. In my own time I was to have died, so there would never have been a love for me there. This time I inhabit now is no my own, so there can be no one fated for me here."

"You have much to learn about the ways of the Fates. Tell me, child, why do you come to me now? What do you wish to do that requires these powers you seek?"

Mairi hesitated. He might deny her right to save her cousin, as her family had. But she needed his help to proceed. And she felt strongly that nothing less than total honesty would sway Pol.

"It is for another of yer daughters. One who lived long ago, whose life was cut short unnecessarily. I want to save her to repay a debt to her mother, the woman who raised me after my own mother's death."

"Is that all? Simply to repay a debt?"

"To repay a debt and to find my place in the world. I feel it's my destiny to do this."

Pol watched her, silently mulling over her request, long enough that she grew uncomfortable. If he planned to refuse, he should just do it, not prolong the agony. When she thought she could stand the silence no more, he spoke.

"Very well, Daughter of my Heart, I have searched your soul and seen your need. I grant you all you ask. And more."

Before she could reply, a tingling sensation started in her toes, like tiny butterfly wings brushing over her skin. It traveled up to her head, to the very roots of her hair, and out to the tips of her fingers, growing, pulsing, heating her skin. The sensations overwhelmed her, continuing to build and swirl around and through her. She felt them center in her chest, burning and expanding until, with one final burst of power, there was nothing.

It left her breathless, weak, exhilarated.

Pol smiled at her. "The Fates have a way of bringing you what you need when you least expect it." He gently kissed her temple. "The Fates and the Fae. Go seek your destiny, child."

"What?" She drew back in surprise but he was gone, the warm tingling of her skin the only reminder that he had been there at all.

She walked to the pond's edge and retrieved her backpack from the spot where she had dropped it. She picked up the water bottle, which had rolled to the side, and placed it in her pack. A moment later, she stuffed her boots in beside the bottle.

The pond was still, the Glen silent, as if nothing had happened at all. Maybe it hadn't. Maybe she wanted it so badly she had allowed her imagination to control her reality.

Slinging the pack onto her back, she turned to leave the Faerie Glen.

The leaves rustled with a wind she couldn't feel and words drifted through her mind, vibrating in her chest:

"Remember, my daughter, with power comes responsibility. Playing with time is a most dangerous game. One whose rules you must never break. You cannot change the outcome of history. You can only alter the circumstances. To do otherwise would invite disaster of a magnitude you cannot imagine."

Lifting a hand to her breast, she felt the vibrations resonating there long after the words were gone.

She hadn't imagined that. It was real.

She was free to do what needed to be done. To fulfill her destiny.

Four

SITHEAN FARDACH
SCOTLAND
PRESENT DAY

*B*reathing was the only sound in the small rental car. Her breathing. Unnaturally fast in the otherwise silent space. The old, familiar panic was taking hold, tensing her muscles, knotting her stomach, paralyzing her.

What had Jesse told her in their self-defense practice sessions?

"Control your physical and you control your mental. Fear is your greatest enemy, the one only you can defeat."

Mairi leaned back against the seat and consciously fought for control of her body, counting each breath.

One one thousand, inhale, hold. Two one thousand, exhale. Slow down. Relax.

Just like he'd taught her.

"I'm no afraid. I am strong. Nothing here can hurt me."

There had been a time when she had really believed that. Hadn't needed to reassure herself by saying it out loud. Seven hundred years in the past. But then her world had turned upside down, she'd been betrayed by a cousin she thought loved her, someone she had trusted to protect her. Lyall had proven to her how vulnerable she really was. How much there was to fear in the world. His actions and her knowledge of what her fate was supposed to have been had undone her, had stripped all confidence from her seventeen-year-old self.

For the last nine years she'd worked hard, trying to recapture some portion of that confidence.

"I'm no afraid. Nothing here can hurt me."

The words echoed back to her in the small metal interior, sounding hollow to her ears. Before she could allow the fear time to return, she opened the door and faced the obstacle at hand.

Sithean Fardach. The new version.

Looking up at it now, she had to admit Connor had done an excellent job in restoring the family castle to its original state. Of course, the grounds were nothing like those of its predecessor. No one had lawns then. But the building, the castle itself, even the outer wall, looked as it had; a massive square structure with a large tower at each of its four corners.

When she'd first arrived in this time, everything had overwhelmed her. Her first exposure to the pile of crumbled rock that had been her home was devastating. It had symbolized to her all she had lost, all that was gone. She had never wanted to see it again.

Even when her brother bought the land, designed and rebuilt the castle, urged her to come with his family each summer, she had refused, using school as an excuse to avoid facing this place.

Now, here she was.

And . . . it wasn't actually so bad.

She opened the trunk of the car and pulled out her suitcase, setting its wheels on the rock walk that led from the driveway to the great stairs. Framing the stairs on either side were long stretches of rosebushes of all kinds and colors.

"Rock under the second rose on the right," she murmured.

Yes, there it was, just as Jesse had described. Connor kept a key to the front door hidden in a fake rock under the second rosebush on the right. He'd chosen that spot to make it easier for all the family to remember where to look, assuming everyone would be able to remember his second child, Rose. Mairi smiled. Yes, little Rosie made an impression that was hard to forget!

After retrieving the key, Mairi climbed the stairs and let herself in the massive front door.

"By my soul!"

The rooms appeared to be the same basic size and shape as in her time, but her sister-in-law had done a much better job of decorating. The massive Great Hall now housed a family room with comfortable leather furniture, an entertainment center, and a dining area rather than rows of wooden tables as it had in the past, although the dining table, with its massive chairs, did look as if it could have come straight from the original castle.

Mairi touched the switch at the doorway and lights, cleverly hidden in recessed areas of the walls and high ceiling, sprang to life.

Doorways arched over staircases on both the left and right of the Great Hall, two on either side, leading to the towers at each corner of the castle, just as they always had. The farthest one on the right would take her to the master wing, Cate and Connor's quarters. The nearest to the children's tower. The closest one on the left should lead to the guest rooms, the farthest, to where her room and Rosalyn's had been.

She chose that doorway.

The main floor had held their sitting room. She opened the door to find a room very similar to what she had known in the past, but more comfortable-looking, furnished with a small desk placed under a large window, a plush loveseat and matching chairs facing a beautiful rock fireplace.

Closing the door, she headed up to the first landing. She reached for the knob of the door, only absently noting that her hand shook as she turned it.

Her room.

"Oh." The sigh escaped without thought.

Cate had outdone herself. It was beautiful, inviting her in, making her want to stay. A large four-poster bed inhabited one wall. It was draped in silky, sheer curtains tied back with cheerful ribbons, the whole of it done in her favorite light blues and yellows. The room seemed somewhat smaller than it had in her time and, looking around, she spied a door in the wall. Peeking inside, she found a full bathroom, decorated in the same colors. She'd have to remember to compliment her sister-in-law on her excellent choice of décor, and her brother on some wise architectural updating. While it wasn't by any means a duplicate of the way it had been, it certainly was the way she would have wanted it.

She backed out of the room and continued up the stairs, already knowing that whatever the top room held now, it was the place she needed to start from. It had been Rosalyn's tower room, the place she kept her herbs and salves, her library, her bedroom, the place in the castle where her magic was strongest.

As the door swung open, Mairi was again delighted with what Cate had done. It was a library now, the walls lined with filled bookshelves. In the center was a large table, a place to lay your books or papers. Centered down the table were jars of dried herbs, and hanging in the windows were dried stalks of lavender. The smell evoked the memory of her aunt.

She smiled. If she were the weepy kind of female, this would have done it.

Kicking off her shoes, Mairi hoisted her suitcase up onto the table, opened it and pulled out a large cloth bag and several garments she had sewn by hand. Shaking out the first, she spread it across the back of the nearest chair and paused, taking a moment to consider what she was about to do.

While she should only be gone from this time for a few minutes, there was no telling how long she would have to be in the other time. And although she had carefully prepared what to take with her, it suddenly struck her that there were many things she couldn't take.

Like that beautiful bathroom on the floor below.

With a shrug of her shoulders, she picked up the

shift she had taken from her case and headed toward the door. One last shower before her adventure sounded remarkably appealing.

This she would miss.

Mairi leaned her head back, letting the hot water wash over her face and head, flowing down through her hair. After nine years, how much more might she take for granted that she didn't even realize? How soft had she gotten?

No. She wouldn't allow herself to go there, to second-guess her plan. She had taken two months to prepare, gathering everything she would need, double-checking her research. True, there were gaps in what she'd been able to find. Documentation and record keeping hadn't always been a priority through-out the years between then and now, but she had all the basics. And she would be traveling to her own time. Well, very nearly her own.

Besides, she couldn't have changed that much in nine years.

She stepped out of the shower, sinking her toes into a fluffy woven cotton rug, and wrapped her hair in a soft towel, warm from the heated rack. The sec-ond towel she wrapped around her body before step-ping up to the sink and mirror.

She automatically reached for the hair dryer and turned it on. No sense going on her adventure with wet hair and giving herself pneumonia.

When her hair was dry, she pulled it back into a loose braid, tying it with a ribbon. She wore it the same today as she always had. Perhaps a bit shorter, she conceded, remembering her first trip to a beauty salon and the squeals from the women there over the length of her hair. Even now the braid brushed just below her waist, but was a good foot shorter than it had been.

She unwrapped the towel from around her body and scrubbed it against her skin, liking the rosy glow it brought to her arms. She glanced at herself in the mirror and gasped, her hand flying to her chest as the towel fell unheeded at her feet.

What is that?

On her breast, directly above her heart, a deep, dark red mark, shaped exactly like a rose.

"It canna be." She traced the pattern with her finger. "It's no possible." The pattern she traced felt warm under her hand, the skin starting to tingle.

"But it is possible," Pol's voice whispered in her mind, resonating in the mark on her chest. "You wanted that which was owed you as my daughter. I granted it. All that you asked for. And more, Mairi Rose."

"That's not my name—" she started.

"It is now, Daughter of my Heart."

The voice disappeared and the tingling sensation ceased. An involuntary shiver ran the length of her.

"Whoa," she breathed, then hastily bent and retrieved her towel, wrapping it around her body. "Are you still here?"

The tingling returned and musical laughter drifted around her, through her.

"You needn't worry. I'm not there with you. I can't see you."

"Then how did you know what I did?" She glanced at the mirror, her reflection showing the suspicion she felt.

"I can feel your thoughts when I choose to."

"Oh." He could just dip into her mind? "Can I do that?"

The laughter again, gentle as a caress. "I don't yet know what you can do, Mairi Rose. I won't know until you know."

This time when he left, she felt it, recognized it. She wouldn't be caught by surprise the next time he came. She knew what to feel for now. The Fae blood had always made her an exceptionally quick learner. Obviously these were simply more skills to learn.

With considerably more confidence, she reached for the shift she would wear. But didn't drop the towel until she had checked behind the shower curtain.

Just in case.

A girl couldn't be too careful.

Mairi hoisted the straps of the cloth bag on her shoulder and brushed her hands nervously down the front of her overdress once more.

This was it.

She took a deep breath and consciously relaxed her muscles. She'd know shortly if the powers she'd been granted included what she needed most—the ability to travel through time.

"Take me back, to the time I must reach to save Marsali Rose, to help Rosalyn. Take me back to this very room." She waited.

Nothing.

"I am not a patient woman," she grumbled, adjusting the straps of her bag. "Why isn't this working?"

She felt his presence a moment before she heard

his voice. "Center yourself, Daughter of my Heart. Work from your source of power."

"My source of . . ." She looked around. What on earth could he mean? Unless . . .

She placed her hand over her heart, over the birthmark she now bore. The skin warmed, tingled and then pulsed under her fingers, as if it gave off little sparks of electricity.

"Take me back. Allow me to find my destiny."

A green sphere of light formed around her, pulsing in tandem with the spot on her chest. The heat under her fingers grew until she wanted to pull her hand away, but knew she couldn't. She glanced around, watching the room waver through a shimmering green curtain.

"Oh, damnation!"

By the door she spotted the shoes she'd forgotten to put on. A moment later her view of the room was obscured as the shimmering curtain turned to multicolored lights, flashing and dancing around her.

"I remember this," she murmured, just before the lights went out.

Five

Give me the paperwork." Ian hung up the telephone and held out his hand.

"Why? What are you going to do?" Sarah had dreaded this moment since she had opened the envelope Mairi had left in her keeping. "You aren't going to . . . to go after her, are you?" Damn. She was going to cry again. She could feel it.

Ian laughed and crossed the room, enfolding her in his arms. "Have you gone daft, woman? Yer brain addled by the hormones?" He held her tightly to him.

In all probability, the honest answer to that would have to be a resounding yes. The only reply she was capable of, without bursting into tears, was a single affirmative nod of her head.

"No, luv, I'm no leaving yer side now—no before the babes arrive—so dinna fret yerself." He stroked her hair. "I'm going to ask Dallyn's help. You read through the information in that envelope while we spoke to Cate and Connor. And you heard what Cate had to say about traveling through time. If Mairi's little adventure had gone as planned, she would have returned to this time only moments after she left, no matter how long she spent in the past. Obviously something's gone wrong and she's no able to return. Based on what we saw in here"—he tapped his index finger against the papers lying on the bed—"I'm sure you know as well as I do there's only one logical person to send after her." He leaned back, cupping her face in his hands and using his thumbs to wipe the tears she hadn't been able to stop.

"Of course! Why didn't I think of that?" She smiled up at him. Damn hormones were turning her brain to sponge, that's why. "You're a genius, Ian." He truly was. Or else she was completely besotted by him.

He kissed her on the head and turned her around by her shoulders, pushing her toward the bed as if she were an errant child up past her bedtime.

"It's after midnight. You need yer rest. Put on yer nightie, snuggle into bed, and I'll be back to rub yer feet before you know it. And here." He handed her the little electronic device on a key chain and she laughed in spite of herself.

"I sincerely doubt I'll go into labor while you deliver these things to Dallyn."

He held up a hand to stop her. "We're taking no chances. If you feel anything, and I do mean anything, you press that and my beeper will alert me."

"Okay, fine. Go. The sooner you speak to him, the sooner all of us can stop worrying."

He kissed her forehead again, scooped the paperwork back into its brown envelope and trotted out of the bedroom. She had no doubt but that he would run all the way there and back.

Poor Cate. The woman was sitting at her home in the States right now with a ranting husband flat on his back, unable to do anything. Sarah knew her friend. Cate would be feeling a world of guilt over this, though they all understood there would have been no way to stop Mairi from going through with her plan.

Sarah thought of her husband's suggestion on how to approach this problem as she slipped into her nightgown and brushed her teeth. It truly was the perfect solution. For everyone.

Now if Dallyn would only agree.

What a delightfully interesting night this was turning out to be.

Dallyn leaned back in his chair, propping his feet on the table, arms behind his head.

First there was the visit from Pol demanding, in his uniquely Prince–like way, that a Guardian be assigned to protect one of his recently discovered "daughters." Apparently the infallible blessing Pol had used to guarantee protection to his descendants had somehow failed this particular female.

"Oh, one more thing." The Prince had stopped at the door as if he'd just remembered an inconsequential little tidbit of information. "She could be somewhat difficult for the Guardian to locate since there is a relatively good chance she is time traveling." He raised an eyebrow before adding, "Naturally we will want to keep that little fact to ourselves."

Naturally.

At the time, Dallyn would have sworn nothing could possibly top the Prince's appearance and request.

Of course, that was before the midnight visit from Ian.

Seems the lovely young woman Ian had introduced him to day before yesterday at dinner was in trouble—time-travel trouble of all things.

What were the chances of a coincidence like that? Slim—unless you happened to be a believer in the Fates playing right into your hands. And Dallyn certainly believed.

He had known when he met the woman there was something special about her, something that just begged him to get to know her better.

She was one of Pol's descendants. One of those the Prince thought to keep secret from the High Council and all the other Fae. One of those he thought to keep separate from the Guardians.

Until now.

Dallyn looked down at the thick brown envelope in his lap. The information he held in his hands indicated they were embarking on a quest such as none of them had encountered before. He could only guess at the ire of the High Council—and the Earth Mother—should they find out about this.

At least the woman was smart enough to leave them a thorough trail in case she needed help. And

Ian's assessment of the best course of action had been spot-on, as usual, though his reasons were not the same as Dallyn's own. Ian sought only a solution to the single problem at hand. Dallyn sought resolution to a much larger issue.

A brisk knock at the door interrupted his musing.

"Come in."

"You sent for me?"

Dallyn's latest recruit. The man was six feet, four inches of honed muscle, coiled to strike at an unknown enemy. Long, shining black hair pulled back from his face highlighted intense blue-green eyes, haunted by a past no one could change. Though he had grown to adulthood in the lap of luxury, he'd taken to the training like a warrior born, and excelled at it.

The means of resolution had arrived.

"I did. I have an assignment for you."

"Already?" As he approached the High General of the Faerie Realm, Ramos Servans watched closely for any indication of the man's true feelings. As usual, he saw none. Dallyn was a master at masking his thoughts and emotions. Even when Ramos used his inner sight, only the incandescent glow of a full Fae was ever visible. "We'd discussed it taking several more months to establish the necessary security clearances in the States."

"Something else has come up, Ramos. Something with more urgency." Dallyn tapped his finger against the large brown envelope he held in his lap. "Something requiring the utmost discretion. Only one of my Elite Guard can be trusted with this particular assignment."

"You have others. Better trained and more experienced than I." Ramos had been grateful when Dallyn offered him the opportunity to train as a Guardian. When, after his second week of training, Dallyn had proposed his transfer to the highly skilled Elite Guard, he'd been honored.

"True. But none quite so well suited for this particular situation as yourself." Dallyn's smile sent a jolt of foreboding through Ramos. "Besides, you were specifically requested."

Now that was truly unexpected.

"Who would request me?" Who would even know of him? "And why?"

"Have a seat." Dallyn motioned to a chair across from him as he slapped the thick envelope onto the table. "How good are you at history?" That smile again. The one that hinted of things to come.

"I had some classes at university." Ramos's mind raced, trying to figure out where Dallyn was going with this line of questioning. "Why?"

"Do you remember Sarah's friends, the MacKiernans? You met them once, I believe?"

"Yes." It seemed so long ago when he'd met them, almost a different lifetime. Almost a different him. Before Sarah's marriage to Ian, before his life had changed, before he had learned what his father really was. What *he* really was. All they'd been responsible for causing. "I remember them."

"You know they're descended from the Fae, yes?"

"Yes. There was some discussion of it just before I left to come here."

"Connor has a sister. Did you know?" Dallyn waited until Ramos shook his head. "A rather headstrong young woman, who has gotten herself into a bit of a bind. Sarah and Ian have requested that you be the one sent to get her out of it."

That answered the question of *who*. Now he just needed to know *why*. Needed to know how this could be worth pulling him away from what he had been training to do.

"What's so important about this particular woman?"

Dallyn's eyebrow rose and smoothed so quickly Ramos might have missed it had he not been watching closely. Again the man's finger tapped the envelope lying between them. Nervously tapped it, Ramos realized with a start.

"These people are descendants of Pol."

"*Prince* Pol? Pol of the High Council?" He should have guessed. Politics. Some things were the same no matter which world you were in.

"The very one. Of course, you know of my . . . arrangement with the Prince."

Ramos nodded. The Elite Guard had been formed specifically because of that arrangement. An arrangement designed to benefit both the Realm of Faerie and the World of Mortals. A secret arrangement, neither condoned nor known about by the ruling council of the Realm of Faerie. "I thought Pol had taken steps to insure the safety of his descendants."

This time when Dallyn's eyebrow arched, it remained in that position. "Yes, well, Prince Pol thought so as well. As it turns out, he was mistaken."

"Then I'm to be assigned as a Guardian to this woman?"

"In a manner of speaking. After you locate her."

"Locate her? Has she gone missing? Kidnapped?"

The vague apprehension he'd felt earlier returned. The General was leading him somewhere unpleasant. He could sense it.

"No, not kidnapped. At least I don't believe so. Not when you're going."

"*When* I'm going?" That caught his attention. Though Dallyn was known to slaughter modern sayings on a regular basis, it was unlike him to misspeak in a situation such as this. "Don't you mean *where* I'm going?"

"No. I meant *when*. You see, there are a few minor details I hadn't yet felt it necessary to disclose to all the Elite Guard. One of those details is that some of Pol's descendants have regained the ability to travel through time."

Time travel. An ability lost to the Fae after the Earth Mother had removed their powers on the Mortal Plain in an attempt to end the fighting between the Fae and the Nuadians. Hardly Ramos's idea of a *minor* detail.

A myriad of contradictory thoughts fought to be voiced, but only one made it.

"Time travel is forbidden."

Dallyn merely nodded. "Yes, forbidden and thought to be impossible. But"—he lifted his hands in a helpless gesture—"obviously not impossible any longer. And as to the forbidden part, well, that's why I need someone I can trust to send after young Mairi MacKiernan. Someone who doesn't mind breaking the council's law, but who would never break the binding Fae commandment."

"What commandment?"

"In the farthest reaches of our people's history,

when all Fae had the power to move through time, one rule existed to prevent utter chaos in both the Realm of Faerie and the Mortal Plain. You cannot change the outcome of history. You can only alter the circumstances."

"Isn't that the same thing? Aren't you merely dancing the edge of a blade with your wordplay?" Wasn't that always what the Fae did?

Dallyn shrugged. "View it as you like, but it is the ultimate mandate that must never be broken."

"Where?" Ramos stopped and shook his head. No, not where. "*When* has this woman gone to?" He would concentrate on the task at hand, what he needed to do, where he needed to go, not the unthinkable process or the possible consequences.

"Any of those university classes cover details of the late thirteenth century?"

"Christ. Enough for me to know that's not a place I'd be particularly fond of spending a great deal of time. What was she thinking?"

A smile of amusement lit the Faerie General's eyes. "The young lady in question knows a considerable bit about the time. She's learned through her studies—and quite diligent personal research, I might add—of a cousin who died at the hands of some rather unpleasant people. It would seem she's taken it upon herself to go save her cousin from the villains."

"And the rescuer now needs rescuing," Ramos summed up. "So I'm somehow to travel back in time to the thirteenth century to save this woman from her own self-appointed task. But how do we even know she needs our help? If she's gone to the past, shouldn't we just wait for her return?" There was more. He could feel it, a tension hanging in the air between them, growing.

Dallyn looked down, tapped the paper once more before he straightened, pursing his lips as if preparing to share some more bad news. He shoved the envelope toward Ramos.

"We know she needs help because we have this. She left it to be opened if she hadn't contacted Sarah by last night. As I understand the process, Mairi should have gone, done what she planned, and returned to our time in the space of mere minutes, regardless of how long she actually spent in the past. Since she's been gone for more than twenty-four hours, we can only assume something has happened to prevent her return. You'll want to read through this carefully. It will give you all the basic details of what Miss MacKiernan discovered, what she theorized, and what she planned to do. We'll meet with Ian tomorrow to get you started on preparations."

Ramos stared at the bulging envelope, the feeling strong that there was something inside the packet he wouldn't like. He would prefer to know what it was now. He still didn't understand why he was more suited to this task than any of the other Elite Guard. Dallyn hadn't hesitated to tell him anything except . . .

"What do we know about the cousin this girl's gone to rescue? What exactly is this cousin being rescued from?"

Dallyn stood and walked to the large window at the end of the room, staring out into the daybreak before finally turning.

"In the year 1295, a small footnote to human history tells of a minor Swiss noble having participated in rabble rousing and general havoc creation in a small portion of the Scottish Highlands. It's this particularly brutal man who's thought responsible for the death of Mairi's cousin."

A feeling of dread clawed at Ramos's throat. "Who was this villain?"

Dallyn paused for a moment, narrowing his eyes before continuing. "It appears he may have been one of your people, Ramos. A Nuadian. We know only that his name was recorded as Servans."

Six

SITHEAN FARDACH
SCOTLAND
1295

*I*t was cold, dark and—Mairi lifted her hand to her face—wet? She pushed herself up to a sitting position, every muscle in her body protesting. How did her hair get wet? She was sure she had dried it completely before . . .

Her eyes flew wide open, straining to see through the gloom that surrounded her.

The room was empty, a misty rain whipping through the open hole in the wall where glass should be. Or shutters. If she'd gone back, there should be wooden shutters.

Her mind scrambled to understand what had happened. No fire in the fireplace, not even wood stacked for one. In fact, it looked as though none had been there for years. She stood and backed to the wall, stepping on something sharp in her path. She bit her lip to keep from crying out.

Things were not as they should be.

No herbs, no salves, no books in the room. Not even the smell of her aunt's things lingered. Only a pile of busted wood that might have been a piece of furniture at one time remained in the middle of the floor.

The smell of mold and dirt permeated her senses. And the sound of metal on metal. She hadn't heard that for a while, but one didn't forget the sound of swordplay ringing within stone walls.

She took a step toward the window and was brought up short by the pain in her foot. Whatever sharp thing she'd stepped on had imbedded itself in her heel.

Keeping her weight balanced on her toes, she slid to the window, stretching up to look out. In the moonlight she could see the corral Connor had built was gone, leaving a wide, open space. The wooden outbuildings he and Duncan had taken such care in erecting now leaned precariously.

Again she heard the clash of swords, followed by distinctly male laughter.

If this room was any indication, it was apparent the castle had been abandoned for some time. Obviously her aunt was no longer in residence. More important, she had the sneaking suspicion that she didn't want to meet whoever was living here.

She limped to the door of the room and quietly closed it. Leaning her body against it, she listened for any sounds from inside the castle. More laughter, singing—drinking songs—from the Great Hall below.

Not many voices, she thought with relief, four, maybe five.

The relief changed to horror as she realized one of the voices was headed this direction.

"I'm no afeard of the Witches' Tower. I'll show ye all. Hear that, banshees? Ranald MacPherson is afeard of no ghosties. Make way." This was followed by the clank of metal on stone as someone, loudly, made their way up the winding stairs from below.

"Damnation," she breathed.

A MacPherson. Hadn't she just barely escaped being murdered by one of them the last time she'd been here?

Her muscles tensed as the door pushed against her, someone on the other side, obviously wanting in.

Now what?

It seemed so wrong to have avoided death at the hands of a MacPherson nine years ago, only to be captured by one as soon as she set foot back in this time.

Or perhaps it wasn't wrong. Perhaps it was her fate.

SITHEAN FARDACH
SCOTLAND
PRESENT DAY

Ramos drummed his fingers against the table in irritation. These people, both the ones on the telephone and the ones in the room with him, droned on and on, covering and re-covering the same ground. Their endless speculation was a waste of his time. He already knew what he needed to know.

There was a Nuadian Fae loose in the Highlands

of Scotland in 1295, searching for a female descendant of the Fae. Searching for a woman who would have the ability to show them the way back into the Realm of Faerie, the home from which they'd been exiled. A Nuadian Fae who would stop at nothing in his pursuit of that goal. Nothing. His people would kidnap, torture, murder without remorse if they thought it would gain them entrance to the Realm of Faerie and access to the Fountain of Souls.

He had to prevent that from happening and rescue the woman he'd been assigned as Guardian to protect. And he could only do those things once he reached his destination.

He had no time, no patience for any more of this theoretical bickering.

"Enough."

He rose from his chair to pace the room.

Sarah and Ian looked at him in surprise. The voices on the telephone, Cate and Connor MacKiernan, ceased as abruptly. Dallyn merely turned a knowing smile his direction.

"It doesn't matter what any of us think. We've determined what to do. Let's get on with it."

"But we've no idea whether or not it will work at all." Cate's concern radiated through the speaker on the desk. "I've never tried to do anything from this far away. Never over the phone. I don't even know if I can."

"And we never will know if we continue to do nothing but talk. Everything is ready. I'm going upstairs to wait for the lot of you to finish your back-and-forth on the subject. Send me when you will." Ramos felt his patience at its end.

"Keep one thing in mind, Servans," a deep voice growled from the speaker.

"My name is not Servans," Ramos interrupted, the sharp pain of betrayal lancing through him like a flash fire. "It's Navarro. My mother's name." He would never claim the other name again. And, as his father had never seen fit to marry his mother anyway, Navarro was his true name.

Only a small pause preceded the continued warning. "Verra well, then. Just you remember, *Navarro*, there's no room for mistakes on this. It's the life of my baby sister we're discussing here."

"Have no fear, MacKiernan. I'll see to it that your sister gets back safely. I swear it."

Ramos leaned down to grab the misshapen cloth bag containing his provisions. After hoisting it to his shoulder, he bounded up the stairs. If the magic worked properly, he should arrive in the past within minutes of Mairi's arrival. Timing was important since they had no idea what might have happened to prevent her return—or when it might have happened.

He reached the top landing and paused, his hand on the doorknob of the room from which he would depart. The room where he should find the woman he had come to think of in the last week of preparation as his own personal enigma, Mairi MacKiernan.

He had learned all he could about her, about her family and their history. Still, as well as he felt he knew her now, the thing that motivated her, that drove her to this action eluded him. Why would she send herself hurtling all those centuries into the past to save her cousin? Why save that particular girl?

He thought of all he'd read and been told about

Mairi, but at this moment, paused outside the room from which he would travel to find her, what came back to him were the words in the letter she'd left behind. He closed his eyes and the flowery handwriting appeared, burned into his memory as if she'd written the words directly to him.

If you're reading this, I'm in trouble and I need help. But know this before you come charging in to my rescue: I'll not come back until I've accomplished my task. I stay until I do what needs to be done. I stay until I've fulfilled my destiny.

His sentiments exactly.

While he'd make sure she got home—regardless of what she wanted—he intended to stay to do what needed to be done. Though his way back was through Mairi's power, he had other intentions. He planned to find whichever of his people was responsible for the horrors taking place and deal with them.

And if in the process he found clues leading to the location of his father? So much the better. He would embrace the opportunity to deal with Reynard Servans as well. He would do anything to prevent the centuries of Mortal suffering at his father's hand, prevent the deaths his father had caused in his all-consuming quest to retake the Realm of Faerie. He would prevent the damage he himself had unwittingly helped inflict as he'd blindly sought his father's approval.

A slight tingle along his skin warned him of the presence of magic. He'd delayed too long on the landing. Cate had started the spell. He straightened, laid his hand on the sword he wore strapped to his body and readied himself for whatever he might encounter.

Knowing the beginning of a spell was the most powerful moment, he spoke into the void as a faint green sphere began to take shape around him. Mairi's words suited his purpose as well as her own.

"Grant me only that I might stay until I fulfill my destiny."

Outside the sphere, the walls, the floor, everything shimmered with a green hue. For a moment, Ramos could swear he heard laughter, a floating, musical sound, followed by a man's voice.

"Bargain struck."

Ramos had only an instant to consider whether what he heard was real or imagined before the gently pulsing green light burst into a million fractured colors all around him, rushing at him and away from him at the same time, disorienting him with the feeling of rapid forward momentum and the accompanying sensation of falling a great distance.

He tried to concentrate on what was happening, but the colors and the lights swirling around him, through him, blanketed his thoughts, making his mind fuzzy as he fought the desire to succumb to the siren call of sleep.

As suddenly as it began, it stopped, leaving him dizzy, disoriented and completely in the dark.

Seven

SITHEAN FARDACH
SCOTLAND
1295

Mairi braced her back against the heavy wooden door.

What to do, what to do?

Her mind raced but found nothing. She could feel the rate of her breathing steadily increasing. Her heart pounded in her ears and her foot throbbed in time with the pulsing of her heart. She needed to think clearly, but that seemed beyond her at the moment.

Wait. Calm down. Don't let the fear control you.

Jesse had taught her self-defense. Made her run through the drills over and over until she'd thought her body would give out on her. Why couldn't she remember even one of the moves he'd made her learn? She'd practiced them countless times.

She scanned the room, fighting back the encroaching panic. Though shadows masked the corners, she seriously doubted she'd find anything there to help her. No weapons, nothing. She briefly considered going for a piece of the rubble in the center of the floor, but quickly remembered how the rotted wood had crumbled under her step.

"Think, dammit!"

As soon as the words slipped out, she clamped a hand over her mouth. She was losing what little sense she had. They mustn't think anyone was in here.

"Open the door," a hoarse whisper hissed at her.

She held her breath. How could the MacPherson already have reached the top of the stairs? His voice had sounded too far away.

"Open the bloody door and let me in before it's too late, Mairi."

That didn't sound like any MacPherson. And he knew her name? Impossible. There was no way . . .

"Now." The sharp whisper was accompanied by a huge push against the heavy oak that sent her tumbling.

From the floor where she'd landed, she peered up at the man who'd come through the door, watching him as he quickly closed it behind him. He was tall, but he blended so well with the dark of the room, she couldn't make out any of his features.

"Mairi? Are you hurt?"

"How do you know my name?" Her head spun, making it hard to concentrate.

"I'm here to take you home. Are you hurt?"

"Home? But who are you? How do you know—"

"Are. You. Hurt."

He ground the words out slowly, one at a time, as he narrowed the distance between them, speaking to her as if she were a simpleton. Whoever he was, she wasn't sure she liked him very much.

"No. Not really. But who—"

This time the interruption came from outside the door, metal pounding on the wood.

"Open up, you wee ghosties! Ranald MacPherson has come to drive you out."

Her breath froze in her throat. "A MacPherson," she squeaked.

The man in front of her dropped something from his shoulder, leaned down, grabbed her by her elbows and hoisted her to her feet, all in one quick movement.

"I need you to trust me, Mairi," he whispered as he pulled her close. "Trust me and follow my lead. I'll protect you. I swear it. Okay?"

She couldn't think, and when she stood, the room seemed to swirl around her. Trust him? Hardly. Still, if the choice were this man or a MacPherson, there was no choice at all.

"But who are you?"

"I am Ramos," he whispered, sliding his hands to her back and down.

Down lower still, lifting her up as he walked. She threw her arms around his neck to secure her perch. Holding her sandwiched between his hard body and the stone wall, he used one hand to lift her skirt, pulling it up between them, before dropping his hands back down to encourage both her legs up around his waist. Without thought, she hooked her ankles behind him.

"Perfect," he murmured as he slanted his mouth over hers.

Sensation exploded through her body, overwhelming her. The wall, hard and cold behind her. The man, hard and hot in front of her. The way his hands felt, moving up her arms, across her shoulders, onto her neck, cupping her face. She breathed him in and wanted more.

A taste. One tiny taste.

Her tongue darted out, as if it had a mind of its own, tentatively testing his lips, only to be captured by his and drawn into the warmth of his mouth an instant before the door crashed in.

Her eyes flew open in time to see a brief smile dance across a smoothly handsome face bathed in the glow of the moonlight before he turned and yelled at their intruder.

"Out, you filthy heathen pig. Can you not see I've my arms full here?" He lowered his lips back to hers, but now she could only think of the hulking man swaying in the doorway, torch in one hand, sword drawn in the other.

"And who might you be?" their unwelcome visitor demanded.

Ramos lifted his head only slightly. "A guest of the MacKiernan and Lady MacAlister. Now go away."

Over his shoulder, Mairi watched the figure watching them. She didn't like the fact that he kept the sword in his hand. Or that she could smell the alcohol on him clear across the room. You couldn't reason with a drunk.

"If yer such a high and mighty guest of such as the likes of them, what are you doing here?"

Again Ramos barely lifted his mouth from her lips. "I've come here for privacy. Something I'm finding to be in short supply in this part of the country."

"Who's the strumpet? How do I ken yer no the castle ghostie trying to fool me?" The man pointed his sword their general direction.

This time, as Ramos lifted his head he let go of her face and slid his hands to her legs, lowering them, and her skirt, to the floor. Eyes like liquid turquoise caught and reflected the moonlight, holding her in thrall. Before he turned to face their intruder, he winked at her.

"You'll know I'm no ghostie because of this."

This turned out to be the tip of Ramos's sword held at the man's throat. Mairi blinked. He had moved so quickly she hadn't been able to follow the action. The dark shadows in the room and the fear must be clouding her mind. That and the man, Ramos.

"As for the *lady*," Ramos said the word with emphasis, holding the man at sword point, "she is no concern of yours. She belongs to me. Are we clear on that?"

Mairi's legs shook as she leaned back against the cold stone. Whoever this Ramos was, she would have to remember to be irritated with him later over that remark, as well as for the strumpet routine. But for right now, she simply felt grateful for his protection.

"Aye. Begging yer pardon, sir, but we—the lads and me—dinna think to find anyone here at the auld castle."

"Neither did I." Ramos nudged the man with his sword and nodded toward the weapon MacPherson still held. "I'd advise you to drop that. Now."

"Och, aye, of course." The man's sword clattered to the floor.

Without lowering his own weapon or turning, Ramos held out a hand Mairi's direction. "It's gotten far too crowded here for my taste, my sweet. Shall we leave now?"

With effort, she pushed herself away from the wall and tried unsuccessfully not to limp as she walked over to take the hand he offered.

He gave her fingers a quick reassuring squeeze and then let go long enough to pick up the bag he had dropped earlier, hoisting it by the strap onto his shoulder before drawing her close, his sword still held in front of him.

"After you, my good man." He angled the point of his weapon toward the door.

It was all the encouragement MacPherson needed. He scurried out of the room and down the stairs ahead of them.

"Yours?" Ramos motioned with the tip of his sword to the bag she'd completely forgotten. At her nod, he let go of her once more, adding her bag to his shoulder before reclaiming her hand.

"Can you walk?" he asked into her ear.

Apparently he saw much better in the dark than she did, noticing every detail.

"I'll be fine." If only she didn't feel so dizzy and disoriented.

He grimaced as he glanced down at her feet, again dropping her hand. This time he slid his arm around her waist, lifting her, carrying her down the stairs with her feet dangling above the ground.

She wrapped her arms around his neck, putting her

cheek to his shoulder. The man was totally amazing. At only two inches under six feet, Mairi had never deluded herself about being petite. Yet Ramos carried her with one arm as if she were tiny.

When they reached the bottom of the stairs, he set her back on her feet, pulling her by the elbow to keep his body between her and the five men standing together in the room watching them.

A wave of sadness hit her at the sight of the Great Hall. Only a couple of the long tables remained, along with the massive one on the dais at the front of the room. It looked as though some of them had been chopped up, probably waiting their turn as kindling in the huge fireplace.

Mairi brought her attention to the men approaching them as Ramos backed her toward the entrance. One of them pointed at her feet.

"Some fierce spectre you cornered, Ranald." He laughed. "I've no seen a ghostie bleeding before. How did you manage that?"

Ranald, still swaying as he tried to stand straight, shrugged. "I had naught to do with the lady's injury. And they sounded like ghosties to me, being in the Witches' Tower and all."

"You've a name?" A large man with a white scar the length of his face leaned toward them, his hand on his sword.

"I do," Ramos replied, a look of assurance on his face that Mairi certainly didn't feel. "But I believe all you need to know is that I'm taking my lady and leaving your company now, pleasant as it is. I trust that our mounts are still below?"

Mounts? We have mounts?

"There were none to be seen when we arrived. And besides, what makes you think we'll be allowing you to scamper off so quickly? I'm of a mind our new employer may be interested in the likes of you, come from the MacKiernans' as you have. You may have noticed, there's more of us than you."

Ramos chuckled but with his free hand pushed Mairi farther behind him. They were almost at the door. She reached out to touch it, using it to gain her balance as another wave of dizziness washed over her.

"There may be more of you now, but very soon there won't be. I can promise you that, gents. I've had one sport interrupted tonight. I'd enjoy the opportunity to engage in another." He swung the sword up in a mock salute and then held it straight out, pointed directly at the speaker. "Shall we have a go at it? See what you and the lads can do?"

Ranald stumbled back away from the group, shaking his head. "No," he mumbled. "I'll no fight a demon."

The larger man, the one who had spoken earlier, looked assessingly at Ramos and then smiled, holding his hands up and away from his weapon.

"I dinna believe that would be the best thing right now. We'll let you go without a fight. You can tell the MacKiernan he owes Davit Graham a boon."

"Wise choice. We'll pass that message along." Ramos began to back toward Mairi. "Can you open the door?"

"Of course." What did he think? That she was helpless?

She pulled open the massive door and stepped through, only to have him fasten his arm around her, once again lifting her off her feet to carry her down the stairs.

"Now what?" She looked around. Five horses were tied to the posts at the bottom landing. "Do we walk to Dun Ard?"

"I don't think I like the sound of that." Ramos slid the bags off his shoulder and hooked them onto the saddle of the closest horse. "I believe those nice men up there would be more than happy to lend us a couple of these animals, don't you?"

"I seriously doubt it. I think it much more likely they'll come after us and bash your brains out for stealing their mounts."

"I can only hope they'll try exactly that," he murmured as he picked her up and tossed her onto the back of the second horse.

After untying all the animals, he mounted the first and grinned at her just before he slapped her horse on the rump. The animal leaped into action, startling all the others into running as well.

She barely had time to grab a tight hold on the reins. The trees whipping past only increased her sense of disorientation. Ramos caught up to and moved just a little ahead of her. She clutched the straps in her hands and closed her eyes, praying her horse would follow his. She jerked as his hand grabbed her reins, his shout seeming to come from very far away.

"Are you okay?" He tugged at her reins, slowing her horse. "Open your eyes and answer me."

"Damnation," she muttered. "I should have known." She'd just recognized Ramos for what he was. How could it have taken her so long? She'd been surrounded by them her whole life.

Travel seven hundred years and she still couldn't escape the controlling men who thought they could take care of everything better than she could. Although perhaps just this once it wasn't such a bad thing to have one of them around.

"Fine," she mumbled, or tried to. "You deal with it, he-man." She closed her eyes again and allowed the darkness to overtake her.

"Ah, bloody hell!"

Ramos dropped the reins and grabbed for the falling woman, scooping her onto the saddle in front of him. Using his knees, he brought his horse to a walk.

He looked around him, trying to decide which option was best. There had been a time not so long ago when he would have been thrilled to hold a beauty like her in his arms, but this wasn't one of them.

Well, that wasn't completely true. He did enjoy holding her. He simply would enjoy it more if there weren't so many other pressing matters.

Like the wound on her foot that obviously needed tending.

Like the men they'd just left who could even now be after them.

Like getting this woman home in one piece.

The wound would wait for another hour or so. He couldn't say the same with any certainty about the warriors whose horses he had "borrowed." He sighed and urged his mount forward, opting to head directly for Dun Ard.

Though he didn't need the backward glance to verify they were not pursued, he looked anyway. Just in case. He would feel it if anyone followed, but this whole time-change thing gave him the willies.

No need for nerves, he reassured himself. She couldn't be hurt too badly. The bleeding hadn't been profuse, just enough to leave smudges where she stepped. He would check her foot carefully and deal with it when they reached her cousin's castle.

The thought of some medieval healer attempting to patch her up gave him momentary pause. Not a problem. He could handle anyone who thought to interfere with his care of her. The antibiotic he had brought along would be all she would need. He would see to her. After all, she was his responsibility. He was her Guardian.

A quick glance down confirmed that his charge still slept. Sleep was apparently a common side effect of the time-travel experience. Cate had warned him to be prepared for that eventuality. She had also promised to prevent that from happening to him.

His mind wandered back to the woman in his arms as he stole another glimpse at her. He had seen her photograph, studied her notes, learned everything he could about her in preparation for this mission. But none of it had adequately prepared him for the real, live Mairi MacKiernan.

He had expected some sort of shy, studious woman who would certainly raise a protest at his little deception to fool those drunken idiots at the castle. Instead, when he'd backed her up against that wall, she'd played right along. She had taken him completely by surprise when her sweet little tongue had danced across his lips and into his mouth.

"Any other time, Mairi, my dear," he murmured into the wind. "Any other place."

He shook his head to evict such thoughts. Not that someone like her would be interested in a man like him. Besides, he had other plans for his life. And those plans began with patching her up, sending her safely home, locating whichever of his relatives was causing trouble here in this time and neutralizing him.

His agenda was way too full for him to be distracted by a blond-haired, blue-eyed Faerie princess. No matter how sexy and appealing he might find her.

"Who goes there? Halt and be recognized." The order rang out into the dim light of the approaching dawn.

Ramos pulled on the reins to stop the horse. He'd pushed the exhausted animal as fast as he dared all the way here. He was sure no one followed, yet he had the uncomfortable feeling that all was not as it should be. Perhaps it was only his perceptive senses dulled by magic overload. Still, he had never been one to doubt his gift of sensory guidance, so he remained on full alert as he called out to the men above him.

"I'm a guest your laird will want to see immediately. This woman is a relative of his, and of Lady MacAlister's, and she's been hurt."

Ramos could picture the consternation and confusion his announcement caused among the guards standing up along the battlement. After what seemed an inordinately long time, he heard the clang of metal and the large grate in front of him began to rise.

Not a moment too soon, to his way of thinking. The bundle in his lap was beginning to wiggle.

* * *

The first thing Mairi noticed was that aroma. She was surrounded by it. Floating in it. Clean and fresh like a good herbal soap, yet entwined with another scent. A strong and soothing smell. A smell that called to her, drew her to it. It crept into her nostrils, cradled her, made her feel safe. She rolled her head, pressing her nose into the fragrance. Of its own accord, her hand lifted, searching, wanting to draw it closer. Her fingers encountered their quarry, flexed, and opened, exploring a massive plane. It was warm, firm and moving.

Moving?

She jerked awake as she realized it wasn't a smell at all that cradled her but a pair of strong arms, attached to a wall of chest into which she'd buried her face, and which she was even now fondling. She looked up into a pair of the most intensely hypnotic pale green eyes she'd ever seen. She pulled her hand back down to her lap as if she'd been burned, not at all sure she hadn't.

Ramos smiled at her.

"Good morning, my sweet. Sleep well?"

She felt her mouth fall open, but couldn't seem to do anything about it as she continued to stare, enthralled. Not really pale green, more of a turquoise, those eyes reminded her of something. Something important, but she couldn't concentrate enough to remember what it was. All sorts of things swam just out of reach in her memory, like a grainy film all out of focus.

The horse moved forward and she threw her arms around his waist, an involuntary gasp escaping her lips.

"Don't worry. I haven't dropped a damsel in distress yet."

A chuckle rumbled in his chest, but now that she'd managed to lower her gaze, she couldn't force herself to meet those eyes again. Fortunately someone yelled and attracted his attention, removing the necessity of her having to respond. She felt as though she'd been saved since she wasn't sure she would have been able to form words. Or that she could have thought of any to form.

"Hang on. We're going in," he murmured as he tightened his arm around her.

She risked another quick look up at the man who held her, taking him in. Long black hair tied back from his face emphasized his light skin, as did the heavy, dark five-o'clock shadow. The rising sun glinted off a small diamond stud in his earlobe and her fingers fairly itched to reach up and touch the small jewel.

Guiltily she dropped her gaze as she realized it was the man, not the jewel, she wanted to touch. Slowly, unable to resist, her eyes tracked upward, moving from his strong chin to his full lips. Those lips parted slightly, allowing straight white teeth to peek out.

"You know," he whispered, "I only convinced them to let us in by telling them you were hurt. You might try looking at least a little pathetic."

His words brought it all rushing back: where she was, why she was here. Everything except who this man was. She knew nothing about him except his first name and that he had rescued her from a MacPherson. Granted, that alone spoke in his favor. She wanted to question him, to know everything about him, but it looked like that particular conversation was going to have to wait for a bit.

"Here they are, yer lairdship. Just as I told you."

"Well, let us have a look, then, at this mysterious lass who's supposed to be a relative of ours, shall we?"

Though she didn't recognize the first voice, there was no mistaking the second. Even nine years away hadn't dulled her memory to that arrogant lilt.

Blane MacKiernan.

The arms around her tightened as she tried to turn to face her cousin. Ramos pulled her close, using the opportunity of dismounting to whisper in her ear.

"Think hard before you speak. Remember where we are and choose your words wisely."

She bit back the growl rising in her throat.

Who does he think he is? Where does he get off giving me orders like some kind of . . .

The thought died a rapid death as it rammed up against another memory. A memory of his hoisting her off the floor with one arm and carrying her downstairs, of his pushing her behind him in the castle entryway, of his total take-charge attitude.

He was one of those overprotective he-men, determined he was the only one who knew what needed to be done. Just like her brother. Just like Jesse. Just like every man she'd been surrounded by her whole life.

Ugh.

She'd be tempted to tell him what she thought right now if not for the strength of the arms that held her. The smell of soap and leather that emanated from his skin. The soft feel of his hair against her cheek.

And, she hastily added to herself, the current situation.

It wasn't because of *him* she held her tongue. It was the people who listened.

Sure. That was it.

"This woman is your cousin. We've traveled a great distance to bring her here to meet with her kin. She's been hurt on the journey and I need a place to attend to her wounds."

Ramos spoke as he held her face against his shoulder, apparently not trusting her to have the good sense to speak for herself. It was only his hand at the base of her neck, massaging lightly, that kept her there, but somehow that touch had the power to hold her speechless.

"Verra well. Bring her inside. Lady Rosalyn should be down by now. She'll attend to the lass's injury."

"No. She's my responsibility. I'll deal with her injuries. I simply need a safe place to do so." Though Ramos walked rapidly, there was no effort betrayed in his voice, as if he were carrying nothing at all.

Up the stairs and into the Great Hall, Mairi knew from memory the route they took.

"Ready?" His breath against her ear sent shivers over her skin.

"Damn straight, caveman. Put me down," she mumbled against his shoulder, irritated when she once again felt a chuckle rumble through his chest.

He gently sat her on a bench and backed away, kneeling at her side. She barely had time to register surprise at the sense of loss she felt when his touch was withdrawn before she looked up into a face she had thought she would never see again. Her aunt had aged since the last time Mairi had seen her, was a bit heavier, but was still a beautiful woman.

"Rosalyn," she exclaimed, surging to her feet, only to be brought up short by a sharp stab of pain in her foot.

"Mairi?" Her aunt's hand flew to her mouth and just as quickly returned to her side. Her face betrayed no emotion as her eyes flickered from Mairi to Ramos. "You must bring her to my chambers immediately, young man. Blane"—she turned to her nephew—"quit gaping. Our . . . *cousin* requires our assistance. Follow me." She turned and marched out of the room, quite clearly expecting her instructions to be heeded.

Ramos, who had leaped up as Mairi had risen, now swept her off her feet, bringing her face close to his. There was no humor in his eyes when hers met them.

"Dammit, you're bleeding again." He shook his head and took the stairs two at a time. "Stupid," he muttered under his breath.

His classically bossy remark deserved some sort of snippy response, but she simply didn't have it in her. Instead she laid her head against his shoulder and sniffled rather loudly. It was the closest she would allow herself to come to crying in front of anyone.

So far her quest hadn't gone all that well. She was tired and dirty, her foot throbbed like crazy, and she had some macho man lecturing her. Still, she thought as she snuggled her head a little closer, things could be a lot worse.

How could I have been so stupid?

Ramos shook his head again. He knew Mairi had

only just come to. The magic had taken its toll on her. He should have had more sense than to have let go of her. Now look what his carelessness had caused.

Mairi sat on a low stool in front of a large fireplace in what appeared to be a sitting room. The woman, her aunt Rosalyn, was across the room at last, still sniffling, sorting through dried plants and bandages and who knew what else, speaking softly to Blane.

It had taken a good five minutes to pull her and Mairi apart once they had reached the privacy of this room. He had neither the time nor the patience to deal with their emotional reunion. Mairi's injury was his first priority.

Ramos glanced down at the foot propped on his knee. Blood oozed from the wound on her heel, freshly broken open. It was swollen and dirty and, based on her reaction when he brushed his thumb across it, whatever had caused the injury was still imbedded in the flesh.

"Any idea what you stepped on?" Might as well get as much information up front as possible. While she could still give it.

"Rotting wood is my guess. I saw a pile of it in the middle of the room." One perfect eyebrow arched. "Unfortunately I dinna see it in time."

"Wood." Rotted, at that. Probably counted for bonus points in the Germ and Disease category. "I sure hope your shots are up-to-date, my sweet."

"As a matter of fact, I've been inoculated for just about every disease you can imagine that has a preventative immunization."

"Really? How did you manage something like that?"

Her cheeks turned an attractive pink before she answered. "I spent months preparing for this . . . this trip. Quite simply, I lied. I told the doctor I would be visiting several third-world countries this summer."

"Good planning." She was proving to be as intelligent as everyone had told him. "Too bad you didn't include shoes in the process."

Her lips compressed into a thin line. "It's no like I *planned* to leave them behind. No wearing them is just such a habit."

He pressed on the sides of her heel and she flinched, grabbing the edges of the stool on which she sat. Before he continued, he glanced at her fingers, already changing color with the strength of the grip she had on the seat.

"Whatever it is, it's going to have to come out." He spoke quietly, for her benefit only.

"I know." She shrugged one shoulder nonchalantly, as if she had no cares. "In spite of what you may think, I'm no stupid."

"I didn't think you were. This is going to hurt." He watched her face for any reaction.

There was none. "Naturally. It hurt going in. I would expect it to hurt coming out."

"It doesn't have to."

"What do you mean?" Her eyes narrowed in suspicion.

He glanced over his shoulder at Rosalyn and Blane. They were still in the far corner of the room, carrying on a quiet argument, by the looks of it. They were busy and that was what he needed right now. He quickly untied the bag he'd brought with him, removed a smaller leather pouch and, with one last assessing glance toward the others, pulled from it a small syringe.

"No." Her voice wavered slightly. "Just go ahead and take it out. I dinna want any of that . . . whatever it is."

Ramos bit the inside of his cheek to keep from smiling. Like he was asking her permission. "I don't suppose you'd be willing to zap yourself home right now?"

She shook her head. "No way. I'm here for a purpose. I'll go home when I've completed what I came to do and no one second before that."

He gently lay her foot on top of his pack and leaned close, as if to whisper his response. At least he hoped she would assume that's what he was doing as he slipped one arm around her shoulders.

"I was afraid that was what you were going to say," he murmured in her ear as he slipped the point of the needle into her muscle.

"Hey." She looked down at her arm as he backed off, then glared at him. "What was that?"

"A very small dose of Ketamine and a wide-spectrum antibiotic."

Her eyes began to blink slowly. "Ketamine," she murmured. "A sedative? You drugged me? After I told you no to? What if I'm allergic? You dinna even ask."

"I don't have to ask, my sweet. I know everything about you. Don't worry." He pulled her forward, laying her face-first on her stomach on the floor.

"What do you think you're doing?" she mumbled, trying to lift her head.

The drugs were already taking effect.

"This position makes it much easier to deal with

your foot. Now just relax, and in a couple of minutes you won't feel a thing."

"We are having one serious talk about your attitude when I . . ." The sedative kicked in before she could finish, her lovely blue eyes fluttering shut.

He didn't need to stifle his smile this time. She was out, but he was willing to bet there'd be hell to pay when she woke up. The real, live Mairi MacKiernan had spirit. That little fact hadn't been anywhere in the paperwork he'd studied on her.

He pulled several small disposable packets of antibiotic wash from his bag, opened one and doused his hands with it. Next he took a sterile bag from his leather case and ripped it open, removing a small, sharp surgical knife and clamp.

"Well, young man, as you've got yer hands all over my niece's bare leg, perhaps you'd like to tell me exactly who you are?"

Ramos barely spared a glance to the woman who stood beside him, but her being so close rattled him. He hadn't heard her approach. More important, he hadn't *sensed* it. He continued to work on the foot he held.

"I need boiled, salted water to clean this wound."

"And you'll have whatever you need as soon as you answer my aunt's question. By what right do you handle my cousin in this familiar manner?" Blane's fingers tapped on the handle of his sword.

Ramos sighed in irritation. It wouldn't do well at all to begin by injuring these people. He started to explain why he and Mairi were there.

No words would come.

He tried again, but no matter what he thought to

say, he physically could not utter a single word of his purpose.

There must be some sort of logical reason for his inability. Or at least as close to logical as Faerie magic ever got. He paused, regrouped and made a quick decision.

If he couldn't tell the truth of why he was there, perhaps he could tell a version of the truth.

"By what right? By the right of a Guardian, her life and well-being entrusted to my care by her brother."

Eight

Mairi was floating. Floating in the most perfect aquamarine water. Floating like a leaf, her body rising and falling as the waves washed up on a fine white sandy shore.

She knew this place, recognized the dream that had become so familiar to her in the past few years. It was the island pictured in a snapshot she kept pinned to the bulletin board above her desk. That photograph had come to represent her challenge and her goal in life. The promise and temptation of adventure was everything she had always wanted, but her nemesis, the fear she had lived with for the last nine years, kept her from reaching out and capturing her dreams.

The water in the photo, and in this dream, rippled quickly away as she reached for it, just like the things she wanted in life. But the island sat there firmly, not moving, holding out hope that someday she might be herself again, might be brave enough to actually go to that place. To walk on those ivory white beaches, wade into that breathtaking lagoon and immerse herself in those crystalline waters.

She stretched, and a dull throb in her foot brought her awake. For a brief instant, dream and reality overlapped. She thought she must still be dreaming as she looked into the clear blue-green of the Indian sea. But this was no dream.

It was his eyes.

"Morning, my sweet. This is getting to be a habit with us, isn't it?"

Ramos's one-sided grin hit her hard, low in her midsection.

No, no, no, she told herself. This was the man who thought he was in charge of her, who thought her stupid, who drugged her when she had specifically told him not to.

She grabbed at the hand he laid on her forehead, weakly trying to push it away. If her mouth didn't feel dry enough for a grass fire, she'd be giving him a piece of her mind. As it was, she wasn't sure her tongue wasn't permanently stuck to the roof of her mouth.

His grin widened, and she could have sworn the room got brighter. Who could have imagined its impact? She was grateful she wasn't standing. *Not our fault,* her mind babbled at her, *we haven't recovered yet. We're still weak.*

"Bollocks," she managed to croak.

"Now that sounds like the Mairi I remember." Rosalyn's voice.

Mairi stretched to peek over the shoulder of the man who was obviously trying hard not to laugh out loud. That only irritated her more.

Her aunt looked a formidable figure standing in the doorway, a tray in her hands and a frown on her face. "And you, young man, what are you doing back in my niece's bedchamber? Dinna I tell you to remain *outside* the door until I returned?"

Ramos waggled his eyebrows at Mairi, then wiped the grin from his face before turning to greet her aunt with a formal little nod of his head. "That you did, madam. But I heard noises in here and came to check on my ward."

His what?

"Did ye now? All the way through this thick door? Likely it was no more than our lass there snoring."

"Whatever it was, she's awake now so I'm going to examine her foot." Ramos sat on the bed and reached for her cover.

"You'll be doing no such thing." Rosalyn's tone stopped his hand in midair. "I'll get my healing basket and we'll look at the lass's injury together. Guardian or no, the only thing you'll be touching while I'm gone is this mug and possibly the back of her head as you help her drink it down. Do you ken my meaning?"

"Yes, madam, I do." Another almost imperceptible nod to her aunt as he took the mug Rosalyn handed him.

Rosalyn swept out the door, leaving it wide open in her wake.

"Guardian?" It came out as a broken, unrecognizable croak rather than the accusatory yell Mairi had aimed for.

"What?" His brow wrinkled. "Drink this before that damned she-dragon comes back. You've no idea what a force that woman is to deal with."

He slid his arm under her shoulders, turning and lifting her to sit propped against his chest. The steaming mug appeared in front of her face.

"Here. Drink."

She obediently sipped the brew, the hot liquid trickling down her throat, soothing as it went. The flowery taste brought back memories of her childhood and every illness or injury she'd ever had. And how loved and safe her aunt had always made her feel.

She relaxed against the wall of muscle behind her, Ramos's arms around her. His hand held the weight of the mug and hers lay over his, guiding the drink to her mouth at her own speed. Her hand looked small and delicate lying over his large warm fingers.

What an absurd thought.

She tried to sit up, to move away, but he held her firmly.

"Take your time, Mairi. Getting something hot down your throat should make you feel more human soon. What was it you were trying to say before?"

Oh! How could she have forgotten, even for a moment? "You told my aunt that you were my guardian? What on earth were you thinking?"

He chuckled lightly, his breath tickling past her ear. "Yes. I wondered if you'd missed that. I guess you didn't."

"No, I didn't."

"I couldn't tell them the truth. Literally. But we'll talk about that later, when we're not so likely to be interrupted. So I settled for a version of the truth. Something that would give me legitimate cause to stay near you." He placed the mug on the table beside them and took her shoulders, partially turning her so they looked into one another's eyes. "You do realize that I'm here because you didn't come back?"

"Oh." No, she hadn't realized that. Hadn't really had the opportunity to think about why he was here, only to wonder who he was. Now his presence made sense.

"Did my family send you?"

"Technically your sister-in-law, Cate, sent me."

Apparently it was a very good thing she'd left a thorough paper trail for her family to find her. A small tendril of fear crept through her but she pushed the thought aside. She wouldn't worry about what might have occurred that kept her from returning. *About what has yet to occur to keep me from returning.*

If the drugs hadn't fogged her brain, attempting to unravel the confusion of time travel would.

"Obviously we know only that you didn't return the same day you left as you should have. So my arrival was set to coincide as closely as possible to yours since we don't know what happened to prevent your return or when it happened. Because of that, I'm none too keen on letting you out of my sight until I can get you home. I can't protect someone I can't see."

"That awful MacPherson at Sithean Fardach. Do you think he could have . . ." She shuddered just thinking of what might have happened if Ramos hadn't shown up. Perhaps she shouldn't have been so quick to be irritated at his attitude. After all, without his arrival . . . Well, she didn't even want to consider the possibilities.

"Could be." He turned her around, tucking her back up against his chest. The mug once again appeared in front of her face. "Or something entirely different later on. Who knows? Personally I prefer to cover all my bases. You don't get to be a hero by making rash assumptions."

Lord, there's that attitude.

She would roll her eyes if they weren't so heavy. She took a couple more sips of her aunt's brew, feeling it begin to work on her body.

"I'm surprised you dinna tell her you were my husband."

"Such a falsehood would have made me verra angry."

They both jumped at the sound of Rosalyn's voice. She stood in the open doorway, frowning at them again.

"So it's wise you kept to the truth. Dinna I tell you her head was all you were allowed to touch?"

"Sorry. I couldn't figure out how to get this stuff in her mouth and not down her front any other way." He rose from the bed and put the mug back on the table, all business now. "Let's have a look at that foot."

Rosalyn had moved to his side. Mairi looked from Ramos to her aunt. Both waited expectantly, watching her.

She sighed and pulled the covers off, lifting her foot.

Ramos shook his head, making a *tsk*ing noise. "I told you the last time we did this"—he reached down and slipped his arms under her, flipping her onto her stomach—"*this* position makes it much easier to check your injury."

"I give up." She flopped her head down on the bed.

"Good," Ramos and her aunt commented together as one of them began to unwind the bandaging on her foot.

When had she so completely lost control of her quest?

From the very first moment I woke up in the thirteenth century.

"It sounds as though yer new life has been quite an adventure." Rosalyn stroked her fingers down Mairi's cheek before taking Mairi's hands between her own. "For all these years of missing you and yer brother, that's what I've hoped for. That you'd both be happy. And from what you've told me, Connor and Cate, with their wonderful children and their big house, are truly happy. But what about you? I'd imagined you with babes of yer own by now."

They sat on Mairi's bed, where they'd been for the last half hour, visiting about all that had happened to Mairi since she'd last seen her aunt. It felt almost like she'd never left.

"I love my work and school. I'll be teaching soon and I'm looking forward to that. I'm happy." Or she would be as soon as she was able to insure her aunt's happiness.

"But you've no found the man for you?" Rosalyn stood and picked up Mairi's shift, not looking up as she asked the question.

Mairi hesitated before she answered. This would be the one person who would understand the price she had paid for escaping death. But burdening Rosalyn with her sorrows was not what she'd come here to do.

"No."

Mairi crawled from the bed and joined her aunt in the middle of the room, standing on a small fur rug. A damp chill crept up over her bare legs in spite of the cheerful fire.

Rosalyn held up the shift and Mairi lifted her arms, putting her full weight on her injured foot. There was almost no pain now, she noted absently, thankful for how quickly her body always healed, one of the side effects of her Fae heritage.

She was equally thankful to have some diversion from her aunt's questions.

"He's a fine, strong lad, that Ramos." Rosalyn spoke as she dropped the shift over Mairi's head.

"I suppose, if you like that type," Mairi finally answered, clenching her teeth to avoid a mouthful of sleeve. And to avoid saying anything else. Why had her aunt brought Ramos into the conversation? When her head emerged from the clothing, she found Rosalyn staring at her thoughtfully.

"Aye." Her aunt plopped the next layer of clothing over her head. "Do you no think him handsome?"

"Verra well, yes, he is a handsome man." This was, after all, Rosalyn. Mairi had never been able to lie convincingly to the woman who'd raised her. But that didn't make a difference in how she felt about Ramos, what she already knew him to be. "In that stubborn, masculine, take-up-all-the-space-in-a-room kind of way."

This time when her head emerged through the top of the dress, she found her aunt laughing silently.

"What?"

"Ah, Mairi. How I've missed yer lively outlook on

life, child. But answer me this: When yer in a room with him, is he taking up all the space or simply all the air yer trying to breathe? Do you care for the man more than simply as yer guardian? Is that why yer brother chose him to look after you?"

Mairi shrugged and pulled her braid over her shoulder, playing with the ends. "No, Connor didn't pick him because of my feelings for him. As a matter of fact, I'd never even met the man before Connor chose him."

"Ah." Her aunt tilted her head, watching Mairi through narrowed eyes. "But is he no exactly what you would seek in yer man? Handsome, brave, devoted, chosen by yer own brother?"

Mairi glanced down, not wanting to look into her aunt's eyes at the moment, unsure of how to answer.

Even she didn't understand how Ramos could be all the things she'd always known she *didn't* want in a man and yet there was no denying that he stirred something in her.

Not that it made any difference.

If there was one thing she was sure of, it was that the question of what she wanted in a man didn't matter at all because there was no true love waiting for her anywhere. Not a woman like her. Not a woman who didn't belong anywhere, to any time. Not a woman who wasn't supposed to be alive.

But she wouldn't share that with Rosalyn. It would only upset her aunt.

Rosalyn took the braid from her hands and began loosening it, combing the hair as she went.

Her aunt's questions continued as her fingers worked through Mairi's hair. "Is that why you've come here, lass? Something to do with this man?"

"No, I've come to—" The words froze in her throat as if she'd suddenly been struck mute. No matter how she tried, no sound, not even the smallest uttered breath issued from her lips. What was happening to her? *I've come to save yer daughter.* She could think the words, she just couldn't say them.

Mairi knew, when she turned to her aunt, her eyes must reflect the panic flooding her body. Why couldn't she speak?

"Ah," Rosalyn breathed, as a look of understanding passed over her face. "Yer touched by the magic of the Fae, are you no? You canna speak of yer true purpose here. Dinna worry, lass. It's their way. When the conditions of yer visit are met, when you've done what *they* want you to do, you'll be free of that."

"When I've finished what *I've* come to do," Mairi managed to whisper. "Right? That's what you meant."

Rosalyn chuckled, shaking her head. "You should ken better than that. Yer dealing with the Fae, my dear. They're a perverse lot, with minds of their own as to how things should be. It's why using the Faerie power is always such a hard decision. Oh, often as not they'll give you what you ask for, but there's always a price. And it never ends up being exactly what you thought it would be. They've their own way of thinking, their own way of testing a soul." Rosalyn tugged lightly at the hair in her hand so Mairi would again turn her back. "I'll try no to speak on the matter again but to say I'm grateful to have time with my favorite niece."

"I will tell you as soon as I can." Why hadn't she remembered this twisted bit of Faerie lore thinking?

Cate had told her many times of her own frustrations with not having been able to confide in Connor the full details of their situation at the time.

"I'm sure you will." Rosalyn stopped fidgeting with Mairi's hair long enough to enfold her in a hug. "For now, we'd best concentrate on how to explain yer being here. Blane and I have decided we'll go along with yer guardian's story. As far as anyone else will ken, yer my cousin's daughter come to visit." The woman shook her head as she once again busied her fingers with the braid. "We could hardly claim you as who you really are. Announcing yer return from the dead would be impossible, especially with you looking only a few years older than you did when you disappeared."

Mairi nodded her agreement, still thinking of her aunt's comments about the Fae. Pol had agreed to her demands rather easily. What kind of ulterior motive might the Fae Prince have? Her fingers lifted to touch the spot over her heart as she wondered what price he might want from their bargain.

"Nine," she murmured, absently keeping up her end of the conversation. "I've been gone nine years. It's difficult to imagine it's been so long."

"Nine, you say?" Rosalyn shook her head. "That just goes to show the wonder of the Fae, does it no? For you it's been nine years; for us it's been two score and three."

Mairi knew that, had prepared for it. Had chosen the exact date she wanted to return. Still, discussing it with her aunt, hearing the words out loud, brought home the shock of what she had done.

Time travel.

"In some ways it feels as though it's been only

weeks, no years. Then again, I'm certainly no the same girl I was before."

And may never be again.

"There," Rosalyn said with apparent satisfaction as she patted Mairi's hair. "All done and as bonny as ever I saw you." Her hands on Mairi's shoulders forced her niece to turn and look into her face. "It may be yer more yerself than you think, lass. Just the 'you' you've grown to be. Dinna fret. Now come with me."

"What now?" Mairi took her aunt's outstretched hand.

"Down to have yer midday meal and meet yer cousins. I'm fair anxious to have you see what Duncan and I accomplished while you were gone." Rosalyn's eyes twinkled proudly. "Did you ken you have cousins?"

"I did, and I'm anxious to meet them. And Duncan—is he here as well?"

A wistful expression crossed Rosalyn's face. "No. I lost my beloved Duncan eight years ago. Blane insisted that we move here under his protection. He never forgot his promise to yer brother to look after me. The children were so young then, our oldest only twelve at the time. To accept Blane's offer of protection seemed wise."

"I'm so sorry. I dinna know." Tears stung Mairi's eyes as she threw her arms around her aunt, hugging the older woman tightly to her.

Duncan hadn't shown up in the few documents she'd found but she had never connected that to his death. There were so few surviving documents from the time, she'd assumed that was why she'd found no mention of him.

The smallest trickle of dread raced through her mind. If she'd missed something as large as Duncan's death, what else might she have missed?

Rosalyn sighed. "Dinna be sad for me, lass. I had the most wonderful fifteen years any woman can imagine with that man. And now I've three fine, strong sons and a lovely daughter to remind me of him for the rest of my days. Come along." She pulled away and tugged at Mairi's hand. "Let's collect yer protector and go down."

Her protector?

"Where is Ramos?" He'd reluctantly left earlier when Rosalyn had insisted they needed privacy to get Mairi ready to meet the family.

"From what I've seen of him so far, he'll be verra close by. Especially if last night was any indication."

"Last night?"

"Aye. After we finished with yer injury and put you to bed, Blane and I insisted that he leave yer room. We gave him the one directly next to you, but he stood guard outside through the day, and last night he slept in the hallway, propped against yer door."

It would seem the man was serious about reaching hero status.

"Though he's no from around here, he has the soul of a Highlander, that one." Her aunt nodded as she pulled at the door, allowing Mairi to go first, but the opening was filled.

With Ramos.

He stood, his back to them, arms crossed, feet spread apart. He looked like a man ready for anything.

As the door opened, he glanced over his shoulder and scowled at her.

"About time. How long does it take one woman to get dressed? I'm so hungry I could eat greasy fish and chips from a street vendor."

Really?

From what she remembered, Mairi suspected he'd be mighty happy to see one of those street vendors after a few meals in this century. She curved her lips into a brightly faked smile and shoved at his immobile back.

"Move it, then. Luncheon awaits."

If he'd thought her smile suspiciously forced when they came down to eat, he knew the one she wore as she watched him now to be absolutely real.

Ramos picked at the food in front of him. Apparently seasoning hadn't yet been invented in any form. The street vendors he'd disparaged earlier would run screaming from the room in abject horror at the presentation of this food, boiled and unrecognizable for the most part.

Even during his training in the Realm of Faerie he'd at least been able to identify what was placed in front of him.

Unbidden, a memory of the elaborate meals served by his staff back home at the chateau floated through his mind, but he brushed the thought away. That was a life he'd left behind.

All that mattered here was that he required nourishment, regardless of how it looked or tasted. And he'd learned to endure hardships of any nature during his training to be a Guardian. This was no more than a minor inconvenience at most.

He pasted a patient smile on his face and forced

down another mouthful, scooping the gummy oats up with a chunk of bread as he saw the others do.

Mairi's smile flickered as she did the same, a look of distaste fleeting across her lovely visage. It happened so quickly, he was sure no one else would have noticed. But he was watching, looking for her reaction. Somehow just knowing she wasn't enjoying this any more than he was made it bearable.

"Cousin Mairi," Caden, the eldest of Rosalyn's sons called out, drawing everyone's attention. "What is it that brings you so far north? You and yer . . . guardian?"

"I sought the opportunity to meet you all, to get to know my family."

"Mairi's mother and I were verra close as young lasses," Rosalyn interrupted. "It only makes sense that Mairi would be sent to stay with me for a time."

"But why now?" Caden pursued. "You never mentioned her or her mother to us before."

"There's many a thing I've no felt the need to mention to you, lad."

"As to why—" Ramos drew the young man's scrutiny from his mother. "It's because her brother has charged me with the responsibility of taking her to my home. This will be her last opportunity to spend time with her family." He was rather pleased with himself, both of his statements more or less the truth.

"I mean no offense, but why is it that her brother sends her off with you, a man who hardly looks old enough to be appointed her guardian? Why would he send her to yer home?"

"No offense is taken, I assure you. I was chosen because I owe a debt of honor—one too great to be easily repaid—and because I've sworn to her brother to see her safely through this journey. As to why she's being sent to my home"—Ramos bit back a smile as a thought struck him—"it's because she's rather old and I'm to find her a husband." No need to point out that their understanding of his duty as "guardian" was somewhat different from his own.

His statement was acknowledged with nodding heads around the table. Mairi's wasn't one of them. The smile he worked at hiding very nearly made an appearance when her foot connected sharply with his shin under the table. Apparently she wasn't impressed with his spur-of-the-moment excuse.

She glared at him for an instant longer before she turned to the woman on her right, quickly engaging her in a conversation.

With Caden's curiosity satisfied, Ramos returned to the food in front of him, taking the opportunity to study the others at the table, assessing strengths and weaknesses.

It was his gift, this being able to size someone up instantly. One look at their aura and he knew all about the basic makeup of that person. Good, bad or indifferent, it had always been useful. His father had been delighted when he'd first discovered Ramos possessed the gift. In fact, it was then, when he was about seven, that his father had insisted Ramos come to live with him. They had practiced the skill constantly, with his father having him use his inner sight on everyone who came to the villa.

Too bad he'd never thought to turn it on his father.

He wondered now what had happened to all those

people he'd told his father meant him harm. He had never seen any of them again. It was likely Reynard would have had them killed.

More deaths laid at Ramos's feet.

No, he wouldn't allow himself to fall back into that depression. This was his opportunity to rectify some of his past mistakes. Perhaps to prevent many future ones.

As servants cleared one course and brought the next, Ramos leaned back in his chair and made an effort to relax his mind. Opening his inner sight, he concentrated on the faces around the table. The majority of them bore the mark of Faerie blood, though it was filtered, as though many centuries had passed and their line diluted.

Of the men, it would be almost impossible to miss the three who were brothers. While Blane bore similarities to Rosalyn and Mairi in his blond good looks, Rosalyn's sons presumably took after their father. They were young, the oldest no more than twenty, but they were all large red-haired boys, though each head bore a slightly different shade of red. Unlike her brothers, the daughter was tiny in stature, with flaming red hair. Ramos had to look intently to find the incandescence in her at all. She hardly shone more than the young woman sitting next to her, a quiet girl with her brown hair severely pulled back into a tight braid. She wore a gown of plain gray, making him think of a large timid mouse, her eyes round and frightened when she did look up. The gold cross hanging around her neck was the only color about the girl. The mouse was betrothed to Caden, and she was clearly all Mortal.

Rosalyn, sitting near the head of the table, emitted a stronger glow than the others, yet nothing like the iridescent light shining from Mairi.

If Ramos didn't know better, he'd think her a full Fae. There was no difference between her glow and those of the full-blooded Faeries he'd grown up around. Something to think on later.

All had auras tinged with determination, varying degrees of integrity, pride and bravery. No aura looked particularly evil or dangerous.

With his inner sight still open, he filtered the conversations from around the table, hoping to learn more.

Caden discussed sheep with Blane, both men intent on a feeding pattern the younger man had been developing. Nothing of interest there.

The younger sons, Andrew and Colin, whispered between them, casting occasional furtive glances at their mother and Blane. No doubt they were up to something. Whether it was something serious or merely young men's pranks, they bore watching, though nothing he could see in their auras indicated anything more dangerous than youthful pride.

Emotion swept the room in a wave, causing Ramos to sharpen his observation. Whoever it came from, it was strong, for he rarely felt others' emotions. A quick scan of the table told him it came from Marsali Rose, and it required no inner sight to discern her irritation. She glared at her brothers over the rim of her goblet. It would appear the girl had some knowledge of what the young men were up to.

Ramos lifted his own drink to his lips and lost the flow of his second sight as he gagged with surprise when the liquid hit his mouth. A bitter, heavily spiced wine coated his tongue.

He was no teetotaler by any means. He owned a winery, for God's sake. But this early in the day? And a nasty version of the stuff at that. He sat the goblet back on the table, pushing it away.

Next to him, though she quickly turned her head, Mairi's shoulders shook with repressed laughter. That explained the earlier grin. She'd been waiting for his reaction.

No napkins to be found. What was he thinking? This *was* the thirteenth century, after all. He wiped the back of his hand across his lips, removing the wine residue before leaning close to Mairi's ear.

"Was that as good as you'd hoped for? You could have warned me, you know."

She jumped, as if he'd surprised her by commenting. When she turned to look up at him, the blue of her eyes gleamed with mischievousness. Another attractive surprise from the learned Ms. MacKiernan.

If he ever got home again, he'd need to remember to look up the researcher who put together his information packet on Mairi. The man might work for her family's company, might be a specialist in information gathering, but he certainly had omitted an awful lot about this woman.

On the other hand, filling in the gaps could prove to be quite interesting.

For someone else, he reminded himself. Not for him. His interest in Mairi MacKiernan was strictly professional.

His thoughts along that line were interrupted when all chatter at the table was silenced by Marsali's slamming her goblet to the table, sloshing wine across the surface.

"I should have ken you both would be too much the coward to ask, but I'm no afraid." She turned her glare from her brothers to her mother and Blane. "You promised you'd make up yer minds. You've kept us waiting for a fortnight now. Will you host the feast or no? Will you invite the man or no? We've only days till Saint Crispin's." Her entire body was rigid with anger.

"Saint Crispin's Day?" The words seemed to slip out of Mairi, drawing her young cousin's ire.

"Aye, Cousin. Saint Crispin's Day. Surely even where yer from it comes every year?"

"Or do Longshanks's people no observe the civilized holidays now?" The youngest boy, Colin, seemed bent on having his voice heard as well, his glare moving from Mairi to Ramos.

Ah, the political naïveté of youth.

"I wouldn't know, boy. Edward isn't my king." Ramos decided this little pup needed to be put in his place.

"*She's* from England." The other half of the whispering duo, Andrew, pointed accusingly at Mairi.

"But not for long. As I said, she'll be returning home with me. To Spain." Ramos arched an eyebrow, giving the boys his haughtiest smile, and reached for his cup, remembering only at the last minute what the offensive vessel held.

Oh well, what we sacrifice for appearances' sake.

He took a small sip and schooled his face not to reflect the distaste he felt. "Besides, she's your kin. It's your blood running through her veins. Or does that mean nothing to a Scotsman?"

Mairi's hand came to rest on his forearm, her fingers tightening ever so slightly, as if to restrain him from pursuing this particular line of conversation. Perhaps she knew best.

"He's right. They're family. And what's more, they're our guests," Caden growled at his brothers. "We'll have no more from either of you, unless you want to settle it with me. In the lists."

"My apologies, s-sir. . . ." Andrew's face was quite red as he stuttered to a stop.

"As your brother says, we're all family here, or very close to it since I'm your cousin's Guardian. Please call me Ramos."

"My apologies, Ramos." Though obviously embarrassed, Andrew did not waver his gaze.

"Mine as well," the younger Colin muttered.

"If it helps at all, my king isn't exactly fond of Edward, either." From what little Ramos remembered of his Middle Ages history, Spain had been fragmented enough to make it a safe place to be from. And it would be quite some time before there were treaties between any of the Spanish rulers and King Edward I of England.

Both boys looked up, surprised interest in their eyes.

"All this blether will no distract me this time." The angry little redhead stood, pushing her chair over in the process. "Tell me now. Give me yer decision."

The mouse, sitting next to her, quickly bowed her head, crossing herself as if to ward off the demon of fury that possessed Marsali.

"Sit down, Sallie Rose," her mother said wearily. "You can cease making a spectacle of yerself. We've already sent riders to announce the feast."

"Oh." The wind momentarily taken from her sails, she turned to right her chair and seat herself. "And when was I to be informed?"

Ramos studied the girl closely. She was . . . what had he read in Mairi's research notes? Sixteen, the youngest of the cousins, all the siblings spaced one or two years apart. What he hadn't found anywhere in those notes was that this girl, the very one Mairi had traveled seven centuries through time to save, was one spoiled little bitch.

It would appear that Mairi hadn't known that tidbit of information, either, he realized as he watched her eyes widen with comprehension.

"There was no reason to inform you earlier, Sallie." Blane smiled indulgently at the girl. "And dinna glare at yer mother so. It was my decision as laird." He nodded as if that were the end of that.

The girl pressed her lips together tightly for a moment before she continued. "Did you invite *him*? Did you even respond to his request?" Her emphasis on the word was unmistakable.

A look passed between Blane and Rosalyn before he replied. "I sent a messenger bearing our invitation."

"Is he coming?"

"An invitation has been sent in response to his request for an audience. We'll have to wait and see, lass, whether or no the man chooses to come to the feast. Now let that be the last of it."

Marsali looked down at her food for a moment before knocking it off the table in a sweeping gesture of her arm. She jumped up from her seat and ran to the doorway, turning at the last moment with tear-filled eyes.

"You dinna want him here. It's no even about his defiance of Edward. You dinna want me ever to meet anyone exciting. You'll keep me locked away here until I'm like her." She pointed Mairi's direction. "Too old for anyone to ever want to wed."

Next to him, Mairi seemed to choke on a drink of her wine, coughing as she put her cup back on the table.

Hands on her hips, Sallie stamped her delicate little foot, turned and ran to the stairs, weeping loudly.

Quiet reigned in her wake, broken only by Caden's little mouse nervously clearing her throat, her eyes closed as her lips moved furiously.

Blane sighed. "My apologies, dear cousins, that you had to sit through that. Our Sallie is a bit"—he paused and looked at Rosalyn, who rolled her eyes— "high strung."

Caden snorted, drawing a glare from Blane.

Only great self-control kept Ramos from shaking his head. That dramatic little exit had convinced him of the accuracy of his earlier opinion. Spoiled, selfish women were one of the things Ramos had learned early on to go out of his way to avoid, thanks to personal experience with his father's courtesan, Adira. He'd had no choice but to deal with her in his childhood. He'd sworn never to do so willingly again. He had no patience for them.

Yet here he was, Guardian to a woman who thought to risk her own life to save one such as this. He had an overwhelming desire to spit the vile taste of truth from his mouth.

Instead he took another drink of the vinegar these people called wine and looked around the table, searching. There was something nagging at the outer edges of his Fae senses. Something he'd missed. Something important.

Again he studied the faces in the room, their emotions still extraordinarily intense as they quietly finished the meal.

Mairi muttered something to herself about Saint Crispin's being a problem. He filed that away to check into later.

Servants bustled back and forth clearing the table. Caden and Blane rose, continuing their sheep discussion as if they'd never been interrupted as they left the room.

"Lady Rosalyn?"

She turned to him with an inquisitive smile when he addressed her.

"Who exactly is it that your daughter so desperately wants invited to this party you're hosting?"

Rosalyn's mouth tightened perceptibly and she glanced toward her two younger sons who remained at the table. Their conversation stopped immediately and they stared at their mother.

Ramos watched as she dropped an emotional curtain over her face, hiding whatever her real feelings might be. The more he saw of this woman, the more he found to admire in her.

"He's the man who will be living at Sithean Fardach for a time. He and his people."

"He's no just any man," Andrew interrupted. "He's the patriot who's come to unite us against that tyrant, Longshanks."

"For pity's sake, lad. He canna be a patriot. He's no even a Scotsman," Rosalyn snapped before catching herself. The tight, thin line of her lips told Ramos she and her sons had been over this ground before.

"And his name?" Ramos pursued, knowing he was on the right track now. The pieces were so close to slipping into place, he could feel it.

"Duke Servans of the Swiss House of Servans," Andrew answered for his mother, his voice hushed with reverence, his eyes gleaming with excitement.

"Damnation." It left Mairi's lips on a whisper of breath, so quiet no one would have recognized it for more than a sigh.

Except Ramos. He heard and understood.

He couldn't have said it better himself.

Nine

No, no, no. How can this be possible?

Mairi closed her eyes and shook her head in disgust. She of all people was questioning the impossible? Yet . . .

Saint Crispin's Day.

This required a rethink of all her plans. Not that she'd actually had any specific plans beyond getting here and saving Marsali, or Sallie, as the family called her. Another glaring gap in her research.

And now that she'd met her cousin, she had even more to think about. The young woman was turning out to be quite different from Mairi's expectations. And why shouldn't she be? It was ridiculous to assume you would know someone simply because you'd found two tiny surviving written references about her. Simply because she was the daughter of the woman you'd always loved as your own mother.

Deep in thought, Mairi rose from her chair and was halfway to the door when a large hand wrapped around her upper arm, stopping her in her tracks.

"We need to talk." Ramos scanned the room as he spoke.

"Aye, that we do." Did he have any idea of their new dilemma?

"Not here. Someplace quiet, private. A spot where we won't be disturbed."

"Come with me."

She led him across the room and through a door onto a large balcony. They crossed to the far side of the terrace, away from the entry, before stopping.

The cool, damp air hit her the moment she stepped into the open. Now she understood why she'd been shivering ever since she arrived in this time.

"You need to take yourself home." Ramos stepped back from her, crossing his arms over his chest as he leaned against the stone railing. "Now."

Of all the things she'd expected him to say, that wasn't one of them.

"You dinna listen verra well, do you? I told you before, I'm no going anywhere yet."

His breath huffed out, his lips a thin, resolute line. "It's not safe for you to stay any longer. Not now that we know the Duke is on his way here."

"Of course it's no safe. But it's even less safe for Marsali. Sallie," she corrected herself. "Especially now that we have so little time."

She drew herself up to her full height and consciously crossed her arms, mimicking his stance. She might not think of herself as a brave woman any longer, but she was determined.

"If you want to speed things up, perhaps you can help me figure out how it all got so off track. Help me talk to these people, to fill in the details I've missed."

A small frown wrinkled his brow and she fought the urge to touch it with her finger, to smooth the furrow away.

"Off track? What are you talking about? I read your research notes and your conclusions were logical, even if your plan to come back here wasn't. The stories of a foreign duke who was involved in the death of a daughter of the house of MacKiernan, the total lack of any further mention of Marsali Rose after that time—it all made sense. You were quite thorough and specific."

"It's what I do. I also chose the time to come back here verra specifically so I'd never have to deal with this Duke Servans. But for some reason, although I'd planned to arrive here in July, it's late October." Surely he'd understand the problem now.

The frown vanished as he seemed to consider her words. "So that explains the significance of Saint Crispin's Day."

"Exactly. October twenty-fifth. We're too close to when she . . . well, when whatever it is happens."

"But from your notes I got the impression you didn't know the exact date of Sallie's death."

He had read carefully.

"No the exact date, but based on the few pieces of evidence, I narrowed it down to a window. Sometime between Samhain and the twenty-first of December. The document I found specifically said the family mourned through the Yule."

"Christmas?" The little forehead furrow between Ramos's eyes had reappeared.

"No. Christmas in this time isna festive like it is now, like it will be . . . you know what I mean." She shook her head in frustration. "Here it's a solemn day. The festive part is the twelve days after Christmas. The Yule, according to old Celtic tradition, is the first full moon nearest the winter solstice. My family, because of our ancestry, continued to recognize many of the old ways." When you know you descend from the Fae, you tend to believe in other, older traditions.

"All right," he said thoughtfully. "So, no later than . . . what? The twenty-first of December? I can see that. But what led you to Samhain as the start of your time window?"

"Samhain is the celebration of summer's end, occurring on the thirty-first of October. It's like the Celtic version of New Year's."

"I know what Samhain is. Why did you choose it? I didn't see anything in your notes about it."

Reason told her he was only seeking information, not challenging her research. Still, she felt on the defensive now, as if she were justifying her research to her professor.

"The first mention I could find of this Duke Servans was his presence at a local celebration in October. I naturally concluded Samhain."

"Any chance the celebration you found mention of could be this Saint Crispin's Day feast your little cousin is carrying on about? The two are only a few days apart."

"Of course it could be." She huffed out her breath. Wasn't he paying attention at all? "Why do you think

I was so bothered by the whole Saint Crispin's Day thing?"

"Listen, my sweet, I have no idea what's going on in that pretty head of yours. But now that we're both on the same page with this, I'm even more convinced. You need to leave." He held up a hand to silence her protests and, leaning toward her, he continued. "This Duke Servans is nothing but bad news. I don't want you here when he shows up."

He was only inches from her face, so she put a hand on his chest to push him away before answering. The feel of solid muscle under her hand brought back the memory of him backing her into the wall at Sithean Fardach. Of his lowering his mouth to hers. Of the taste of his lips. She shivered and jerked her hand back. Lord, he really did suck up all the air around her. And they were outside! This close, she was hard pressed to even speak, let alone answer his questions.

"I dinna plan to be here when he showed up. But I see no way around it now."

"Well, I sure as hell see a way. Chant your little verses or whatever it is you do to invoke your magic and send yourself home."

"I dinna chant verses. And I'll no be leaving without finding a way to save Sallie. It's what I came here to do in the first place. I'll simply have to find a faster way now."

"Here." He grasped her upper arm and began moving toward the door. "Let me show you a faster way. Let's go get your spoiled little cousin right now and you zap the both of you home. Problem solved."

"No, you dinna understand. That'll no solve any-thing. The problem's bigger than that." She jerked her arm from his grasp. "I canna just take her away with no explanation to her family."

"Then explain. To anyone you like. Tell your aunt what's going on, take your little cousin with you, but go. Now."

"I canna!" Mairi yelled, though they stood toe to toe, her looking up into his face.

"Why not?" His quiet response only made her feel guilty for having yelled at him.

"When I try to talk about why I'm here, nothing comes out," she admitted. "No a thing. According to Rosalyn, it's the way of the Faeries. When I've done whatever I'm supposed to do, whatever it is the Fae want of me, I'll be able to speak of it." It sounded so stupid when she said it out loud, she expected him to laugh at her.

To her surprise, he simply nodded and shrugged. "That sounds very like what I experienced. And very like what I would expect from Fae magic. Nothing simple. Ever. There's always a catch of some sort." He smiled grimly and took her upper arm, again leading her to the doorway. "We can't wait for the Fae on this one, Mairi. What you need to do is get your cousin and get out of here. So, this is what's going to happen. You go without any explanation. I'll tell them when I'm able."

"No, Ramos."

Without letting go of her arm, he turned, pulling her close, stealing her air again.

"I swore to your brother I would see you returned home safely. Servans is a very bad man, Mairi, with very bad intentions. I'm sure of it. I need you away from here so I can deal with him without having to worry about anything happening to you."

"I understand that. And I promise I will do my best to be gone before he gets here. But we still have a few days before then. Help me try to figure out what I'm missing. There must be some reason I dinna arrive here when I planned to. Something about this Duke I dinna know. And there must be some way I can make Rosalyn aware of what's going on. She'll be devastated if Sallie simply disappears." *Exactly as I did.*

"And how devastated will she be when this man shows up and kills both her daughter and her niece?"

"We willna let it come to that. We'll learn everything we can about him and then we'll figure out a way to do what needs to be done." She waited, staring up into the clear aquamarine sea of his eyes, hoping the decision he mulled would be the one she needed.

"Very well," he responded at last. "I'll give you three days. But you stay inside the castle while we're here, agreed?"

"Agreed." She glanced at his hand, still wrapped around her arm. "Are you going to let go or do you intend to drag me around with you for the next three days?"

He smiled then, one side of his mouth quirking up before he released her, lifting his hands in surrender as he backed away. "Okay. You work on the hellion and I'll see what I can learn from the brothers." He turned his back and walked to the door, holding it open for her with a sweep of his arm.

She entered with only a small twinge of guilt.

She should probably tell him more, confide in him

her fears that this Duke Servans might have been responsible for more than just the death of Sallie. After all, the document she'd found had said that the family mourned their *losses* through the Yule.

Plural.

Ramos stood, lips pursed in thought, watching as Mairi hurried away, her thick, pale butter-colored braid swinging tantalizingly back and forth like a beacon directing attention down to the perfectly rounded backside it swept above.

As if he needed anything to draw his eye to that particular feature.

Something about his conversation with her had set his senses on alert. Opening his mind, he allowed himself to view her with his inner sight, observing her until she disappeared up the curve of the stairs.

It was more than her luscious backside that had caught his attention. She was radiating some strong emotional response. The pristine white light surrounding her was filled with wildly flickering sparks of color.

He headed the opposite direction, lost in thought as to what that particular display could mean. More likely than not, she was hiding something. Whether she lied or simply omitted some piece of information, his Mairi wasn't being completely honest with him.

His Mairi?

The recognition of that thought brought him up short, but only for a moment. Of course he'd feel possessive. He was, after all, her Guardian. She was his responsibility, her safety his paramount dictate.

Satisfied with his own explanation, he pushed the

thought away and left the building, seeking her cousins and some answers.

"Come in."

Stomach tightening, Mairi pushed open the door and walked into the room that once had been her own. She quickly realized that she had wasted her time worrying that this room would bring back troubling memories. It was so changed, she hardly recognized it. The once bare floor was now completely covered in expensive rugs; the once bare walls, draped with tapestries.

"What do you want?" Sallie stood at the foot of her bed, surrounded by piles of clothing, a look of irritation on her pretty face.

Irritation, Mairi noted, not the dramatic weeping of such a short time ago.

"I thought we could spend some time together, perhaps get to know one another better." If she planned to take this girl with her when she left, it would be a good idea to make friends with her first. "What are you doing with all this? Could I help you?" She looked around at the jumble of clothing on the floor.

"I doubt it," Sallie sighed. "But you can try, I suppose. I'm going through all my dresses, looking for something fit to wear for the Saint Crispin's feast. I'll need to look my verra best and they've left me almost no time to prepare."

Mairi reached down and pulled a light green dress from the pile nearest her and held it up. "This is lovely."

"But it's so plain," Sallie whined. "I want to look elegant when I meet the Duke."

"This Duke of yours could be old, fat, bald and married, for all you know."

Sallie's eyes narrowed and she jerked the dress from Mairi's hands. "He's no any of those things. Ran says he's a fine figure of a man. Besides, fat, bald men aren't heroes. Did my mother send you up here to plant those lies?"

"No. Yer mother disna even know I'm here. Who's Ran?"

"A family friend. He squired here for years." She held the green dress up to her shoulders. "I suppose this color would be good on me."

"A lovely color with your hair," Mairi said absently. She'd need to find out more about this fellow, Ran.

"I dinna know where we'll find anything for you to wear, unless it's my mother's. Yer verra large."

"What?" Mairi's attention snapped back to the conversation.

"My things are all much too small. But, as yer so old, too, her clothing would be best for you." A wicked smile accompanied the comments.

"I have my own things to wear, thank you." Mairi was forming a rather definite dislike of her little cousin. Perhaps when she got her home, she could talk Connor and Cate into letting the girl live with them.

"Oh." The girl picked up a blue gown, dropping the green one. "This one displays my figure to more advantage." She looked up and smiled. "Yer no one of the gifted daughters, are you?"

"What?" It seemed the girl was constantly catching her off guard.

"The Fae gifts. Do you ken the story of them?" At Mairi's nod, she continued. "You dinna have them, do you? You're no the daughter of a daughter, are you? No like me."

"No, I'm no the daughter of a daughter." That much was true.

"I dinna think so. Perhaps we could take that one in." She dropped the blue dress and picked up the green one again. "There was another Mairi who lived here many, many years ago. Long before I was born. She was like you."

"Really?" They knew of her? "How was she like me?"

"She was ungifted." Sallie sighed and shook her head before turning the wicked smile back on. "That Mairi was my mother's favorite niece. A beautiful, carefree lass who tragically died in this verra room, murdered on her wedding night by the groom himself."

Mairi stood in shocked silence. Not this room. It had been the storeroom down below where she'd been held, where she would have met her end.

"I've seen her ghost."

"Oh, really?" Hard to believe. Especially since she hadn't actually died.

"Aye. But you'll never see her. She appears only to me because I have the gifts."

"Just as well. I dinna believe in ghosts. Would you like me to help you alter the green one?"

"You can. We'll take it down to my mother's solar. The light is better there." Sallie paused at the door, turning with a glare. "Best you remember this, Cousin Mairi. You'll have to wait to find yerself a husband when yer guardian takes you to Spain. Dinna be thinking you'll steal my Duke away. You've no gifts, and yer old and large. He'll choose me over you."

With that she flounced out the door, leaving Mairi staring after her.

Sallie would definitely have to live with Connor and Cate. Either that or someone would be seeing *her* ghost.

On top of everything else, Sallie snored.

Mairi cast a disgusted look over at her sleeping cousin, swathed in the blankets beside her like some medieval mummy. And she was a cover hog to boot.

When Rosalyn had first approached her about moving into Sallie's room, Mairi had known it would be a trial. But with houseguests coming for the Saint Crispin's celebrations, rooms were at a premium. After all, it wasn't as if they could just hop in their cars and drive home. And there certainly weren't any nearby hotels in this time.

Mairi rolled her eyes at the noise coming from her cousin. The only positive was that she was sure Sallie slept. At last. The girl had talked forever, right up to the minute she dozed off. Straight from inane chatter to deafening snores.

Mairi had waited all through the afternoon and evening to find an opportunity to sneak away to speak to Ramos. She wanted to tell him about the man Sallie had mentioned. This Ran might provide some useful information for them, if only they could learn more about him. He apparently knew the Duke and was well acquainted with the family, though she remembered no mention of him in any of her research.

Mairi slid from the bed, shivering as her feet hit the cold stone. She wondered briefly if Sallie had purposely moved the rugs from her side of the bed. It seemed to be the only bare spot in the entire room.

The fire was down to embers and the wood basket empty. Obviously her cousin wasn't fond of the little everyday chores. Mairi regretted the clingy silk nightgown she wore, but only for a moment. She had always hated the thick woolen nightdresses. They made her feel as if her arms were bound, and they tangled around her legs. The long, sleeveless silk she wore had been the one concession to modern times she had made when coming back. Sallie had been fascinated by the gown, but Mairi had explained it away as a gift her brother had procured from traders.

Rubbing her hands up and down her chilled arms, she crossed the room and slipped out the door, closing it quietly behind her.

The hallway was much darker than she remembered, a lone torch burning at the far end her only illumination. She trailed her hand along the surface of the wall, wishing for a light switch and some overhead bulbs as she made her way to the bedchamber where Ramos slept.

Reaching his door, she hesitated. It had taken so long for her cousin to finally fall asleep, surely he wouldn't be awake any longer. She could knock, but what if he were a sound sleeper? Pounding could bring others to their doors as well, and she didn't particularly want to invite speculation as to what she was doing at his chamber in the middle of the night.

She bit at her lip as she paused, her hand on the

knob. Sneaking about in the dark was something she might have done long ago when she'd lived in this castle. The reassurance of that thought gave her the courage to push open the door and slip into the room.

Inside, she waited a moment, gathering her bearings. The room was as dark as the hallway, the only illumination coming from the soft glow of the burning wood in the fireplace. She held still and listened. Deep, rhythmic breathing affirmed Ramos's presence in the room.

As she reached his bedside, she saw that he lay on his back, one arm flung above his head, the hand tucked under his pillow, the other arm resting by his side. His hair was unbound, flowing across the pillow like a burn of black silk. The bed woolens were drawn only up to his waist, and his chest—she sucked in her breath—was gloriously bare.

Without thought she leaned closer and reached out, her hand hovering above the rippled plane of his chest. Her finger, as if with a mind of its own, lightly stroked the bronzed muscle just above his heart.

A grip of steel on her wrist was her only warning. Within the space of a heartbeat, she was on the bed, flipped to her back, her arms stretched above her head.

Ramos loomed over her, his body covering hers, holding her immobile. The hair that had reminded her of a stream on the pillow beside him now pooled about their faces like a silken curtain of ebony. His eyes glittered, reflecting the glow of the fire.

"Mairi?" Ramos whispered her name. "What the bloody hell do you think you're doing in here?"

How had he moved so quickly?

"I needed to . . ." The words stuck in her throat as he released one wrist, his hand slowly skimming down her arm.

"To talk to you." Once freed, the words came out in a breathless rush, one tumbling over the other.

Amazingly it wasn't fear wreaking havoc on her senses at the moment. It was attraction. She'd never felt such an immediate and intense response to anyone.

"Talk?" A lazy smile curved his full lips.

Such a fascinating mouth; such mesmerizing lips. The memory of their feel, their taste came rushing back to her. She felt them calling to her, willing her to capture them with her own.

His hand slid lower, toward her ribs, his thumb extending to brush the side of her breast. She sucked in her breath and his head dipped, so close their lips almost touched.

"About?" With the one whispered word, his breath trickled over her face, an inviting tendril of air beckoning her closer.

She couldn't resist its call.

Her free hand wrapped itself in the black silken curtain of hair and pulled him down, her mouth closing over his.

His tongue tested her lips and she opened them, inviting him in, her own dancing with his.

She melted into him, his arms behind her now, one at her shoulders, one at her hips, drawing her into him.

Her hands slid down his chest and around his waist, exploring the back muscles that flexed as he drew her closer still, kissing her as if he wanted to suck her very soul from her body. On her hands traveled, down his back and lower.

His body was all muscle, hard molded stone, covered in warm, inviting skin.

Bare skin.

Her hands froze in place and she gasped as she realized his shirt wasn't the only thing he wasn't wearing.

His eyes were heavy when he lifted his head, a lazy half smile curving his sexy lips. "What is it, my sweet? Remember what you came to talk about?"

What am I doing?

"You're . . . you aren't . . . Ran!" She fought for breath. "I came to talk to you about Ran."

His brow wrinkled in confusion. "Who ran?" He dropped his mouth to her neck, doing something with his tongue that made thought almost impossible.

Both his hands slid to her hips, pressing her into him. It quickly became obvious that every part of his body was hardened. Especially the part that pressed tantalizingly against her now, as he nestled between her legs, the thin silk of her nightgown the only thing separating them.

His mouth moved lower and she sucked in a breath, needing air, needing to clear her head, needing to regain control.

"No, it's no a who. . . . Ran is a who. . . . Holy Christ, Ramos, you've nothing on," she finally managed to sputter. "Get off me." She pushed at his chest. This had to be his fault. She'd never, ever behaved even remotely like this.

"Okay." He leaned on his forearms, his face still above hers. "If you're sure that's what you want."

"That's what I want," she whispered, held captive by his eyes.

"Your words may say stop"—he lowered his head, capturing her bottom lip, sucking it into his mouth, running his tongue over it, forcing a moan from her before letting go—"but your body is telling me something else all together."

Her body was telling her something else, too.

"Yeah, well, listen to my words and get off me." Before words completely failed her again.

He rolled off her and rose from the bed.

"Good Lord!" She slapped her hands over her eyes. "You're naked!"

"I thought we already established that fact, my sweet. I'm okay with it."

"Well I'm not," she muttered as she heard him rustling around the room, his low chuckle sending a shiver through her whole being. He was an overbearing Neanderthal and he'd called her old in front of her entire family. How could she possibly be this attracted to him? "And I'm no yer sweet anything."

The bed dipped next to her, alerting her he had finished whatever he was doing. His hands on hers pulled them from her eyes.

"Okay, since you don't want to finish what you started." He paused. "Do you?" At her emphatic head shake, he grinned. "Then what are you doing in my room at this hour of the night?"

She sat up, discreetly glancing toward his legs. The rustling had obviously been him putting on his pants. But no shirt. She quickly looked down at her hands. That chest view made it hard to concentrate.

"We need to find out about someone named Ran.

He's apparently one who knows this Duke Servans. Sallie has mentioned him several times, but I haven't been able to learn anything about him from her other than that he's a friend of the family and that he squired here."

"Squired here? You mean like an apprenticeship or something?" He leaned back against the head of the bed, swinging his feet into her lap.

"Something like that," she answered. One foot moved methodically up and down her thigh, distracting her. "Stop that."

"Then tomorrow I'll ask one of the boys who this bloke is. No problem."

The foot in her lap moved again, this time against her stomach. She quickly stood, spilling his feet to the floor.

"I need some wood."

"What?" His strangled question stopped her. She turned as he rose from the bed to stand uncomfortably close to her.

"Wood. Our fire was almost out and there's no more in Sallie's room."

"Ah." He chuckled again and walked to the fireplace, squatting down next to the filled wood basket.

As he turned, she caught sight of his shoulder, covered in an elaborate tattoo. "What's that?"

He glanced down to where she pointed and frowned, turning his shoulder away from her. "Nothing. Come on. Let's get you back to your room. And, Mairi?"

Staring at the broad expanse of his back, she almost didn't respond. "Hmm?"

"Once you're in your room, stay there. Wandering

around a dark castle in the middle of the night isn't the sort of thing I want you doing again."

She followed him through the door and into the hallway. He thought nothing of ordering her around, but let her ask him a simple question and what happens? It appeared her curiosity would remain unsatisfied for now.

Just like her body.

Ten

That's no so bad. The bleeding's almost stopped."
Andrew rocked back on his heels, grinning as Ramos
splashed another handful of water over his face.
"Caden's good, aye?"

Not that good. "Shame he wasn't good enough to
miss me." Ramos fingered the cut on his cheek. *My
own damn fault.*

Caden strode into the small room, stopping to
stand over Ramos. "I dinna want to miss. Next time
we spar, you'll remember and pay attention to what
yer doing."

He was right about that, at least.

After nine months of training with Dallyn's Elite
Guard, the swordplay of Caden MacAlister should
have been no challenge to Ramos. But he'd allowed
his mind to wander, automatically returning each attack without concentrating. Let his thoughts drift to a
woman's body so tantalizing, just the memory of it
filled him with need. Thoughts of soft curves draped

in clingy silk that outlined every delicious inch of her. A body that responded to his own with an electric intensity. Mairi's body.

That was his first mistake.

No. Last night was his first mistake.

Allowing himself to daydream like some lovesick teenage girl was his second. And Caden had simply exacted a punishment for that error in judgment.

Caden reached down and placed a finger under Ramos's chin, surveying the damage. "Drew's right. It's no so bad. Naught but a scratch to give yer bonny face some much-needed character."

Ramos pulled his chin away, splashing water over his face again. It was one thing to be bested in battle, entirely another to be sloppy.

"Dinna fash yerself, my friend. I've no ruined yer pretty visage." Caden laughed and moved to lean against the wall, stopping to retrieve his shirt and put it on. "Yer good—I'll give you that, Spaniard. If I dinna know better, I'd say you've the soul of a Highlander in you."

Ramos relaxed and grinned up at him. "Next time," he promised.

"Aye, next time," his opponent agreed. "Perhaps then you'll take me seriously enough to keep yer mind with the fight."

That he'd been so transparent rankled. He was no amateur, though he'd certainly acted as if he were. "Of that you can be sure."

He stood as Colin ran in holding a skin flask he offered to his older brother.

Caden took a long drink and held it out to Ramos.

"Wine?" He didn't think he could stomach another

mouthful of the rank spiced mixture, not even for the sake of bonding.

"No," Caden scoffed. "This is a man's drink, no a ladies' table accompaniment."

Ramos accepted the flask, tipping it back for a quick taste. Strong Scots whisky. Quite good. He downed another swallow, feeling the mixture burn pleasantly along his throat.

Ramos and Caden moved outside the shed, where they sat on benches and leaned against the wall, enjoying the welcome respite after their vigorous workout in the lists. They passed the flask back and forth in companionable silence.

"Who is Ran?"

Caden looked up, suspicion clouding his eyes at the question. "Why do you ask?"

Ramos shrugged. "Your sister spoke of him to Mairi. I wondered about him is all."

"Like as not, if Sallie mentioned his name it came in the same breath as that of the illustrious Duke," he responded sourly.

"I take it you're not as impressed as your brothers with this Servans?"

Caden glanced over his shoulder, assuring himself his brothers were well occupied in their own round of sword practice before answering quietly.

"I dinna begrudge him his political beliefs. I dinna even begrudge him the use of Sithean Fardach. But I'm no in favor of his luring our lads off to serve his purposes with fanciful tales of battle and glory. I dinna want to be burying my brothers. War may be coming, but I want no part of it."

"Is this Ran one of the young men who follow Servans?"

"Aye, sadly enough. Ranald MacPherson is like a brother to me. He spent more time here growing up than he did in his own keep." Caden chuckled and slowly shook his head. "If you'd ever met his family, you'd understand why."

MacPherson. As Ramos recalled, Mairi had been rather upset at the mere mention of the name. "I think I may have met this Ran of yours. Mairi and I originally traveled to Sithean Fardach. There was a young man there by that name, along with several others. It's their horses we, uh, *borrowed*. Since our own were missing, that is."

"Aye, those were MacPherson steeds you rode in on. We sent a messenger letting them know we had them here and would care for them until they came to make claim."

"How did your friend come to be mixed up with the Duke?"

"Ran went to university in Paris for a time." He shrugged. "His father's mother, the first wife of Red Dunald, was a French lass, what can I say? Ran met the Duke in Paris. Servans returned to Scotland with him, sending Ran on ahead to Dun Ard to make arrangements for his use of Sithean Fardach."

Of one thing Ramos was sure: no Fae ever did anything without a good reason. What could this Servans have learned from the boy that brought him here? His father's plan last year to use Sarah Douglas as a means to enter the Realm of Faerie flashed through his mind. Could Servans have heard stories about the

MacKiernans' claim to Faerie ancestors? Could that knowledge be what would lead to Sallie's death?

"Your friend Ran sounds like someone I should meet." *And question.*

Caden chuckled. "I hope yer no setting yer mind on him as a husband for yer ward. He'll have no interest in Cousin Mairi, lovely though she is."

As if. "Why would that be?"

"Ran's been head over heels for Sallie for as long as I can remember. Follows her about like a motherless puppy. She'd do well to have him, too, but the spoiled tart has airs. Ever since she heard of this Duke's visit, she seems to think she needs herself a great man for a husband."

"She did seem rather insistent about meeting the Duke." Her scene at dinner came readily to mind.

Caden made a sound of derision deep in his throat, shaking his head. "She's insistent on everything she wants. Spoiled her beyond her own good, Blane has. Dinna get me wrong. Cousin Blane has been verra good to us all, taking us in after Father's death, even naming me his heir. But I fear Sallie's too much a handful for any good man now. I have my doubts any will want her."

"Any except this Ran," Ramos added distractedly, his attention drawn to a flurry of activity in the far courtyard.

The large gates were drawn up and a party of riders made their way toward the main building.

"Aye, except Ran. And even *he's* tongue-tied around her as often as not. Speak of the devil. It looks as though yer in luck, Ramos." Caden slapped him on the back. "There's Ran and his family arriving now. Let's go make the introductions."

They rose and headed toward the new arrivals.

A whole family of MacPhersons was here? Something told him Mairi wasn't going to be very happy about this.

Mairi had kept to her room for the better part of the morning, hoping to avoid Ramos. She crept quietly down the stairs, stopping at the last turn to peek around the corner, verifying he wasn't in the entrance hallway.

She was mortified by her behavior last night. And even more embarrassed to admit that she would do it again in a heartbeat. For some strange reason, though Ramos epitomized everything she found repugnant in men, her traitorous body didn't seem the least bit repulsed. Quite the contrary.

They had left his room last night, making their way back down the hall to where Sallie slept. When they reached the door, he'd dumped the wood he carried into her arms. With her hands full, he'd taken the opportunity to kiss her again. His hand at the back of her head, he'd pulled her close. When his lips met hers, she'd been unable to resist returning the kiss. His heated look as he'd left her seared into her memory.

Thinking about him, about that kiss, she raised a hand to her fiery cheek.

"And what do you think yer doing?"

Mairi almost leaped off the stairs at the sound of Sallie's voice so close behind her.

"Dinna anyone ever tell you it's no polite to sneak up on people?" she asked irritably.

"What about you? It looked to me like you were doing some sneaking of yer own."

Mairi had no intention of explaining any of her actions to this girl, and was saved the trouble when several servants ran past them out the main door, distracting Sallie.

"Och," the girl breathed, "the guests have started to arrive." She pushed past Mairi, racing down the remaining steps and out the door onto the great landing.

Mairi descended the last of the stairs, casting a glance in both directions before stepping into the hallway. Straight ahead was the entry to the Great Hall. To her right was the entrance where, through the open door, she could see Sallie leaning over the railing.

To her left was the door to Blane's public solar, the room where he conducted business. At the far end of the hall was the entry to the kitchens, and next to that, looming large and threatening, was another, smaller doorway. One that led down three steps to a dark, windowless storage room.

If her ghost were to haunt the room where she supposedly died, that would have been the room. Involuntarily she shuddered and, turning her back to that place and those thoughts, she hurried out to the landing to join Sallie.

Blane and Rosalyn stood at the foot of the great stairs, waiting together to greet their guests. A large man dismounted and approached one of the female riders in the party.

He looked somehow familiar.

Mairi leaned over the railing to get a better view.

"Oh no," she whispered, her stomach lurching.

It was the MacPherson from Sithean Fardach. She was positive of it. What was he doing here? Surely they wouldn't be hosting anyone from the MacPherson clan.

He smiled up at the woman on the horse, and lifted her to the ground. As he did so, her cloak fell back from her head.

"Holy Mother of God." The words escaped Mairi on a breath of panic and her hand flew to her chest.

"What did you say?" Sallie looked up quizzically as she started down the stairs.

She was older, of course, her once raven hair liberally streaked with gray, but there was no mistaking the arrogant tilt of her head or the haughty expression on her face.

Anabella. The hussy who had betrayed Mairi's brother. The harlot who had married her uncle.

There was no chance the woman wouldn't recognize her. They had hated one another with a passion. Mairi had to get out of here. Ramos had been right. It was time to go home.

She grabbed Sallie's hand, dragging her back up the two stairs she'd descended. "Come on. Hurry."

Where to go? Where to find privacy? The parapet. It was the highest point of the castle and the most secluded.

Running up the stairs as quickly as she could, she pulled Sallie along.

"Let go of me! I've guests to greet. What's wrong with you?" The girl tried to pull away, but her petite build was no match for Mairi's strength and panic.

Through the last door, Mairi pushed it shut and leaned against it, both she and Sallie gasping for breath.

"Have you gone completely daft? Move yer great body from the door and let me go." Sallie again attempted to free her hand from Mairi's grip, and when she was unsuccessful, she stamped her foot, obviously expecting to get her way.

Her little cousin had a lot to learn.

"Return us now," Mairi whispered. Holding tightly to Sallie's wrist, she waited for the green sphere and the sparkling lights.

Nothing.

The center of her power. She'd forgotten. She placed her free hand over her breast, over the spot where her new birthmark resided.

"Return us now." More forcefully this time.

Nothing.

No sphere, no lights and, most important, no tingling in her birthmark. It wasn't working.

"Now, now," she cried frantically.

"Now what, you daft cow?" Sallied pulled at her wrist.

Nothing.

"What do you think yer doing?" Sallie's face was pink with exertion and her eyes flashed with anger.

Suddenly Mairi knew—*knew*—it wasn't going to work. It seemed as though Sallie wasn't the only one who had a lot to learn.

She pulled her cousin to the wall to peer over, down into the courtyard. The people looked small from here, but the threat still loomed just as large.

"Look how pretty it is from up here. I wanted us to

view their arrival from this vantage." It was the lamest excuse on the face of the planet, but the only one she could come up with to explain her behavior.

Sallie jerked her hand free as Mairi loosened her grip, making a disgusted *tsk*ing noise in the process. "I dinna care what Mother says, you *are* daft." The girl turned, shaking her head, and left Mairi alone on the high castle walk.

Mairi leaned against the half wall, sliding down until she sat with a thud. The wind picked up, blowing fine hairs about her face, tickling her skin.

The magic hadn't worked. She couldn't go home.

Her task to save her cousin apparently wasn't what kept her here. Her aunt had nailed it. She was here until she accomplished whatever it was the Fae wanted done.

The problem was, she had no earthly idea what that might be.

Ramos shielded his eyes as he peered up, searching the outline of the castle parapet. Something was wrong and his instincts told him it concerned Mairi. A flash of color had caught his eye, or perhaps it was only the prickle of his Fae sense.

She needed him.

He had never put much thought into the why or how of his Fae gifts, and he didn't question them now.

Increasing his speed, he shouldered his way through the collection of people greeting one another at the foot of the stairs. He took the steps two at a time, reaching the door just as Sallie stepped through.

"Have you seen Mairi?"

Her scowl gave him the answer. "I've just left the daft woman on the parapet. You'd best see to her before she throws herself off."

"What?" His stomach knotted at her words. "How do I get there?"

"All the way to the top of the spiral stairs."

He pushed past her and raced up the steps.

Once through the topmost door into the fresh air, he spotted her immediately. She sat huddled into herself, her knees drawn up, head down resting on them.

"Mairi?"

Her head snapped up in response, a myriad of emotions flowing across her features.

"What's wrong?" He reached down, pulling her to her feet when she took the hand he offered.

"There's someone down there. Someone I have to avoid." She stopped, her eyes dark and troubled. "What's happened to your face?" She reached up, her fingers hovering just above the cut on his cheek.

"Nothing serious. Just a bit of carelessness on my part." He captured her hand with his own, surprised to feel her trembling in his grip. "I know about the people in the courtyard, but it's not going to be a problem." Perhaps she thought this MacPherson person was responsible for what had happened to her, whatever it was that had kept her from returning to her own time.

"You dinna understand."

She was shaking her head when he pulled her to him, wrapping his arms about her, stroking her hair. "I know you're afraid of the man in the courtyard. But you don't have to worry. That's Ran, the friend your cousin spoke of."

Her head shot up and she pushed away from him, disbelief evident in her expression. "You're telling me that my cousins are friends with a MacPherson?" Sighing deeply, she turned her back to him, crossing her arms. "Even that disna matter right now. It's no about him. It's the woman with him I must avoid."

Forcing himself to remain silent, he waited for her to continue.

"She was married to my uncle. She'll recognize me."

The quiver in her voice gnawed at him. Fear must be coloring her judgment.

"Use reason, Mairi. Even if the woman down there is your aunt, she'll hardly recognize you. It's been, what? Over twenty years since you supposedly died? She couldn't possibly assume it's you."

"You dinna know her like I do."

"Very well. If you're convinced this woman is a problem, then leave now. Send yourself home and I'll deal with things here."

"I canna."

"Don't you trust me to see to Sallie's safety?" And why should she? He'd done nothing to give her reason to trust him. If anything, his actions last night showed just how untrustworthy he really was. Still, her lack of faith in him stung his pride.

"It has nothing to do with trust. I have no choice but to remain here for now."

Stubborn, hardheaded . . . "Then you've no choice but to go face this woman." At her look of panic, he softened his tone. He'd simply need to earn her confidence. "Come on. Let's go down and we'll meet these people together."

Ignoring her doubt, he took her hand and led her

through the door and down the stairs. Later, once she'd calmed, she would recognize how absurd her idea about this woman really was.

When they reached the main level, the sound of voices told him everyone else had moved into the Great Hall. He thought for a moment that Mairi might resist joining them but, with another deep sigh, she straightened her back, composed her features and followed him. Her rigid hand in his was her only outward indication of the depth of her concern.

"Here they are now," Caden called as they entered the Great Hall.

Mairi's fingers tightened in his and he drew her closer, his hand protectively at her back.

"This is the cousin my mother spoke of and her guardian. Ramos, this is—" Caden's introduction was cut short by a scream ripping through the room.

All heads turned to the woman at Rosalyn's side. She lifted a shaking arm, pointing toward Mairi.

"Holy Mother preserve us," Anabella cried. "Get back, you wicked ghost!" One step forward and she fainted, collapsing to the floor in a heap.

As the room erupted in noisy confusion, Ramos glanced to Mairi, ready to assist her if necessary. Her hands flew to cover her mouth, her eyes stricken.

Apparently her concerns hadn't been so absurd after all.

"I am sorry, dear, I should have warned you she was coming. I'd planned to tell you today, but when they arrived early, I hoped I could avoid Anabella's reaction by telling her I'd a young cousin visiting. As usual, she was so busy talking about herself, she'd hear nothing I had to say." Rosalyn patted her niece's hand. "We'll convince her, dinna fret."

They were in Rosalyn's private solar, the two women seated at a small table. Ramos leaned casually against the fireplace, a mug of ale in his hand, trying to look inconspicuous but failing miserably, as far as Mairi was concerned. It was all she could do to keep from staring at him. Even the wound on his face didn't detract from his raw appeal.

Concentrate. With an effort, she turned her thoughts away from Ramos. There were more urgent things she needed to think about now.

"What I want to know is what Anabella is doing with the MacPhersons. And for that matter, why any MacPherson would ever be welcomed at Dun Ard."

"Things have changed much in the time you've been away, Mairi. It was all verra confusing in the days after you . . . well, after yer *death*," Rosalyn began. "Red Dunald dinna appreciate being accused of murdering his new bride."

"Not that he would have minded actually murdering his new bride—only being accused of it," Mairi muttered. The very memory of the man sent shivers down her back.

"Verra likely," her aunt agreed. "Though he was also quite angry to find Artair dead and his debt no paid. He sent a raiding party, bent on retribution. Blane and Duncan had both received injuries at the hands of Lyall's men and we'd all remained at Sithean Fardach, waiting for them to regain their strength. When the MacPherson's men stormed Dun Ard, the only MacKiernan woman they found was Anabella, so they took her and sent a messenger to Blane demanding a ransom."

"Blane should have been thrilled to have her out of his home." Mairi knew she would have been.

"Aye, well, as the new head of the MacKiernan clan, Blane couldna afford to indulge any personal feelings."

Of course her aunt was right. She should have thought of that. Would have if she hadn't been so rattled by all this.

"So he negotiated a deal. Anabella would remain with the MacPhersons in payment of Artair's debt. Only fair as she was the man's widow. But, young as she was, she ended up wed to Red Dunald's oldest son, Angus. The following year, she provided Angus with an heir, Ranald. No long after, the MacPherson himself died, leaving Angus to assume responsibility for the clan. Anabella was, once again, wife of a laird."

"That may explain why she's with the MacPhersons, but not what all of them are doing here."

"The negotiations included an alliance. Once Angus became laird, he and Blane found they got on verra well. Blane's offer for young Ranald to squire here cemented the relationship. They're more family now than no. It's the same with the Maxwells. Their sons, Steafan and Alasdair, have been with us for years, and Alycie is betrothed to Caden."

Mairi leaned back in her chair. "That's entirely different. Grizel Maxwell has been your friend forever," she mumbled. *The MacPhersons are considered family?* Things had certainly changed in the time she'd been gone. Somehow she'd have to learn to deal with them.

"What do we do about the woman, this Anabella?"

Ramos spoke for the first time, drawing her attention. He left his spot by the fire and moved to her side, laying his hand protectively on her shoulder.

Though he spoke to her aunt, his eyes were on her. Gazing into them made her think of last night and she quickly turned to face her aunt, her cheeks uncomfortably warm.

"I'll deal with Anabella. I've already acknowledged to her the family resemblance." Rosalyn smiled. "Now it's only a matter of distraction. The vain woman is almost as excited to meet this Duke as my own Sallie. You'll just need to mind what you say and do." She looked pointedly at Mairi.

"I think I'd rather simply avoid her altogether." Hateful, horrible woman.

"Unfortunately I dinna see that as a possibility, lass." Rosalyn shook her head. "In fact, I'd best go check on her now, see what I can do to calm her. You two feel free to stay and finish yer drinks." She rose and left the room, leaving the door discreetly open.

Mairi turned to find Ramos stroking his chin, still staring directly at her. "What?"

"I was just thinking. If you can't avoid her, you'll need to throw her off track. You say you got on badly with this Anabella when you were here before, so perhaps you should pretend to like her now. That would be completely different from the old Mairi, wouldn't it?"

Mairi snorted. "Totally different. And so not going to happen. I'd rather do anything than try to be friendly with that bitch."

Ramos raised an eyebrow and one side of his mouth lifted in a half smile. "Anything? You could go home."

No, she couldn't.

"Fine. I'll try to be friendly."

She took one last drink from her goblet and placed it on the table with a shaking hand. It galled her to say those words, but she wasn't ready to admit her little problem to Ramos.

Guilt gnawed at her as she stood to leave the room, and she risked a quick glance at the man. He watched her closely, a frown on his face.

If he was irritated with her now, what would he be like when he learned they were stuck here?

Eleven

I'm going up to check on the lads in the far pastures today. Would you care to ride along?"

Caden's invitation had come as a surprise to Ramos, out of the blue at the finish of their morning meal. His first thought had been to refuse, to stay at Dun Ard close to Mairi, where he could protect her from Ranald MacPherson.

"Ran and Drew are coming. As you wanted to get better acquainted with the lad, this seems a good time, aye?"

It had seemed so indeed.

Sitting on his mount, staring at the small huts used by the shepherds, Ramos pulled the woolen plaid Mairi had given him tighter about himself.

"Take this." She'd pushed the bundle into his hands, her cheeks pink from having raced upstairs to her room and back again. With a quick glance as if to assure herself no one watched, she'd held the end of the plaid and expertly wrapped it around his shoulders and head. "Yer best off to wear it like this. It'll help to keep you warm and dry if the need arises. The cold will creep up on you out there, catching you unawares if you're no prepared."

She had been right. Even at the height of the sun's swing across the sky it had been a chill day. Now, nearing late afternoon, the damp air had begun to seep into his bones.

"It's fair clever what Caden's done up here, is it no?" Ran looked admiringly out over the pastures and the healthy animals grazing there. "They alternate the pastures regularly, and they have shelters scattered about all over the countryside so they're never caught out unawares. He's made life much better for the shepherds."

Ramos nodded his head in agreement, studying the young man intently. Early in their journey, he'd opened himself to his inner sight, probing for information. There was little to find. Ran was a decent sort, though easily led and, in the case of Servans, easily misled.

Talk throughout the day had frequently turned to the much-touted Duke and his desire to aid the Scots in seizing their independence. Andrew had asked one question after another, saving Ramos the need to interrogate young MacPherson himself. It had quickly become apparent that Ran knew only the barest details about the Duke's background.

Ramos sifted through the day's conversations, searching for some useful clue but finding none. Time was running out and he was frustrated at being no closer to deciphering which of his Nuadian relations would be responsible for what was about to happen here.

Ran cleared his throat nervously, pulling Ramos from his thoughts to find the young man watching him closely.

"Is there something on your mind?" It struck Ramos that the color rising in Ran's cheeks was from more than the cold.

"Aye, there is, sir. I've a question to ask, but I've no intent to insult, only a curiosity."

"There's nothing wrong with curiosity, Ran. Ask away."

"Caden tells me yer responsible for the welfare of his cousin. That you travel to yer homeland to seek a husband for the lass." The young man paused, his eyes narrowing in a scowl.

"This is true."

Ran looked off to the distance, as if gathering his thoughts before continuing. "These people are as my own family. I'd lay down my life for any one of them. While I've never met this brother who entrusted the lass to you, they are family as well."

"Yes?"

His next words came out in a rush. "What are yer intentions toward the lass, Mairi? Though I've no yet spoken to Caden of the matter, I'm no at all pleased with the idea of what you were about to do to the lass before I interrupted at the auld castle. Yer responsible for her safety, no to ruin the lass. I want to know, what were you doing at Sithean Fardach?"

Ramos had wondered if Ran had been too overcome with drink to remember the incident. Apparently not.

"I was protecting Mairi the only way I could think of at the time."

Ran snorted. "What you were doing dinna look like protecting to me."

"Exactly." Ramos stopped, waiting as Ran's expression changed to confusion. "Mairi was injured. We took shelter in what we thought was a deserted building. When the lot of you arrived, with you stomping up the stairs issuing threats, I had no idea what *your* intent might be. I did what was necessary to distract you so I could get her out of there. It worked, did it not?"

Ran nodded his head slowly.

"As to my intentions toward Mairi, they are to see her safely home. Curiosity satisfied?"

"I suppose," the young man replied slowly. "I would never have thought of that deception myself."

Ramos shrugged. "Then perhaps you've learned a new trick that will help you one day."

Ran merely continued to nod thoughtfully as Drew rejoined them to wait for Caden's return.

"It's a shame Steafan couldna be with us today, eh, Ran? Would be like the old times."

"Steafan?" The new name caught Ramos's attention.

"Aye," Ran replied. "Steafan Maxwell. If Caden is Blane's right hand, Steafan is Caden's. He's brother to Caden's betrothed."

"But no the pious pain in the—" Drew began.

"Andrew! Mind what you say. She's to be yer sister soon," Ran reprimanded.

"No if she has a say in the matter. You ken as well as I do, she's no love for Caden. More's the pity that he and Mother are too dense to see it."

"I'll hear no more of this from you. It's no matter

what we think. The betrothal is done." Ran shook his head and turned back to Ramos as if he'd not been interrupted. "Steafan and his younger brother, Alasdair, have gone home to bring their family for Saint Crispins."

In the wake of Ran's rebuke, Drew pulled his mount away to the edge of the path and conversation died as they waited for Caden.

A fine mist was falling by the time Caden finished his conversation with the old man who appeared to be in charge of the shepherds in this section.

Caden returned to their little group, bringing his horse to a halt next to Ramos. He tugged at the end of his plaid, pulling it up to protect his head as the others had already done.

"Old Kenneth says his bones are aching something fierce. He's sent the lads to gather the sheep into cover." Caden stopped and scanned the heavy clouds overhead, wiping the mist from his face before continuing. "We'd best forgo the higher pastures and get back to Dun Ard. The old man is almost never wrong about the weather. If he says snows are coming, we'll see them soon."

They turned their horses and started the long trip back, allowing the animals to pick their way down the slick, steep incline to the wider path below. The fine mist had gotten heavier, stinging the skin now where it hit.

"I hope the Duke makes it to Dun Ard before the snow sets in," Andrew mumbled, his mouth covered by the plaid.

"Dinna fash yerself, Drew. They'll be here soon enough." Ran didn't bother to turn as he spoke.

"They?" Ramos pulled even with Ran.

"Aye. The Duke and his brother. It's my guess they will be here by the morrow."

The chill that gripped Ramos had nothing to do with the rain or the cold.

Two of them? That certainly wasn't anywhere in Mairi's notes. And arriving tomorrow.

He had been wrong. Time wasn't running out. It was already gone.

Tiny sensations shot up from the base of Ramos's skull. The tingling started there and spread through his body, his Fae senses on high alert in his own version of an early warning system.

It began before he could even see the gate or the thick walls of Dun Ard and grew increasingly stronger as they drew closer. By the time they cleared the gates, he felt like a tightly wound coil, ready to spring.

"I'll take yer horse. I'm going to check on the animals and the men." Caden reached for his reins as Ramos dismounted. "I've need to make sure everything is readied for whatever this weather brings. Drew, you'll come with me."

"I'll come as well," Ran offered, following after the others.

Ramos raced up the stairs. Whatever danger it was he sensed, he knew it was behind the door his hand rested upon; it was somewhere within the great house.

And the woman whose safety was his responsibility? Mairi was somewhere in there with it.

He pushed the door open and stepped quietly inside. The scene that greeted him immediately relieved one of his concerns.

Pressed tightly against the wall, Mairi peeked around the corner into the Great Hall, completely engrossed in watching the activity unfolding before her.

She's safe.

It was an easy task for him to glide silently into place behind her. Perhaps he moved in closer than necessary, but he enjoyed the feel of her body trapped between the wall and his own, delighted in her startled gasp when he pressed his mouth to her ear. He paused just long enough to breathe in the essence of her before he spoke.

"Hello, my sweet. What have I caught you doing this time?"

To her credit, she didn't scream, but she did jump.

While he waited for her answer, he leaned closer into the curve of her, feeling not the least bit of guilt when he realized her heart hammered in her chest. The woman had already mastered stubborn. If he couldn't convince her to leave immediately, he needed her to learn caution, even if it required scaring the lesson into her.

"What does it look like I'm doing? I'm spying." She attempted to shove an elbow at him, but he'd left her no room. "Get off me," she hissed. "You're drenched."

He ignored her command as he ignored the discomfort of his cold, muddy clothing. "Spying on whom?"

"The Duke arrived about an hour ago. I wanted a look at him before I actually have to face him."

An hour ago. That fit with the warning signals his Fae senses had been sounding. He shoved her aside so that he could take her place.

"Hey!"

He spared her a quick glance, and she glared at him, her hand rubbing at her chest. He had only a quickly passing thought as to whether or not he had pressed her too tightly against the wall when his attention was fully captured by the scene in the Great Hall.

Blane spoke with two men, one of whom had his back to Ramos; the other he could see in profile. That they were Fae he had no doubt. He could recognize his own kind even without using his inner sight. There was something familiar about the profile he studied, though he was sure he had never met the man.

Ramos allowed himself only a moment of distraction. He had been so certain he would know the Fae who showed up. He needed to see the other's face, convinced he would recognize him as one of his Nuadian family.

"Please join me in my solar, yer grace. We can discuss our business in privacy there." Blane moved toward the door, his hand extended in invitation. "And yer brother, of course," he added, nodding toward the man Ramos had studied.

"But of course, *mon ami*," the Duke answered, turning to lead the way.

Ramos jerked back behind the entry, his heart pounding in his chest.

"What is it?" Mairi asked, his panic reflected in her whisper.

They'd both known the Duke could be a threat to her; Ramos just hadn't realized how great a threat until now.

He had to get her out of here.

They couldn't take the stairs; that would require passing in front of the Great Hall's entry and they'd be seen by the men coming this direction. Scanning the empty hallway, he grabbed Mairi's hand and started toward the farthest door at a run.

"Wait," she hissed, trying to pull her hand from his. "Where are we going?"

As the voices behind them drew closer, the door just ahead began to swing open.

He wouldn't risk having her caught. Not yet. He needed a moment to think—to decide what to do, to convince her to go home. Pushing open the door next to them, he grabbed her around the waist, hoisting her from her feet. He clamped a hand over her mouth, stifling her protest as he slipped into the dark, windowless room. Once he had pushed the door shut, he leaned against it.

She fought him and he tightened his hold, crushing her back to his chest, her wildly pounding heart a match for his own.

Nothing was as he had planned. Nothing had prepared him for this.

Ramos had expected to know the Duke, to recognize him as one of the Nuadian Fae. He had thought he might even learn something from the man regarding the whereabouts of his father in this time.

Unfortunately the one thing he had never even considered was the possibility that the Duke would actually *be* his father.

Panic clawed at Mairi's throat. It was just like the dream, just like the reality had been.

It was happening all over again.

The room smelled the same, the dank odor of grain and wood filtering to her. A large hand clamped over her mouth, her arms pinned to her sides, her body crushed back against her captor's. The harder she struggled, the tighter he held her.

It was exactly the same.

Any moment now, he would bind her hands, tie the gag over her mouth, and shove her down the steps, laughing as she fell to the floor. He would kneel over her, the stench of him filling her nostrils as he ran his hands over her body. She would be helpless to stop him from touching her, humiliating her when he trailed his tongue over her flesh. Only his fear of Red Dunald's wrath would keep him from doing more, but he would explain to her, in detail, what the old laird would do when he arrived. The man's rancid breath would curl over her skin as he described the indignities that awaited her.

There was no one to hear her, no one to help her.

It was exactly the same.

She struggled against the strong arms, trying to bite the fingers covering her mouth.

"Shh," her captor cautioned, urgency in his voice. "Be quiet."

In the silence of the impenetrable dark, she stilled.

The brute had never tried to silence her before. He hadn't cared if she screamed. Why should he? There was no one to come to her aid.

Mairi fought to control her emotions. She could overcome this fear, could take charge of her life. What had Jesse taught her? Embrace the calm. Center yourself.

The same words Pol had used.

As she slowed her breathing and relaxed her body, the arms that held her loosened. The hand that covered her mouth slid down to her shoulder, the thumb massaged the back of her neck. The breath that ruffled through her hair wasn't fetid and stale; it was warm and sweet.

No, this wasn't the same at all.

It wasn't happening again. It wasn't even the horrible dream that repeatedly consumed her. This time she hadn't waited for the terror to slowly ebb away, leaving her weak and trembling. She had taken charge and defeated the paralyzing panic on her own.

She knew where she was and, more important, who it was that held her.

"Ramos?"

"Shh," he warned again.

Slowly she turned in the loosened circle of his arms, laying her head against his chest as he stroked her hair almost absently. He breathed so quietly, she couldn't hear him at all, but his heart pounded under her ear, the beat strong and reassuring in the dark.

He drew back from her, his hands rising to caress either side of her face. "You have to go home, Mairi. The Duke is here and we're out of time. You must leave now."

Her stomach sank even as his thumbs feathered over her cheeks. How would she tell him she had no way to leave even if she wanted to go? She suspected he wasn't going to take the news well. After all, he wouldn't have counted on being stranded in this time when her brother had somehow convinced him to come after her.

"I canna."

His hands stilled. "Look, you agreed to be gone before the Duke showed up. Well, he's here now. You need to honor your end of the arrangement. The time for amateur hour has passed. Go home and leave this to me."

"Amateur hour?" Indignation flooded her, replacing all the guilt she'd felt just a moment before. "Maybe you've forgotten, but I'm the one who searched out all the information on these people in the first place. I'm the one who managed to find my way back here unaided. I'm the one—"

"You're the one who didn't return home," he interrupted, placing a finger over her lips. "Which is why I'm here. To see to it that you do get back. Right now. I'm through playing games with you."

"Games?" she sputtered. Like he could just lay down the law and she would obey? "I told you, I canna leave now."

His hands slid down to her shoulders. "Well, then, you'd better prepare yourself to spend some time right here, because you're not walking out of this room. At least not in the thirteenth century, you're not. So you decide. Go home now or stay in here."

To think she'd wasted her time and energy worrying about his feelings. She should have remembered that he had the mentality of a caveman so he couldn't possibly have feelings.

"Then we're going to be in this room an awfully long time, because I said *canna*, no *willna*."

"Semantics," he scoffed.

"No semantics. Faeries."

His grip on her shoulders tightened. "What are you saying?"

"They're no letting me go back. I already tried." She wished it weren't so dark; his expression must be priceless. On the other hand, perhaps it was best he couldn't see her gloating. Threaten to keep her in a storage room, would he?

"When?"

"When Anabella arrived. That's why I was up on the parapet with Sallie. But it did no good. Nothing worked."

"You're sure?" He sounded doubtful.

"I think I should know what's supposed to happen, thank you very much." She shoved at his chest, wanting some distance.

It might as well have been the cold stone wall she pushed against.

"Perverse bloody Fae," he muttered under his breath.

Instead of giving her more space, he pulled her closer, enclosing her in his embrace. The heart pounded again under her ear. At first the beat seemed faster than before, but that must have been only her imagination.

With the steady sound comforting her and strong arms soothing her, she closed her eyes and relaxed against the broad wall of muscle. Dimly she acknowledged that she shouldn't allow herself to think of Ramos as her security blanket, but it was so hard not to. Yes, he could be frustrating and horribly bossy, but when he held her like this, it was difficult to think of those things.

In fact, it was almost impossible to think of any-thing but the way his warm, smooth skin felt under her fingers. Or the way he smelled, like . . . wet, muddy horse?

Mairi shivered and pulled back from him.

"We should get out of this storage room. It's freez-ing in here and you're soaked to the skin."

"We'll wait a few more minutes. Now be quiet." He pulled her back against him, his chin resting on her head.

"You'll catch cold."

"I don't get sick."

Of course he would say that; she should have known. He was a first-rate he-man, after all.

"Maybe you dinna, but I do. And right now I feel like my fingers are turning blue." A slight exaggera-tion, perhaps, but she hadn't dealt with his kind all her life without learning a thing or two about how to manipulate their behavior.

"Bloody hell," he muttered, running his hands vig-orously up and down her arms. "You are cold. How'd you get so wet anyway?"

"Maybe having you drip all over me had something to do with it?"

With a noncommittal grunt, he turned and cracked the door open. A silent hallway greeted them. Taking her hand, Ramos pulled her along behind him.

The door to Blane's solar was closed, shielding them from the men inside. As they passed by, Mairi once again felt a sharp sting in her chest, just as she had earlier standing at the door to the Great Room. It lasted only a second this time, but she rubbed at the spot anyway.

At the foot of the stairs, Ramos released her hand. She should say something, or turn and go, but she found herself unable to do either as she stared into the blue-green clarity of his eyes. She felt herself held captive.

He lifted his palm to her face, feathering his thumb over her cheek. "I can't allow anything to happen to you. We'll figure out a way to get you home."

His hand slid from her cheek to the back of her head and he pulled her close. The lips that met hers were soft and warm, but the contact much too brief to suit her.

"Go on to your room. I'll send one of the maids to start a hot bath for you. That'll warm you up." He gave her a little shove up the stairs before he strode back down the hall toward the kitchen entrance.

Warm her up? She lifted her fingers to her lips and then to her cheek. She felt plenty warmed up every time Ramos touched her.

Mairi thought of how much she missed hot showers as she poured the pitcher of lukewarm water over her hair to rinse out the last of the soap. Changing position in the large wooden tub, she drew up her knees and leaned back against the scratchy edge, allowing the now tepid water to slosh over her.

She ran her hand over her chest, half expecting to feel something when her fingers encountered her new birthmark. There was nothing she could distinguish by touch, just the normal feel of smooth, wet flesh. It was the birthmark that had stung when she was downstairs. It wasn't the pleasant electric tingles she'd experienced when the magic surrounded her, but instead was painful, more like when, as a child, she'd fallen into a patch of nettles. Puzzled, she looked down at the skin, unblemished except for the deep, dark red shape of a rose. Another Faerie mystery. One of many, she was beginning to suspect.

Her relaxing bath time was almost at an end. The water had grown cool enough to become uncomfortable. Besides, Sallie would be back soon and the momentary bliss of silence would be broken. The teenager made more noise than anyone Mairi had ever known. Even little Rose would be a quieter roommate.

The thought of her niece gave her a chill to match that of the water. She didn't want to think about not seeing the little girl again.

She shook her head in wonder as she stood and stepped out of the tub, squeezing the water from her hair. Not so long ago she hadn't been sure which time was her home. Now that her choice to leave had been taken away, she found she had the answer. She would simply have to figure out what it was the Fae wanted of her and do it so that she could go home.

The drying cloth lay on the floor next to her. It was larger than the heavy towels in her bathroom back home, but much thinner and scratchier. She shook the cloth out and had just draped it around her body when she heard the door open.

"I thought you'd be back soon, Sallie."

"I'm hardly Sallie."

Mairi whirled around at the sound of Anabella's voice, clutching the ends of the cloth tightly in front of her as if it were her shield.

"What are you doing here?"

Anabella stood just inside the room, the door wide open behind her. "I wanted to see you again for myself. I know yer aunt Rosalyn says you're not who I think you are, but . . ." The woman narrowed her eyes as she stopped speaking.

"My aunt? I'm afraid yer mistaken, Lady MacPherson. Rosalyn is my cousin." Mairi's voice shook, but whether from the stress of the moment or the cold air whipping into the room she wasn't sure.

"So you say," the woman murmured, moving slowly toward where Mairi stood. "And yet . . ." She tilted her head and studied Mairi.

The air eddied around Mairi's feet and flowed up her wet legs, raising a trail of goose bumps on her skin. "Do you think we might finish this conversation another time?" She shivered and clasped the drying cloth tighter around her.

"I knew it," Anabella hissed, pointing down at Mairi's feet. "I was right," she screamed. "It *is* you."

Mairi glanced down and her stomach dropped. There on her toe was the emerald ring Cate had given her so long ago. The ring she wore now out of habit and friendship. The same ring she had originally worn simply to irritate this very woman.

From Anabella's bloodcurdling shrieks, it seemed that the ring was still doing its job.

Ramos pulled back his damp hair, securing it with a strip of leather before sitting down in front of the fireplace. A wet wool smell steamed from the clothing he'd worn today, now freshly washed and draped over the chair he'd placed close to the fire. He doubted any of it would be dry by morning.

He stretched his long, breeches-clad legs, bringing his bare feet closer to the fire. Ignoring the dank chill of his room, he rested his head against the back of the hard chair and let his mind wander.

Down the dark hallway to the last room on the left. Would Mairi have completed her bath, too? Or would she even now be finishing up in the large wooden tub, a match to the one sitting in the center of his room? His imagination painted a vivid picture of her, water sheeting down her body as she rose, caressing her curves as he wanted to. Droplets of water clinging to her incredibly long legs—legs he could almost feel wrapped around him.

"No."

Abruptly he leaned forward, head in his hands, elbows propped on his knees. He had to stop this mental journey before it went any farther.

Being around Mairi seriously messed with his mind. He'd never experienced this type of lust for a woman. All-consuming lust that seemed to take over his actions as well as his good sense.

But lust was all it was, and control it he would. Indulging his desires with this woman wasn't in the cards. Besides, whatever attraction they felt would fade. Once she returned to her home, her family, she'd forget all about him. He was nothing more than her appointed Guardian. Sworn to protect her.

The day he'd accepted the offer to become a Guardian was the day he'd given up the right to thoughts of a life with someone like Mairi. On that day he'd pledged himself to one goal and one goal only. He had wanted nothing more than to hunt down and eliminate every Nuadian Fae he could find, starting with Reynard Servans.

Even if that weren't the case, what kind of Guardian wouldn't realize that issues far more important than his own personal desires came first. Issues like how he would get Mairi home and how he would keep her safe with his father in the keep.

His father.

Reynard Servans.

The man who had betrayed his trust, lied to him for twenty-eight years and deceived him into doing untold damage to the World of Mortals. His father was responsible for thousands of deaths and centuries of chaos in the Mortal World, all without the slightest thought to those around him.

Reynard Servans was within these very walls.

Ramos rubbed his temples in a futile attempt to drive away the agony he always felt when thinking of his father.

Agony? No. Guilt.

Guilt for turning a blind eye to what he should have seen, should have felt, should have known.

On the day he walked through the Faerie Portal, Ramos had devoted himself to doing everything in his power to atone for his father's sins. And for his own. He had dreamed of what he would do if he were ever able to confront his father again.

Now that confrontation was imminent.

"And my hands are tied," he muttered. He couldn't risk challenging Reynard—at least not until he had Mairi safely out of here. As her Guardian, she was his priority, his primary responsibility.

The first shriek brought him out of his ruminations, out of his chair. By the second, he'd pulled his shirt over his head and was racing down the hallway, following the sound.

To the last door on the left.

It felt as though everything happened at once.

The turmoil inundated Mairi's senses, paralyzing her. Bodies crowded through the open doorway, drawn by Anabella's screams. Sallie stood next to the bed, her eyes wide, mirroring the expression worn by the maids. Ran, at his mother's side, tried to quiet the woman to no avail.

Relief filled Mairi at the sight of Ramos framed in the doorway like some dark avenging angel. His hair was wet, his shirt askew and his feet bare. He'd never looked better to her.

"What the bloody hell is going on?" He shouted to be heard over the noise in the room, pushing his way past the Duke and his brother, who both stood just inside the entry.

Ramos gripped her shoulders when he reached her, the warmth of his hands releasing her from the shock that had held her frozen in place.

"Out," he bellowed, barely sparing a glance to the clamor behind him. "Everyone out of here."

Anabella lunged for her, grabbing at the drying cloth as Mairi tried to dodge the woman's outswept hand. Only Ramos's quick intervention saved her from enormous embarrassment. She grappled to rearrange the cloth, which had slipped dangerously low.

When she looked up at Ramos, the eyes that met

hers were stormy, reminding her once again of the photograph on her bulletin board back home.

He reached past Sallie, pulled a blanket from the bed and wrapped it around Mairi's body before turning to face the growing throng. "Get that woman out of here or I will."

"Mother," Ran began, gently pulling at his mother's shoulders.

"Dinna 'Mother' me, lad. I'm no leaving," Anabella yelled. "No now that I have my proof."

"And what proof might that be?" Blane's voice cut through the noise.

A peek over Ramos's shoulder showed Mairi several other people had squeezed into the room. She lowered her head, not wanting to see the servants, her cousins, and even the Duke and his brother, all staring at her.

"There. On her foot," Anabella accused. "The jewel Connor's heathen gave to her. She wears it still."

How stupid. Now, because of her carelessness, they would both be exposed, with the Duke looking on. There was no excuse for it, no way to explain . . .

Ramos's calm voice interrupted her thoughts. "I beg your pardon? That ring?" He pointed to her toe.

"Aye, the very one given her by that filthy heathen, right here in my very own home."

"I'm afraid you're mistaken, my good woman. As Navarro family tradition dictates, I myself put that very ring on Mairi's foot the day she was declared my ward. It will remain there until she marries and is no longer under my protection."

Mairi leaned her head against his back and closed

her eyes, not daring to look over his shoulder now, not with that inventive piece of fiction hanging in the air.

"I dinna believe you."

"I don't particularly care what you believe, Lady MacPherson. Now, if you'd all be so kind, I must insist that everyone leave my ward's room."

The words rumbled in his body, their vibrations comforting against Mairi's cheek, lulling her so that she almost missed Blane's parting words.

"There's an uncanny resemblance, to be sure, Anabella, but she's no our Mairi. I wish it were true, but it's no. Our Mairi is lost to us, many years gone past."

"But I was so certain." The woman's voice faltered to a stop.

"Would our Mairi stand meekly behind the shoulder of some lad and allow you to attack her that way? I dinna think so. No, back in the day, it would have taken the lot of us to pull our own Mairi off you."

"I suppose yer right. I hadna even thought of that. Mairi was never one to shirk a fight. More likely to seek one out, in fact."

"Aye, that she was," Blane agreed. "Our own Mairi was a fearless, independent lass, no like this one."

The words floated through the door to Mairi, assaulting her like a slap of cold water as Ramos walked her over to her bed. He assisted her off her feet and left detailed instructions for Sallie to see to her comfort, but she barely noticed.

Her cousin was correct. The Mairi he had known would never have huddled behind some man's back, waiting for him to defend her. That Mairi would have handled the situation without help.

Unfortunately that Mairi had long ago turned into something very different.

Fearless and independent? They wouldn't think that if they'd seen her when Cody and Cass had come to her rescue, huddled in the corner of the dark little storeroom downstairs, crying like a lost lamb awaiting its slaughter.

No, Blane was right. She wasn't that Mairi anymore.

The very walls closed in on him.

Leaving Mairi in Sallie's care, Ramos strode the length of the dark hallway, past his room and down the narrow stone steps. The need to escape was strong, but he maintained an even stride down the wide hallway to the great entrance and out into the cold, wet night.

Once there, he moved to the far edge of the landing, grasping the railing with shaking hands. He drew great draughts of the cold, damp air into his lungs, waiting for the queasy, claustrophobic feeling to pass.

When he'd raced into Mairi's room, the first face he'd seen had been his father's. He'd brushed past Reynard, their shoulders actually touching as he rushed to get to Mairi's side. To shield her from the man his friend Sarah had called *pure evil*.

His father.

He'd looked into Reynard's eyes and seen . . . nothing. His own father.

"What the bloody hell did I expect?" He muttered. After all, how could his father know him? He wouldn't even be born for another six centuries.

No, he couldn't blame Reynard's lack of recognition for the weight on his soul or for the curdling in his stomach. It was the fact that he'd seen that empty look before. It was the same void he'd seen in the woods of Thistle Down Manor the day his father had ordered the woman under his compulsion to fire her weapon.

There had been nothing in those eyes that day, either, and whether the bullet was aimed at his enemy or his son had made no difference to him.

Ramos backed up against the hard stone wall of the castle and allowed the cold rain to wash over him, taking with it his gut-twisting need to retch.

If only it could as easily wash away the pain in his heart.

Twelve

That was interesting." Reynard smiled as he poured himself a drink from the decanter on the table.

"Yes it was," Wyn agreed. One of the best performances he'd seen in quite some time.

"Did you see the girl's chest?"

"I could hardly miss it. Most impressive." Wyn took the cup Reynard offered him. "Though I wouldn't have minded seeing a bit more." He'd actually intended to see more when he'd mind-pushed the screamer to snatch the drying cloth away. Too bad the girl's guardian had been there to intercede.

"Keep your mind on business, Wyn. I was referring to the mark there. Did you see it? I think we may have stumbled onto the real thing this time."

"Perhaps." More likely another false trail. How many times had Rey dragged him along, chasing after some rumor, some legend, some worthless Mortal superstition? "But I thought the boy said the mark was to be found on the back."

"So he did. Perhaps he was mistaken about that."

Wyn didn't respond. He needed to keep his irritation in check. If the boy was mistaken about the location of the Fae mark, what else might he be mistaken about? Here they were once again in the middle of nowhere, pursuing some local legend, all because of Reynard's obsession to find a female descendant of their people.

Wyn tipped back his head and drained the goblet, though it would do nothing to settle the feeling of unease that had crept over him in the girl's room. Not even the strongest of Mortal spirits would have any effect on him. What he wouldn't give for one small glass of Faerie nectar. It had been so very long.

"Still"—Reynard stroked his chin thoughtfully— "it is the little redhead who's supposed to have the gift."

Wyn chuckled. "I'd have thought you'd had your fill of redheads by now."

Reynard sneered. "Hardly. Besides, this is business, not pleasure."

"No reason we shouldn't enjoy ourselves." Rey's foolhardy plan was unlikely to work anyway. And from what he'd seen on display of that blond beauty down the hall, it looked like there might be some enjoyment to be had in this outpost of humanity, after all.

"That's your problem, Wyn. You waste your energies on the pursuit of pleasure whereas I channel my energies into purpose and planning. That's why I'm in command and you're merely my second." Reynard removed his jacket and tossed it to the foot of the bed. "Having either female should be easy enough.

I'll be patient and make my decision when the time is right."

"Having either female easy? I shouldn't think Adira would be at all pleased to hear you say those words. What would your own dear redhead think of your latest plan?" He knew the answer to that question without having to ask. The vindictive bitch would be furious if she knew what was going on here.

"Please, my dear Wyn." Reynard arranged himself on the bed, one foot propped atop the other, arms behind his head. "When have you ever known me to be concerned about what anyone thinks? Least of all my fair courtesan."

True. Wyn rose from his chair and sauntered to the door. "On that note, *your grace*, I'll take my leave of you." He bowed low on his way out, knowing Reynard would never notice the sarcasm in his action. The Fae wasn't patient; he was oblivious. Reynard had grown so full of himself over the centuries, he actually expected to be treated as royalty.

Wyn, on the other hand, understood patience. He'd learned its cruel lessons in the time since he'd left the Faerie Realm. He wasn't second in command because of misdirected energies; he was second because he chose that position. He would be patient, too. Like Reynard, when the time was right, he'd be making his own decision because, unlike Reynard, Wyn had no desire to conquer the Realm of Faerie, to rule it. He only wanted the right to go home. And what was he willing to do, to sacrifice to gain that right?

He shook his head, pausing at the entry to his room, taking one last look down the hallway to where the two women in question were even now sleeping.

As he closed the door, he noted with satisfaction the fire, the fresh decanter on the table and the turned-down bedcovers. There were advantages to his station. All the benefits bestowed upon the Duke, with none of the responsibility. How fortunate for him Reynard was so ambitious.

Still, this pittance was no match for what he'd lost.

No match for what he might stand to regain if there actually were some truth to this particular family legend.

As he lowered his body into the chair by the fire, he acknowledged that, unlike so many times in the past, there was something unusual about this family, some energy he could sense.

He leaned his head against the back of his seat, staring into the flames. Yes, this whole experience *felt* different.

Perhaps it was time he did a little investigating on his own.

Thirteen

The minute Mairi seated herself at the great table, she knew it was going to be a long and trying session.

"I dinna expect to see you at main meal today." Sallie's opening shot was innocent, yet just loud enough to garner the attention of those present.

"And why is that?" Mairi would have preferred to bite off her own tongue rather than hand over the perfect opening to that spoiled brat. But she didn't. She fell right into the trap.

"Weel . . ." The girl opened her eyes wide and looked knowingly around the table. "I wouldna have the courage to show my face if I'd made a spectacle of myself the way you did yestereve." Sallie lifted her goblet, a sly smile lighting her face as she looked over the rim. "Baring yer great body for all the world to see."

"Sallie," Blane reprimanded sharply. "What happened yestereve was no fault of Mairi's."

"And you'll apologize immediately," her mother added.

"My apologies, Cousin Mairi."

The insincerity of the quick apology matched the young woman's expression.

Mairi's mouth dropped open. She felt it happen and snapped it shut. The red that flooded her face had as much to do with fury as humiliation. But before she could respond, a sharp blow to her ankle diverted her attention.

Ramos's warning kick went unnoticed by any but her, as did the laughter he hid by lifting his goblet to his mouth for a drink of wine. When he started to cough, she pounded his back a bit harder than necessary, though he appeared not to notice.

"Blane is right, Sallie." Anabella cast a sympathetic glance toward Mairi. "I'm responsible for poor Mairi's embarrassment. I'm no sure what came over me to make me behave so badly, but I am sorry for it." She smiled brightly before leaning in to pat Blane's hand. "As you said, dear Blane, I only have to pay attention to see how verra different this one is from our Mairi. I canna imagine her sitting here quietly through such as this. Unlike our Mairi, this lass has been raised to be a lady."

Pity from Anabella. It couldn't possibly get any worse than this.

Mairi tried to disappear into her seat as an awkward silence gradually gave way to normal conversation. Ramos attempted small talk, but she ignored him. When his fingers feathered over her arm, she jerked away from his touch without looking at him, angry with him for not defending her. Angry with herself for expecting him to do so.

The stinging pain in her chest, when it began, was

small and might have gone unnoticed had she been engaged in conversation. Mairi glanced up from her meal to find the Duke studying her intently.

When he spoke, everyone at the table gave him their undivided attention. "My brother and I are extremely grateful for the kind hospitality you've extended us. During our time in Edinburgh, Ran told us so much about you, we almost felt as if we knew you. Isn't that so, Wyn?"

The Duke's brother nodded and lifted his cup in a toast to all his dining companions.

"Thank you, yer grace," Blane acknowledged.

"It's an honor to have you in our home," Drew quickly added, adoration shining in his eyes.

The Duke smiled indulgently at the young man before turning his gaze back to Mairi. "Ran told us many family stories, but one in particular we found quite entertaining. I wonder, Laird MacKiernan, if I might impose upon you to indulge my curiosity about the Faerie legend?"

Next to Mairi, Ramos tensed. Though there was no outward indication of it, she felt it all the same. It was as if the air between them grew suddenly heavy.

"I'd be the one to answer those questions, yer grace."

"Sallie," both Blane and Rosalyn admonished at the same time.

"I *am* the only one at this table—other than my mother, of course—who carries the blessing, am I no?" She smiled at the Duke and touched a hand artfully to her hair. "What would you like to know?"

"So it's true? Your family claims to descend from the fabled Fae?"

"Aye. As a female descendant of the Fae, I bear their mark myself."

"Their mark? I'm afraid I don't understand, *ma fille chérie.*" The Duke looked first to his brother and then around the table.

Sallie's laughter trilled. "A birthmark. I have the mark of my Fae ancestor on my back."

Reynard Servans sipped from his goblet before glancing around the table. "Do all *les belles dames . . .*" He smiled apologetically. "Please, pardon my lapse. Do all the lovely ladies here bear such a mark?"

"No!" Caden's fiancée blurted out, her face turning a bright crimson as she nervously fingered the ornate cross she wore about her neck.

"Alycie speaks the truth," Sallie added, irritation fleeting across her delicate features as she glanced at the girl. It was gone before she faced the Duke. "Neither she nor Lady MacPherson are related by blood."

Mairi kept her eyes on the trencher in front of her, slowly eating the food, which had lost all flavor. Her little cousin prattled on, flirting with the Duke, a person who was so awful his presence rattled even a man like Ramos.

A covert glance at the Duke and his brother told her nothing. They looked perfectly innocent, like any other highborn gentlemen of their time. Both, in fact, were extremely handsome men, with long blond hair pulled back and tied at the neck. The Duke was perhaps a bit shorter than his brother, but both men had equally elegant features and manners.

The annoying sting intensified and she fought the urge to rub the spot. She looked up from her food to find the Duke staring at her once more.

"And you, mademoiselle? You are related by blood, are you not?"

From the corner of her eye, she saw Ramos's hand freeze as he reached for the meat in his trencher.

"I am, yer grace."

"But Mairi disna bear the mark, nor does she have the power of the blessing," Sallie interrupted.

The Duke continued to watch her. "This is true?"

"It is, your grace. I was not born with the gifts or with the mark."

"And no with any sort of prospects, either," Sallie added.

"Sallie," her mother reprimanded sharply. "I'll thank you to mind yer tongue, lass."

"We all ken the truth of it, Mother. If she'd any prospects at home, her guardian would no have to drag her all the way to Spain to find someone daft enough to wed her."

Next to Mairi, Ramos at last lifted a piece of meat to his mouth, awkwardly bumping his goblet in the process. The cup tilted sideways and tumbled, splashing spiced wine down Mairi's front and into her lap.

She gasped as the cold liquid hit her.

"Oh no," he said. "How unforgivably clumsy of me. I am so sorry. Now you'll have to leave us to tidy yourself up."

"It's no a problem. Dinna worry yerself about it," she mumbled quickly, hoping to avoid becoming the center of unwanted attention yet again.

"No, my dear, as your Guardian, I must be firm about this. You'll return to your room at once." He stood, one hand on the back of her chair, the other gently grasping her upper arm, pulling her up.

How dare he think he could send her from the table like a child.

"It's of no consequence, Mairi," Blane spoke up. "I believe we've all finished here, aye? Perhaps the gentlemen would care to join me in my solar?"

The ladies rose, murmuring of adjourning to Rosalyn's solar. Sallie stopped on her way out, an obviously feigned look of pity on her lovely face.

"Too bad you'll have to miss the remainder of the evening. We are to finish details for the feast. If only you'd inherited the Fae grace of yer MacKiernan blood instead of that great clumsy body, eh?"

Anabella waited for the girl, watching closely, so Mairi clenched her mouth shut, saying nothing.

Sallie smiled sweetly and walked out.

"Shall I accompany you upstairs?" Ramos leaned close, interrupting the thoughts of what she'd like to do to her little cousin.

"That willna be at all necessary," she snapped.

"Good. Then I'll join the other men. I expect you to go straight to your room."

If the others weren't passing by at the moment, she'd tell him exactly what he could do with those expectations of his.

Ramos took one last look over his shoulder before walking out of the room. Mairi had risen from her seat and was headed toward the door.

If looks could kill . . .

Her expression could easily serve as early warning for major thunderstorms.

So be it. His task wasn't to become her favorite

person, only to keep her safe until he could get her home.

Perhaps the dark, wet stain covering her dress should evoke some guilt, but it didn't. He'd hated to embarrass her, to draw more attention to her, but it was the best he could do on short notice. This way, she'd be in her room. Safe. That, after all, was his primary concern.

He nodded absently to himself as he entered Blane's solar. Yes, it was for the best.

The way Sallie was pushing her this evening, anything might happen. One outburst was all it would take to have the MacPherson woman up in arms again. It was only Mairi's docile behavior that had finally convinced the woman she was mistaken about Mairi's identity.

And he didn't for one minute believe docility was inherent in Mairi's nature. No, she was a woman filled with barely checked emotion. Fire. Passion. He had seen it in her eyes, tasted it on her lips. Under other circumstances, he would already have . . .

"Whisky?"

Ramos started guiltily, turning his attention to Caden. "Pardon?"

"Did you want some whisky or no, man?" Caden smiled and glanced toward the door. "Yer mind is above stairs, is it no?"

Ramos frowned as he reached for the glass, ignoring the younger man's chuckle.

"Navarro, is it?"

A chill raced down Ramos's spine at the sound of the all-too-familiar accented voice. He could handle this. This man was no different from any other lowlife he'd come in contact with. Except, of course, that around six and a half centuries from now this particular lowlife would be his father.

"Yes, your grace?" He turned and forced the words past frozen lips, covering his hesitation with a quick drink.

Even up close, Reynard Servans was unchanged. Or rather, Ramos reminded himself, this man would change very little over the next several centuries.

"Laird MacKiernan tells us your home is in Spain?"

Reynard tilted his head as he spoke in a move Ramos recognized well. His father wasn't making casual small talk. He was seeking something specific from this conversation. The realization sharpened Ramos's senses, allowing him to push away any shreds of emotional reaction he might have had to the man. He needed to be on his toes. This was the enemy.

"It is."

"You'll forgive my presumption, but have we met before? There is something . . . familiar about you."

"We have not met in the past." Ramos danced on the fine edge of truth. "Unless you've spent time in Spain. Or perhaps while I was at university in London?"

Reynard pursed his lips. "No. And yet . . ."

Ramos resisted the urge to fidget under Reynard's scrutiny. He would not be made to feel like the frightened seven-year-old who had gone to live with this formidable man, the boy who had spent his youth so desperately seeking his father's rarely given approval.

"So it's true you're taking the MacKiernan woman to Spain to arrange a suitable marriage for her?"

Ramos acknowledged the arrival of Wyn Servans with a nod of his head. He met that man's eyes as he answered his question. "That is correct, your lordship."

The Duke's brother held up a hand. "Just Wyn." He chuckled. "As a younger son, I hold no titles."

"And what about you, Navarro?" Reynard's eyes scanned the room as he spoke, resting once again on Ramos. "Were you chosen as Mademoiselle MacKiernan's guardian based on your family connections?"

"Like Wyn, your grace, I hold no titles. Although"—he smiled when the thought struck him—"my father is a duke. As eldest son, I suppose that one day I will inherit the title."

"*Lord* Navarro." Caden slapped him on the back as he joined them. "Son of a duke. You should have corrected us."

"No need. As I've said before, Ramos will do just fine." Ramos shook his head, his attention momentarily distracted as Reynard wandered away to join another group and launch into a discussion about King Edward's policies toward France and Scotland.

Clearly he had just overlooked something important.

His father was nothing if not relentless. Once in pursuit of a goal, the Reynard Servans he had grown up with wouldn't stop until he reached it. That must mean that whatever information he had sought from Ramos he had found.

Lifting the cup to his lips, Ramos frowned as he watched the Duke. What could Reynard possibly have wanted to know?

More important, what had he told the man?

* * *

The relentless rain had stopped for the moment, easing into a light mist.

Mairi leaned against the door she had passed through only moments before, breathing in great gulps of the cold, wet air.

Escape to the balcony had been the only option she could think of when she'd come this way. She hadn't even cared if it was pouring rain. After the horrible meal she'd just endured, she needed peace and quiet or she would very likely wring her little cousin's scrawny neck.

And Ramos? She wouldn't mind having a go at his neck while she was at it.

Arrogant, overbearing bastard.

Though her room would be quiet without Sallie there, it was the last place she wanted to be now. Send her to her room, would he? Well, she'd just see about that.

The cold wind whipped around her, molding the stained, wet bodice to her chest. She did her best to ignore it as she made her way to the far end of the balcony, leaning out over the thick wall as if the air would be fresher there.

The moisture carried on the stiff breeze stung her face, but she welcomed it. Concentrating on the physical sensation cleared her mind.

Once she calmed, she was able to view the situation more objectively. She was nearing her breaking point with Sallie and that could be very bad. Out here, in the quiet, it was easy to understand why Ramos had insisted she leave the group.

He'd been right, of course. And that, more than anything, was what frustrated her at the moment.

No, that wasn't quite true. If nothing else, Mairi had always tried to be honest with herself, and she could do no less now.

She turned, leaned against the balcony wall, and slid to the ground, drawing her knees up with her arms around them. Sighing, she dropped her head to her arms.

Her frustrations with Ramos went much deeper than simply his being right all the time. There was something about him that got to the very core of her, something she couldn't begin to pretend to understand.

She could feel her world brighten when he entered a room, like some sort of warming cloak laid about her shoulders. She felt his mood changes as if they were her own. When she was near him, she could barely keep herself from touching him, as if she needed the physical contact like she needed her next breath.

And when he touched her, she wanted . . .

Her breath caught and her face flamed. *Want.* That described exactly the root of her frustrations with Ramos. He made her feel things she'd never felt before, want things she'd never wanted before. Somewhere along the way, she was going to have to deal with all these troublesome emotions.

But not right now.

For now, she was too busy dealing with the one other emotion she had regarding Ramos.

Guilt.

He gave her friendship and protection, and what had she done for him?

Stranded him in the thirteenth century, that's what. Stuck there until she could figure out what it was her

Faerie ancestors wanted her to do so that she could return them both to their own time.

She groaned and lifted her head, only to find herself the object of intense scrutiny. The Duke's brother leaned against the door, quietly watching her.

"Do you make a habit of spying on women, yer grace?"

A look of surprise flitted across his face, quickly masked. Apparently he wasn't used to being called to task for his actions, not even the rude ones.

"Please call me Wyn, my dear." He walked forward slowly. "I apologize for intruding on your privacy. I had only thought to escape the incessant talk of the coming war when I stepped through the door. Too late, I saw you sitting here and realized the terrace was already occupied."

"Should you no have thought leaving me alone the polite thing to do?"

He smiled down at her before lithely hoisting himself up to sit on the wall behind her, his own knees drawn up as he balanced there.

She glanced up to see him shrug before he answered, the smile still on his lips.

"If you'll forgive my being so forward, my dear, you appeared to be in some distress. I couldn't very well walk away and leave you like that."

"So instead you chose to stand there, silently watching me?"

"I've never been particularly good at dealing with the ladies."

"I find that hard to believe." From his attitude and looks, it was much more likely that this man knew exactly how to deal with the ladies.

The musical notes of his laughter lilted through the air. "Nevertheless, my dear, what could possibly torment you enough to drive you out here on a day such as this?"

Mairi rose to her feet, making a great show of dusting herself off as she stalled for time. It wasn't as if Wyn Servans were the type of person she would actually confide in. She squared her shoulders and readied herself to turn and tell him exactly that when the door opened once again.

Who could have imagined she'd actually be happy to see Sallie?

"I went up to my room, but you were no to be found," the girl said accusingly.

Perhaps *happy* was too strong a word. Mairi waited, hoping there wouldn't be another scene in front of the Duke's brother.

"'Tis just as weel. We have need to talk, you and I, Cousin, so it's good I've found you here alone."

"Alone? I rather think his being here counts as something, dinna you?" Mairi gestured toward the low wall behind her. From the rustle of sound, she assumed Wyn had stood.

"Who?" Sallie put her hands on her hips and strode directly over to stand in front of her cousin.

"*Who?*" What was wrong with the girl now? Mairi turned and suddenly felt as if the air had been squeezed from her lungs.

The wall behind her was empty.

She surged to the rail and leaned over, peering through the gloom, searching.

Nothing.

"I dinna understand," she whispered to herself.

They were on the second level. It would be over a full story's drop to the ground. If he'd jumped . . . She caught herself and stopped. Why on earth would he do something like that?

"It disna matter, Mairi, what you meant. I dinna care. There's none here but you and me now."

Mairi turned to find her cousin glaring at her through narrowed eyes. "What?"

"I watched yer performance at dinner, playing the modest lass. I'm telling you now, it willna work."

"What are you talking about?"

"You ken verra weel what I'm speaking about." Sallie paced back and forth. "The pink cheeks and the eyes cast down to the table—you acted the perfect wee maiden. But I'm warning you now, dinna you even think of going after the Duke. Or anyone else at that table. I've plans of my own for him."

It took every bit of Mairi's self-control to keep from grabbing the silly girl and shaking her. The only plans she had for that man were the ones to prevent his causing Sallie's death.

"If my face was red in there, it was because I was embarrassed by yer hateful remarks. But you can relax. I've no the slightest bit of romantic interest in that Duke."

"It's difficult to believe yer no trying to entice a man like him." Sallie came to a stop in front of her, hands back on her hips.

"Well, I'm no interested in him. And you, of all people, should know better than to chase a man simply for his position. For all yer talk of yer Fae heritage, yer completely ignoring the importance of the legacy, the whole reason for that birthmark on yer back. It's there because of the Fae Prince's blessing. The blessing that insures his female descendants the right to choose their own true love. The blessing that promises dire consequences to any who harm those female descendants or keep them from choosing the man they want. You should settle for nothing less than finding yer own true love."

Sallie glanced away, her pearly teeth worrying at her bottom lip.

Mairi had to make her understand. "Yet here you are, chasing after some man for no reason other than he has a title. Why on earth would you do something like that?" If only Sallie could be convinced to give up this idea of pursuing the Duke. Maybe that would change things enough to allow the magic to work.

A little shiver passed through Mairi as she remembered Pol's warning about the importance of her not changing the outcome of history. Still, the Fae had stranded her here for some reason. Perhaps this was it.

"It's no what you think. I've no desire to waste my life like my mother." Sallie's words were barely above a whisper, her eyes filled with tears when she faced Mairi again. "She waited more than thirty years for her true love to declare himself. She spent her youth raising her brothers' children. I dinna want that future. I'll no wait my youth away for the right man to come asking for my hand. I'm no so patient as all that."

"But Rosalyn was so happy with yer father. She told me those were the best years of her life."

"Aye, they may have been so. But those following

his death must have been the worst. You dinna see her then, her suffering. I remember it weel. I've no intent to watch my life pass me by as she did."

"Yer a beautiful young woman, Sallie. I canna imagine that your true love will take so long to find you."

"It's no the finding that's the problem. And I can promise you, looks have nothing to do with it. My mother was more than beautiful, tall and elegant with fine hair like the sunrise. In her youth, she would have looked verra much like you do now."

"Really? I seem to recall yer comparing me to a great cow."

The girl sniffled loudly before lifting her chin in defiance. "Aye, weel, it's easier to compete with a cow than a great beauty, is it no? I spent my youth hearing stories of my cousin Mairi—the one who was murdered here, mind you. About what a free-spirited beauty she was and how my mother had loved her as a daughter. Stories about how much my mother missed the lass. I could close my eyes and see Mairi, I'd had her described so many times and in such great detail. I felt as if I knew her. And I hated her with a passion. Have you any idea what it's like to compete with a ghost?"

Her cousin was jealous? Of her?

"Then I wake one morning to find a new Mairi has come to stay. A Mairi my mother canna stop talking about, canna keep from touching when she enters a room. A woman who looks so like her namesake, it's as if that first Mairi has returned to haunt me in truth. To compete for the attention of those I hold dear. First to steal my own mother and then to win the man I've decided to claim."

"There is no a competition between us for any-thing, Sallie. Though I can honestly say Rosalyn is very special to me, I could never mean as much to her as you do—we both ken the truth of that. And that's as it should be. I only want both of you to be happy. As for the Duke, I have no desire to marry that man. None."

"I would if I were you. He's handsome and he's ti-tled. I'd no want to be dragged off to Spain to have someone find a husband for me. A husband no of my own choosing. Are you no terrified of who yer guardian plans to give you to?" Sallie shook her head, her eyes large.

"I dinna have any worries about my guardian mar-rying me off to someone horrible." That much was true. "I have complete faith in him. I'd go anywhere and do anything that Ramos asked of me."

"Then why didn't you go to your room like I told you to?"

Mairi turned sharply at the sound of his voice. He stood just inside the door, an angry scowl on his face. How did he constantly manage to sneak up on her like that?

"Dinna be vexed with Mairi," Sallie interjected. "It's my fault she's out here. I asked her to come with me. But we'll go up to our room now, as you wish."

The look on Ramos's face conveyed his utter lack of belief, but he said nothing as Sallie grabbed Mairi's hand and pulled her past him into the empty hallway.

The evening had been full of surprises.

From the bottom stair, Mairi took one last look over her shoulder. Ramos watched their retreat, a scowl still lining his handsome features.

She needed to tell him about her experience with Wyn Servans, about what she'd seen tonight, but now, with Sallie dragging her to their shared room, was not the time. She just hoped that when the opportunity did present itself, his irritation would have passed.

If not? Well, she'd just have to see what she could do to change that.

Fourteen

Ramos pulled his shirt over his head and tossed it to the floor before sitting to pull off his boots. The first boot dangled loosely in his hands as he stared into the fire, lost in thought.

He'd always been a man of strong emotion, but he'd learned early the importance of controlling those emotions, of never allowing anyone access to his soft underbelly. Unfortunately burying his feelings deeply didn't mean he didn't have them.

And he wasn't at all pleased with the particular emotion he wrestled now. He tossed the boot to the floor and began to unlace the second one.

Earlier this evening, as he'd tried to determine what Reynard was up to, he'd suddenly realized Wyn Servans was no longer in the room. He'd hurried upstairs to check on Mairi only to find her chamber empty.

For the briefest second, an emotion very like fear had gripped him, gnawing at his gut.

"I am a Guardian. I fear nothing," he said aloud,

tugging off the second boot and throwing it to the floor.

The feeling had grown, an emptiness clawing at his stomach interfering with his ability to breathe, as he peered into Rosalyn's solar, still finding no sign of Mairi. Not until he stepped out onto the balcony and saw her safe did the feeling change, morphing into something familiar and comfortable.

Anger.

But even the anger had gradually faded until now he was left to grapple with the foreign, uneasy emotion he chose not to name. He had to get her out of his thoughts. She was under his protection, nothing more.

He jerked the leather tie from his hair as he stood. The remainder of his clothing joined his boots in a pile before he crossed to the bed and climbed in.

Without thought, his hand slid up and under his pillow. A grim smile played briefly across his lips as he realized what he did and consciously brought his hand to rest on his chest. The habit he'd developed as a child clung to him still, though he no longer needed the little dagger he'd slept with then. His body was weapon enough now.

When he'd first gone to live in his father's chateau, he'd believed his life would be a true Faerie tale. It hadn't taken long for him to realize the life of a real Fae, particularly a Nuadian Fae, had a dark, twisted side.

He'd had the best tutors and schools, the most expensive clothing. But his free time had been spent in what Reynard had called The Training. His father had personally seen to shaping his son's mind and body to create the perfect weapon to fight their enemy, the

Fae. The same Fae who had driven them from their rightful homes, who'd supposedly hunted them with no thought other than the complete annihilation of the Nuadians and the destruction of the Mortal World.

Indoctrination, he now realized. Brainwashing.

His father had never demonstrated affection of any kind, though Ramos had sought it, finally settling for approval when it was all there was to be had.

To show emotion was to show weakness. Ramos had learned that lesson early. He shared his feelings with no one.

The days had been hard, but the nights . . . the nights were terrifying. As Reynard's "favorite," Ramos was envied by many. Many who wanted him dead. Or so his father had told him.

Reynard had driven him to strengthen his body to defend himself against those who would come after him. Cowards who would come under cover of dark. Each night his father would caution him to sleep lightly. To be prepared.

Night after night, he had lain awake waiting, waiting for someone to come into his room, until at last exhaustion would overtake his body.

Until the day his father taught him to fight with weapons, that is. When he'd first wrapped his hand around the hilt of the little dagger, he had known his life would be different. He'd hidden it in his clothing, claimed it as his own and slept with it every night as most children might a stuffed animal.

He hadn't been afraid any longer.

Why think of these things now?

The memories he'd all but driven from his mind

assaulted him. He clamped his eyes shut and forced the memories from his thoughts, but they left in their wake a disturbing sense of unease.

This nagging disquiet prickling at the back of his mind was no more than lack of sleep and frustration. Once he determined what needed to be done to satisfy the Faerie magic that kept Mairi here, he could send her home and be free of this turmoil.

Tomorrow he would speak to her, quiz her on what exactly she had said as she'd invoked the magic to travel back through time. He should have thought of it earlier. Her words at the moment the magic built, when the power was greatest, would hold the key. It was one of the things the Fae did best, using your own words to ensnare you, catching you up like a helpless gnat in their spiderweb of plans.

Closing his eyes, he counted on the discipline of his training to replace his agitation with the welcome void of sleep. Instead the doors of his subconscious mind opened, to visions of Mairi.

He fought them, pushing them back, vainly trying to reshape his thoughts until, at last, he gave in to them, allowing them to wash over him. Flow through him.

It was then he heard the quiet tap on his door.

Maybe this wasn't such a good idea.

Mairi leaned her forehead against the cool, smooth wood of the heavy door. She'd done this once before, this midnight trek to Ramos's room. The last time had showed her how little self-control she actually possessed.

What was it about this man?

She couldn't imagine how she could be so drawn to someone who epitomized everything she found most irritating. His typical he-man mentality prevented him from having any emotions more complex than anger or arrogance. More important, it made no sense that she could have feelings for any man when she knew there was no hope of finding her one true love.

Everything about Ramos confused her. She wanted—needed—to understand exactly what her feelings for him were.

Perhaps it was that reason, even more than her desire to tell him about the strange incident with Wyn Servans, that drew her to his door tonight.

She had good cause to be here.

Her resolve strengthened, she turned the handle and pushed, opening the door only wide enough to allow her access, closing it quietly behind her.

Mairi remained where she'd entered, her back to the door, while she identified the sounds in the room. Flames crackled in the fireplace, their dancing light doing little to pierce the dark or the cold. Outside, the rains had returned, beating fiercely against the walls of the keep. The winds forced their cold mist between the cracks in the shutters, permeating the air with a damp chill.

A shiver made its way down her spine as she moved tentatively across the floor. She could see the dark outline of covers mounded on the bed and felt a pang of regret. The way he huddled under his blankets, she wouldn't be treated to the sight of that magnificent chest tonight.

At least she wouldn't make the mistake of touching

him without thought again, of startling him so that she ended up pinned beneath his body.

Although that hadn't exactly been unpleasant.

She shook her head in irritation. *Get on with it.*

Reaching out, she lay her hand lightly on what she assumed was his shoulder. Hard to tell, buried as he was beneath all those covers.

"Ramos?" she whispered.

Leaning forward, she pushed against the mound, only to have her hand sink into the empty pile of woolens.

Her surprised gasp was cut short by a pair of large arms encircling her, pulling her back against a very hard body.

"You have got to stop sneaking into this room, my sweet."

He spoke the quiet words next to her ear, his warm breath tickling down her cheek and neck.

"I need to talk to you, to tell you what happened this evening."

His hands stroked slowly up from her wrists to her shoulders. Silken strands of his hair flowed over her bare arms as he bent his head and grazed his teeth lightly over her earlobe. She could feel herself melting back against him and knew the shiver that went through her now had nothing to do with the cold.

"Apology accepted. Just don't let it happen again."

"What?" The haze of her sensory fog slowly evaporated. "What apology? Don't let what happen again?" She couldn't be around him for two minutes without his attitude starting up.

She tried to turn, to face him, but his hands gripping her shoulders held her firmly against him while he trailed his lips from her earlobe down the side of her neck.

"Your apology for not doing what I told you to do. Don't make me worry about you again. I don't like it." His lips began the reverse trip up her neck.

He cared enough to worry about her? How could she be angry with him when he worried about her? Sure he was arrogant, but he couldn't help that. He was a caveman. A caveman with the lips of a Greek god.

She met no resistance when she moved this time, turning in the circle of his arms to face him. The firelight sparkled in his eyes and once again she felt herself drifting in a sea of turquoise.

"You were worried about me?"

"Only because you weren't where you were supposed to be and I couldn't find you," he growled, his hands sliding up her shoulders and onto her neck, his thumbs following the path his lips had traversed earlier.

He was going all he-man on her now, frowning and grumbling. She recognized the signs. To admit he worried was like admitting a weakness and these cavemen types never liked to appear weak.

In that moment, gazing up into his eyes as she stood in his embrace, she had the answer to her question. She might not understand why or how, but she no longer had any confusion about *what* she felt for Ramos Navarro.

He was in trouble.

Ramos realized it the minute Mairi turned in his arms and looked up at him like that.

As her Guardian, the scope of his actions was clear. He was here to rescue Mairi, to keep her safe until he could find a way to get her home. Nothing more. Anything else was confined to that area between waking and sleep, the place where his subconscious ruled and he had no control.

But she had floated into his room as if straight out of his dreams, wearing that next-to-nothing silk nightgown. It was all he could do to limit himself to a few stolen kisses on the pretext of trying to scare her away.

And now . . .

Her soft hands skimmed his chest, leaving a trail of fire in their wake. Onto his shoulders and up, her fingers sliding into his hair, twining in its length.

She smiled and slowly rose up on her toes, pulling his head down until their lips met. With the surge of adrenaline flooding his body, all his good intentions were swept aside, falling away like the strap on her shoulder sliding down.

He pulled her closer, deepening the kiss when her lips parted willingly for him. He delighted in the taste of her, her tongue darting to meet his, move for move.

Her hands wandered down his chest, leaving a new trail of fire, burning their way to his waist and around to his back, her fingers sliding lower. She broke the kiss, pulling away to look up at him with soft, dreamy eyes.

"Yer no wearing anything, are you?" She didn't look the least bit shocked this time. In fact, she was smiling.

He lowered his head to claim her mouth again, but she moved back from him, climbing up onto the bed. When she turned to face him, she knelt, her gown pooling around her, its shiny material reflecting the light of the flickering fire. Not even the women he'd seen in the land of Fae looked half as good.

She lifted her arms to him in an invitation he couldn't refuse, no matter that he knew he should.

Joining her, he reached for her heavy braid, freeing its fastening and running his fingers through the golden waves, fanning the hair out around her shoulders. It felt exactly as he had known it would.

He pulled her to him, kissing her mouth, her neck and lower. Her quick intake of breath as his hands covered her breasts only excited him more. He ran the pad of his thumb gently back and forth over her nipple, delighting in her body's immediate response to him.

Lowering his head, he covered the hardened bud with his mouth, the silk of her gown seeming to melt under the warm moisture of his tongue.

Her tiny moan of pleasure incited him. He wanted more.

Reaching for the hem of the gown, he slid his hands underneath, up the sides of her thighs to her waist. She lifted her arms and he continued on, his fingers gliding up the soft, smooth flesh, pulling the silky material over her head and tossing it away.

He straightened, his breath catching at the sight of her.

"Lord, but you're beautiful, Mairi."

She touched his arm, her hand tentatively skimming up over his shoulder and onto his chest.

"Me? You're the beautiful one."

He smiled down at her. No one had ever called him that before. Handsome, yes, but beautiful? Innocence and boldness warred in this woman in a way that completely enchanted him.

Once more he trailed his hands to her breasts. They fit his palms as if they had been created to be there. Her hands explored up his back and into his hair as he lowered his head, once again taking her into his mouth, this time without the impediment of the silky gown. The taste of her was more exquisite than he could have imagined. He couldn't get enough.

Her hands fisted in his hair as he pulled her close, his tongue flicking back and forth before swirling round and round the pebbled nipple.

Beneath his fingers, her back was like satin. A tremor ran through her as he slid his hands lower, under her perfect bottom, to lift her, knees spread, bringing her closer to him.

Her long legs locked behind him, fitting her against him perfectly. He lifted his head and took a deep breath, only to find her head thrown back, her long lovely neck tantalizingly bared to him.

In that moment, he wanted her more than he had ever wanted a woman in his entire existence. At this rate, he'd need to start listing players on all his favorite rugby team rosters just to maintain.

Cradling her head in his palms, he leaned her back, gently lowering them both to the bed. He buried his face against the welcoming curve of her neck, kissing, tasting, moving lower. Between her amazing breasts and down, onto her smooth stomach, he nibbled his way, his pleasure growing as her skin trembled under his lips, his tongue.

Her thighs, soft and inviting, tensed as he trailed kisses across them. Her eyes flew open as he pressed his mouth against her, sampling the outer limits of the moist heat he wanted so badly to enter. Her gasp was all the encouragement he needed. Her body writhing beneath him was his reward.

Back up he moved, across her stomach, stopping to appreciate her beautiful breasts. Delighting in the feel of her, the taste of her, he raised himself over her, pausing to drink in the beauty that was Mairi.

She lay under him, her hair spread around her like a lake of gold. Her eyes opened slowly and he was shocked by the warmth of the invitation he saw in their blue depths.

Once again she locked her legs behind his back and he shuddered. The little game he'd begun as a calculated effort to frighten her into racing back to her room and staying there had backfired, ensnaring him instead. He knew he should stop this now, send her back to her room before it was too late.

As if she read his indecision, she reached out and, with a lazy smile, drew his head down to her. When she clasped his lower lip between her teeth, pulling gently as she ran her tongue back and forth, he knew the truth of the matter.

It was already too late. Not only would he not send her away, he would do everything in his power to convince her to stay.

He moved against her, his body swollen with need. Positioning himself at her opening, he slowly, gently pushed, allowing himself only the smallest of movements.

"Yes," she breathed into his ear. "Now."

Her legs tightened around him, urging him forward, and he obeyed, burying himself deeply in her warm, welcoming sheath. His muscles strained with the effort to hold back, as the in-and-out rhythm of their bodies' movement grew more frenzied.

Not until she clenched around him, shuddering tremors of pleasure gripping her body, did he allow himself his final release.

He lay there, holding her wrapped in his arms, long after their exhausted pants had returned to normal cadence. Long after her breathing had slowed and deepened with sleep.

He shifted onto one arm to look down at the beauty in his bed. The blanket had shifted, baring her breasts of all cover except her long golden hair. Even in the half-light of his room he could see the dark mark over her heart, the shape of a rose, too perfect to be naturally occurring.

It shouldn't be there. Nowhere in the dossier of research he'd read on her was there any mention of scars, tattoos or birthmarks of any kind. He'd have to remember to ask her about it.

For now, he pulled the covers up over her arms. Gently he brushed the tangled web of hair from her face and watched the play of light from the dying fire create the illusion of a smile there. Or perhaps it was real.

Drawing her close, he laid his head next to hers. All he knew for sure was that being with Mairi was like nothing he'd experienced before.

And that he could never allow it to happen again.

Fifteen

How can this be possible?

Mairi studied the man beside her in the first gray haze of predawn light. Relaxed in sleep, his face was a chiseled study in masculine beauty. His mouth held a stubborn set, but those lips, she knew from experience, were soft and warm. Long dark lashes rested against strong high cheeks. Those lashes, when his eyes were open, would frame a sea of aquamarine in which she wanted to lose herself for days at a time.

It made no sense, these emotions, this feeling that engulfed her.

He is the one.

It shouldn't be. By all rights, there should be no one for her. She was a woman without a rightful place, supposedly dead in her own time, living in a future that didn't belong to her.

This can't happen.

But the truth of the matter was undeniable. She knew it as surely as she knew her own name. The man lying next to her was her one true love. She felt the pull and the bond. There could never be another for her.

She could see him more clearly now. Either her eyes were adjusting to the early light or, more likely, the sun would be up soon.

And everyone in the castle would be up, too.

The realization stirred the beginnings of panic. She had to get out of here and back to her own room. Getting caught in Ramos's bedchamber was not something she wanted to explain to anyone.

More important, she wasn't ready to face him just yet. The acknowledgment of her true feelings for him was too new, too raw. She needed time to think about this, to decide what she should do.

She shifted her body and the muscled arm sprawled over her hip tightened as if, even in sleep, Ramos responded to her presence, holding on to her.

With his movement, the long ebony hair that had draped over his shoulder slid back, revealing strange markings on his skin. Mairi had noticed them briefly once before. She leaned closer to get a better look at the tattoo covering Ramos's shoulder and bicep.

She had seen tribal tattoos before. After all, she'd spent the last several years on a university campus. But this didn't look like the ones she was familiar with. What fascinated her most was the symbol at the center of the tattoo. It appeared to be some type of snake with a sideways "Z" slashed through it, reminiscent of the NO ENTRY signs posted by the exits of the university parking lots back home.

There was something about the symbol that drew her, as if she'd seen it somewhere before. Almost beyond her control, her hand lifted and hovered above the unusual markings.

Only with considerable effort was she able to stop herself from tracing the mark with her finger.

If she touched him, his eyes would surely open and then she'd be lost.

She jerked her hand back. She had to get out of here without waking him. Now.

Consciously relaxing her body, she slipped from under his grasp, gently placing his arm on the covers as she crept from the bed. The stone floor was cold against her feet as she hurried to retrieve her night-gown and slide it over her head.

At the door she paused to look back at the peace-fully sleeping figure before scanning the room. There was nothing to show she'd ever been there.

One quick peek to assure herself no one was about and she was into the dark hallway, racing on silent feet to the bedchamber she shared with Sallie. Mairi could hear her cousin's snores as she cracked open the door and once again she was grateful the girl was such a heavy sleeper.

Quietly she let herself into the room, leaning into the door as she shut it. The wood was smooth against her forehead, her sensitive skin feeling each ripple in the pattern of the grain.

Her thoughts and emotions were in turmoil. She needed someone to talk to. Someone who could un-derstand her dilemma and help her make sense of this.

The only two people Mairi could think of who would fit that description were Rosalyn and Cate.

This whole perplexing relationship with Ramos—this might be something her aunt would know how to explain. And yet, she was oddly reluctant to confide in Rosalyn. She really felt as if she'd begun to make friends with Sallie tonight and she didn't want to jeopardize the fragile friendship by igniting the fires of jealousy again.

Besides, confiding in Rosalyn would mean she'd have to admit to her what she'd just done, and she didn't think her aunt would be too happy with those actions unless she was also confiding details of a marriage proposal.

No, Rosalyn wouldn't work as a confidante on this particular problem.

Cate would be much safer.

"That's who I need," Mairi whispered, pressing her cheek into the cool wood of the door, concentrating on the physical sensation in an attempt to forestall imminent tears. The knowledge she might never see that part of her family again weighed heavily on her. Especially now.

"I need to be home."

Her time-traveling sister-in-law would know what to do. The woman who had tamed her brother would surely know how to resolve any relationship problem Mairi might have. If she were home, Cate would brew them a pot of tea and they would huddle together in Cate's cozy living room, where Mairi would confide what troubled her, all her fears and hopes, to her best friend.

Mairi smiled to herself as she turned to go to bed, picturing how Cate would react to her dilemma.

The smile faded from her lips as she realized the sound of snoring had disappeared. She glanced toward the bed and found the room bathed in a gentle green glow.

The realization struck like a physical blow.

"No," she breathed. It wasn't the room. It was her. She was cocooned in a sphere of green light. Just like before.

"No," she said aloud. This couldn't happen now. She couldn't go home. Not without saving Sallie. Not without Ramos.

"No," she screamed, beating her fist against the unrelenting shell surrounding her. "No! I won't go. Not now."

"Why do you resist the magic, Daughter of my Heart?" The whispered words floated around her, echoing off the wavering green walls.

She recognized the ethereal quality of that voice.

"Pol? How can you be here?"

His tinkling laughter fluttered around her, so real she turned in a full circle, expecting to see her Faerie ancestor.

"I am not there with you. But we are joined by the magic, *here*."

As if a finger brushed lightly against her skin, the mark above Mairi's heart began to tingle and pulse in time to her own heartbeat.

"You've been able to do this all along?" A wave of anger roared through her. "Where have you been? Why have you no helped? Why dinna you explain what was going on? Why are you trying to send me back now?"

"I have nothing to do with this. It's not my power invoking this magic. It's yours. Only now in the circle of magic *you've* invoked am I able to connect with you."

"The magic *I* invoked? That makes no sense at all. I thought I could no go back until I'd completed some mysterious Faerie requirement of yers."

"Of mine? No, Daughter, the conditions necessary for your return were all of your own making." Pol paused and the sphere surrounding Mairi glowed more brightly. "You've done what you asked to do, so the magic has responded to your directive to return you to your home."

Mairi battled back the panic threatening to crush her. She couldn't leave now. Not without Ramos. "I've no done anything I came to do. I've no saved Sallie nor even discovered how I'm supposed to save her. And I canna abandon Ramos. It's my fault he's here at all."

"Ramos cannot travel to his own time yet. He has not met the conditions necessary for his return."

Mairi clasped her hands together to stop their shaking. "What are you talking about? He only came here to find me. To take me home, to save me, just as I came here to save Sallie."

"The reasons you state may have been what motivated each of you to travel, but they were not what either of you asked for. Neither were they the conditions agreed upon by the source of the power."

This was insane. "I canna understand any of this. I dinna agree to anything that would have kept me here. I canna imagine that Ramos would have, either."

"But you did. Surrounded by the magic, you set the condition yourself. *Take me back*, you said. *Allow me to find my destiny*. Those were your very words, were they not? The bargain was struck. The magic brought you here, and here you found him, your destiny. Bargain struck, bargain fulfilled."

"Him?" Pol's words took her breath away. "I never meant . . . I wasna talking about . . ." She stammered to a stop. All her life she'd heard stories of the dual nature of Faerie magic, of the price required for its use. How could she have thought she would be immune to that cost.

She straightened herself to her full height, lifting her chin. "What of Ramos? What bargain did he strike?"

A sigh, deep and heavy, surrounded her and she was almost certain she could feel tiny hands patting her back, her head, her shoulders as if something wanted to console her.

"His bargain is his own to know and keep."

"So now that I've found my destiny, my one true love, I'm forced to . . ." Her voice broke, and she paused until she could regain control. "I'm expected to simply walk away from him? Just turn my back and leave him here?"

She waited, but no response came.

"What's wrong with you people?" She hated the tearful crack in her voice, but she didn't let it stop her this time. "Do you no believe in happy endings?"

"*You* people?" Pol's reply snapped back. "You are one of us, Daughter. What do you believe in?"

After nine years of believing in nothing, of trusting so few, what did she believe in? She'd obviously been so wrong about what destiny, and the Fae, had in store for her. Yet she knew, from the bond she felt, from the confirmation Pol had given her, Ramos was meant to be hers. If only she could be strong enough, brave enough to pursue that destiny, perhaps she could be fortunate enough to capture it.

"I believe in true love." Her response was an honest answer, but one completely different from any she would have given twenty-four hours earlier.

"And what would you do for the sake of that belief, Daughter?" The words echoed in the sphere, a hushed version echoing over and over in the confined space, prodding at her.

"Whatever it takes."

"Even though you know he might never fulfill his own requirements to leave here?"

"Even though." It didn't matter. She couldn't allow it to matter. She would deal with whatever came.

"You do understand that he might not recognize his connection to you in this lifetime? Might never acknowledge you as his one true love?"

That one was harder to face. These were stories she knew all too well. Theirs were matched souls, but the legends told of how it happened repeatedly, one not recognizing the other for many lifetimes.

"I'll no turn back now. I have no choice."

"You always have a choice, Daughter. And the one you make is to risk your chance to return to the life you've built. To the family you love. All this for a man who might never offer you more than his protection."

"Ramos is my one true love. I know the truth of that even if he never does. I canna abandon him."

"So be it."

Cold moist air enveloped her as the warm green light winked out. The sound of Sallie's snores pounded at her ears. Her body shivered almost beyond her ability to control it as she tiptoed to the bed. She suspected the physical response was more a reaction to the emotional trauma than to the temperature in the room.

She climbed into bed and burrowed under the heavy covers. She was exhausted. When she awoke she would confront the consequences of the decisions she had made in the last few minutes. Then she would figure out what she needed to do next.

For now she simply wanted to escape in the arms of sleep.

Sixteen

A piercing shriek accompanied the loud clang and clatter of metal on stone.

It was the final straw for Mairi as she looked around the Great Hall in disgust. With only one sympathetic glance back toward the young maid hurriedly wiping up the cider she had spilled, Mairi headed for the doorway, intent on escape. There was no way she could endure the new round of hysteria this latest accident would prompt.

Final preparations for the Saint Crispin's Day feast had been under way since early this morning with everyone going at full speed, anxious to complete all the last-minute tasks. The problem was they were all going in different directions, disagreeing on even the tiniest details.

Granted, Mairi's lack of sleep could have some bearing on her high irritation levels, but she preferred to lump the blame fully on the annoying women running around the Great Hall like crazed hellions.

Mairi had barely drifted off to sleep this morning before Sallie was roughly shaking her awake.

"Come on!" Sallie had tugged on her arm to emphasize her insistence. "I mean it. I've no the patience to tell you again. We've too much to do." The girl had yanked the covers from Mairi's body, leaving her to shiver in the chilled room.

"You could have fed the fire, you know."

"You dinna need the fire on this morn. Drag yer lazy self from the bed and get dressed." She had taken Mairi's hand and pulled her up to sit. "Come on, now. It's no a day to lie abed."

Mairi had groaned as her feet hit the cold floor. It had been a horrible beginning to what promised to be a long day.

Now the Great Hall erupted around her again, as she had known it would, Sallie and Anabella locked in another great shouting match over some unimportant detail. It amazed Mairi how the two women actually seemed to enjoy these arguments, ending each in laughter.

"I dinna for the life of me understand why you insist on tying those ribbons around the legs of the tables. No a one of the beastly men sitting there will ever notice." Anabella glared down at Sallie. "You've no a brain in yer head, lass."

"But *I'll* notice," Sallie replied from her spot on the floor. "And, brain or no, I like them here. Spend yer time decorating the main table if you wish."

Too much for me. I've had it.

Mairi had nearly made it to the door when her escape was blocked by Rosalyn's entrance, her arms full of greenery.

"That's enough from the two of you. Can you no agree on anything at all?" She dumped the evergreen boughs on a table and stood, hands on her hips, looking from Sallie to Anabella. "We'll never finish on time at this rate."

A new round of accusations and counterclaims broke out, nipped in the bud by Rosalyn.

"Stop it! It disna matter in the least who's doing what." She shook her head in irritation. "Yer squabbling nearly made me forget what I came in here for. Sallie, run find Alycie. Her family's at the outer gates."

"Och, Mama. Send Mairi or one of the maids to fetch her." Sallie rose from her spot on the floor and picked up the branches her mother had brought in. "Alycie will be more likely to pay attention to one of them. You ken how much she hates me. She'll likely hide if I go after her."

"That's what you get for encouraging yer son to marry beneath his station, Rosalyn." Anabella shook her finger to emphasize her point. "The impudent little hussy disna appreciate what you've done for her. I'd no allow my Ranald to do the same."

"We've been all through this, Anabella." Rosalyn sighed as though her patience drew near an end. "Alycie's mother has been a friend of mine for many a year." She shook her head and leaned over to look at her daughter. "And she disna hate you, missy, so I'll hear no more of that."

"I'll go," Mairi offered. Anything to escape this madness and avert another argument. "Do you have any idea where Alycie might be?"

"Yer most likely to find her in her chapel," Sallie offered, rolling her eyes at the last.

"You've built a chapel at Dun Ard?" Mairi looked askance of her aunt. Their family had never seen the need for one in the past.

"No a real one. Alycie insisted on a place to pray each day, so Caden and his brothers converted the small bedchamber next to Alycie's until they can finish building a real chapel for her on the grounds."

"Giving us even fewer rooms for guests," Sallie added.

"Aye, that it did," her mother agreed. "I have to say, I was most grateful this morning when Ramos offered his room for today's newcomers."

"Ramos gave up his room this morning?" The news caught Mairi off guard. He hadn't said anything to her about it. Not that they'd really taken the time to *chat* last night. In fact, she realized with a guilty start, she'd never even spoken to him of the concerns that had taken her to his room in the first place.

"Indeed. He said he had no need for the privacy and would be more than happy to share Caden's room. And thank the Fates he did. Without that, I'd no idea where I was going to put all the Maxwells when they arrived. Oh my!" Rosalyn put both hands to the sides of her head. "What am I thinking? I have to get down to the courtyard to greet them."

She turned to Mairi, who stopped her with a lifted hand.

"Go on with you. I'll find Alycie and bring her down." Mairi darted through the door in front of her harried aunt, thoughts of other than Alycie and the Maxwells on her mind.

So Ramos had no further need for privacy. Mairi worried at the inside of her bottom lip as she raced up the stairs, trying to decide what his actions might mean. While it could be as innocent as his trying to be helpful, her gut instinct didn't lead her imagination that direction.

Obviously his reaction to what had happened between them last night hadn't been the same as hers. Even now, if she allowed herself to, she could feel his hands on her body, his lips against her own.

But this was not the time to think on Ramos.

Reaching the top landing, she started down the long dark hallway where daylight never penetrated. She'd gone only a few steps when the hairs on the back of her neck began to prickle, as if someone watched her. Her steps slowed and she glanced around. Straining to see into the depths of the shadows cast by torches on the old stone walls, she finally shook her head in annoyance. Whether it was lack of sleep or her confusion over Ramos, she was letting her imagination run wild again and really needed to rein herself in.

Near the end of the hallway, on the opposite side from the room she shared with Sallie, she reached an open door. Inside, she found Alycie.

The room was bare except for a small table next to the fireplace. A simple wooden cross sat on the table-top, with small lit candles placed on either side. Alycie knelt in front of the cross, her head bowed, her lips moving rapidly in silent prayer.

Memories slammed into Mairi, of the trips she had taken in her youth down to the small church in the village. On her brothers' birthdays each year she had visited the church to light candles in their memory.

Candles exactly like the ones burning on Alycie's altar.

Whatever the girl prayed for, it was obviously something of utmost importance to her.

Mairi hesitated at the doorway, torn between her reluctance to interrupt the private moment and her need to let Alycie know her family had arrived.

Practicality won out.

She cleared her throat, hoping to garner the girl's attention. When that failed, she crossed into the room and placed a hand on the girl's shoulder.

"Alycie?"

Alycie's body jerked and her eyes flew open, unfocused and wild. At first, Mairi thought it was panic she saw reflected there, but the moment passed so quickly she wasn't sure. More than likely her own out-of-control imagination taking flight again.

Mairi withdrew her hand, lacing her fingers together in front of her. "I'm truly sorry to interrupt you. Rosalyn asked me to bring you down to the courtyard. Yer family has arrived."

Alycie nodded her head slowly, leaning against the table to maintain her balance as she pulled herself up to stand.

"Verra well." The girl glanced around the room, fingering the cross at her neck. "I'll come with you."

As Mairi turned to leave, she was surprised to see large crosses painted on either side of the doorway they passed through.

"I suppose Lady Rosalyn and Sallie are waiting with my family?" Alycie pulled the shawl she wore tighter around her shoulders as she accompanied Mairi down the hallway.

"Rosalyn has gone out to greet them, I believe. But Sallie was still working in the Great Hall when I came to get you."

Alycie's steps slowed to a stop.

"I suppose there's naught to be done for it but to go down," the girl mumbled, her fingers still playing over the cross hanging from her neck.

"Is there something amiss here? Are you no anxious to see yer family?"

"Aye, but . . ." Alycie paused, casting a nervous glance back toward her chapel as if she might break and run down the hallway for the safety of that chamber. "Yer no like them, Mairi—you said as much yerself. You should have yer guardian take you away from here as soon as possible."

"I dinna understand yer meaning. I'm no like who?" Mairi turned to look at the girl, reaching out to touch her shoulder.

Alycie flinched at the contact, looking as though she were near tears. "The women of this family, that's who. Yer nothing like them. Yer clearly a refined lady, with good Christian values. You turn the other cheek to Sallie's hateful behavior, bearing it all with quiet dignity. And when Lady MacPherson attacked you with vile accusations, you held yer tongue. It's only because I admire you so that I'm telling you this. Until you leave, yer welcome to join me in my chapel whenever you like. You'll be safe there."

"Safe?"

"Aye. The entryway's protected by the Holy Cross. The evil canna pass through." The girl looked up and down the hallway before lowering her voice even further. "Though you should leave while you can. Before it's too late."

"Too late?" Mairi heard her own voice squeak the question. Surely this girl couldn't have any idea what the future held for Sallie or of the danger presented by the visiting Duke. Crosses painted on a wall would be no deterrent to a man like him.

"Aye." Alycie nodded, her large serious eyes watery with unshed tears. "Can you no feel the vile taint of evil here? It's *them*. The women. It's their unholy magic, born of their Fae ancestry."

Mairi wasn't sure whether to laugh or to sigh in relief. Yet another example of allowing herself to jump to conclusions. The girl was simply overzealous. But what an odd choice for Caden's future wife, considering her feelings about his mother and sister.

"If you feel that way, why do you stay here?"

The girl bowed her head. "I've no choice in the matter. It's what my mother and father have agreed on with Lady Rosalyn as the best thing for me. To marry Caden. To live here. They approve of the joining of our families. Two of my brothers are even apprenticed here at Dun Ard. My family is blinded to the evil."

"There's no evil in my cousins, Alycie. Surely you canna believe there is."

"But it's true! Brother Peter said all who claim unnatural heritage and practice the pagan magic are children of the devil."

"Though I've no idea who this Brother Peter is, I can assure you, he's wrong about my cousins."

"He's a great man, sent from the Archbishop himself to visit our village priest. He spends his life traveling the world, spreading the work of the Church. It was God's own blessing that I had the good fortune to meet him."

"Well, however great a man he is, he's wrong on this count, I'm sure. There's no an evil bone in Rosalyn's body. Surely you feel that? And Sallie is a decent person when you get to know her."

"Aye, well, blood is thicker than water, is it no? But I've done my duty. I've warned you."

Alycie clasped her hands together, her pursed lips announcing the end of their conversation as she turned and headed down the stairs, leaving a bewildered Mairi to follow.

Behind them in the dark hallway a door, which had been open only the tiniest crack, quietly closed.

"The witchwood or the blackthorn. The berries of either will do equally well. I've only to find some."

Sallie clasped her hands together in her lap, a sparkle in her eye as she confided her plan to Mairi.

They sat in Rosalyn's solar, waiting until the proper time to enter the Great Hall for the feast. Alycie had joined them, though she shrank into a chair against the far wall, her hand tightly clasped around her cross as she listened.

All three wore their finest gowns for the evening. Sallie had finally settled on the light green overdress that perfectly complemented the red hair she wore loose this evening. Alycie's gown, an ivory-colored wool, looked all the more plain for her having pulled her light brown hair back into a severe braid. Mairi's overdress of blue perfectly matched her eyes, according to Sallie, who had insisted that she wear her hair loose, too.

"I still dinna see what you hope to accomplish with this . . ." Mairi searched for the right word. ". . . concoction yer thinking to make."

"A love potion," the girl announced dramatically, scooting to the edge of her seat. "What do you think?"

Mairi's heart sank. Had she gotten nothing through to her little cousin? She'd almost convinced herself the girl had given up on marrying the Duke.

"Sallie," she began, but was surprised to silence as Alycie sprang from her chair.

The girl ran to the door, but stopped before she went out, speaking to them without turning to look their direction.

"'Tis the devil's own magic you think to use."

The smile on Sallie's face grew. "It's no such thing, *Sister*. It's Faerie magic."

Alycie's back stiffened at the words. "Yer no a sister of mine, Sallie Rose. And well you ken magic of any kind is evil."

"But I will be yer sister as soon as Caden weds you. Then you'll be part of the Faerie family as well."

Alycie didn't look back as she slammed the heavy wooden door behind her.

Wyn Servans leaned against the door to the balcony, watching as the timid little Mortal stormed into the hallway, her cheeks pink with emotion. It was the first time he'd seen any life at all in the dull wench.

It was also exactly the opportunity he had waited for. After what he had heard this afternoon, he wouldn't miss this chance. While he still preferred the more direct approach he intended for later this evening, he knew the value of a good backup plan.

Alycie jumped, barely containing a squeal, when he stepped from the shadows and into her path. Just as he'd known she would. Her kind were so easy to predict.

"Och, but you frightened me, yer grace," she stammered, her hand on her chest.

"I beg your pardon, good lady. I'd no intent to alarm you, but I do have need to speak to you in private."

"I'm no sure that would be at all proper, sir." The girl glanced around as if looking for someone she might call to her aid.

"I understand your reluctance, but I assure you, I've nothing other than the highest purposes in mind."

"Aye?" She laced her hands primly together at her waist and waited.

"I've observed you, Mistress Maxwell, and it's apparent to me—and to the Duke, I might add—that you're a devout, God-fearing young woman."

Her chin rose and he knew he was on the right track.

"It's the others here we'd like to help. You see, on our travels we met a man named Brother Peter, who told us of this place."

Her little gasp delighted him.

"You know Brother Peter?"

"Oh yes." He smiled. Mortals were so easily convinced of what they wanted to believe anyway. "And, at his request, we decided to do what we could to make a difference."

"You feel the evil in this keep? You and the Duke himself?" Her eyes shone with her fervor.

Yes, he'd read this situation correctly.

"Indeed. And we have a plan to cleanse it, if we could but count on your assistance."

"Of course, yer grace. I'll do whatever I can to help."

He took her elbow, steering her out onto the balcony where they wouldn't be overheard. She accompanied him through the door eagerly.

Wyn smiled to himself. Patience was indeed a virtue. And all of his was getting ready to pay off at long last.

"Sometimes I dinna understand you at all, Sallie. Why do you do that?" Mairi shook her head at her grinning cousin. It was as if the girl intentionally went out of her way to be disagreeable.

"Bait Alycie, you mean?" When Mairi nodded, she continued. "She disna belong here. I ken that Mother is good friends with Grizel Maxwell, but the two of them forcing this marriage is a great mistake. Caden deserves better than a woman who wants nothing more than a life spent in prayer. My brother should have a wife who loves him."

"A fine one you are to be talking about love in one breath and making some potion to snare the Duke in the next."

Sallie's eyebrows drew together in a frown. "Whatever are you babbling about? I'm no making a potion for the Duke."

Mairi felt her own frown mirroring her cousin's.

"But you said you planned to make a love potion."

Sallie's burst of laughter was totally unexpected.

"Aye, a love potion, but no for the Duke." She tilted her head, a dreamy, far-off expression in her eyes. "No, you were right, Cousin. I'd thought it myself, but yer words convinced me to action. I dinna want the Duke. I'd only considered him to make another jealous, anyway, but it dinna work."

"Then who?"

Sallie leaned close, lowering her voice. "My own true love, of course. I decided I'd settle for no less. But I'm no willing for the man to take till my youth is gone to come asking for my hand. I'm going to hurry him along a bit."

"That's wonderful news." Mairi threw her arms around her cousin's small shoulders, hugging her close. "What can I do to help?"

"I was hoping you'd ask." The girl sat back in her chair, grinning conspiratorially. "On the morrow, we'll slip out to the woods. It's no yet Samhain, so we should be able to find the berries I need."

A knock sounded at the door just before it opened, bringing an end to their planning session.

Drew entered, but stood still in the doorway, his mouth open as he stared at them.

"What?" Sallie asked sharply as she rose from her chair.

Her brother shook his head and grinned. "Dinna take that tone with me, Sister. You surprised me, is all. Come along with me now. They're gathering in the Great Hall."

"And how is it that we surprised you?"

He stretched out his arms in an obvious invitation

to join him, waiting until they reached his side before answering.

"To walk in expecting to find my plain little sister and cousin, but instead to be confronted by the sight of two beautiful women—well, it fair took my breath away."

"Och, Drew. At times I truly believe yer my favorite brother." Sallie curtsied and favored the young man with a dazzling smile.

Mairi took the arm Drew offered, feeling a strong sense of relief and accomplishment. For the first time since she'd arrived, she no longer had to worry about the Duke having an opportunity to harm Sallie. She had accomplished her purpose in keeping the girl safe.

As she accompanied her cousins toward the Great Hall, she allowed herself to relax and grow excited about the festivities. There would be music and food, and she would have the opportunity to spend time with Ramos, whom she'd not seen all day.

They stopped at the entryway to admire the scene before them. The Great Hall sparkled. All the torches were lit, as were the candles on the great hanging candelabra. The room was already filling with people, all visiting and laughing. The musicians were taking their place in the far corner of the room.

Mairi smiled as the smell of evergreen and dried herbs tickled sweetly at her nose.

"Oh, it's going to be a wonderful evening," she breathed, just before the sharp stinging started in her chest.

Seventeen

She's here.

Ramos had no need to look to the doorway to know the precise moment Mairi entered the room. He could *feel* her presence.

After the disaster he'd made of last night, he had lain awake berating himself for his colossal lack of self-control.

When he first realized it was Mairi in his room again, he had decided to frighten her enough to ensure this would be the last time she showed up in the middle of the night, certain his actions would scare her into staying safely in her room in the future.

But he hadn't counted on his own weakness.

He was a Guardian. Her safety and well-being was his paramount responsibility. And what had he done? He'd taken advantage of her.

Dallyn should have chosen someone else to look after her.

She was too good for someone like him. No matter how hard he tried, he was still tainted with the evil of his father. Still his father's son, corrupting everything he touched.

Nearing dawn, he'd finally dozed off, only to wake moments later as Mairi had slipped from his bed.

It was then it had begun.

Without opening his eyes, he had *felt* her passage across the room, as if some internal tracking device had been planted in his brain. Though he pretended to sleep, he could clearly see her movement in his mind's eye as she silently let herself out and hurried down the dark hallway. He had lost her for a few moments after she'd entered her room, a black void descending that had filled him with an unexplained sense of loss. But then she was back, a tiny blip on the screen of his thoughts, and there she remained. At any given time during the course of the day he had but to think of her and he knew her exact whereabouts. He'd never experienced anything like it.

Suppressing the confusion his acknowledgment of this new connection brought, he forced himself to concentrate on his conversation with Caden and Ran. He kept his back turned toward the door.

This awareness was surely nothing more than a temporary aberration and would pass soon.

It had to.

"By Heaven," Ran breathed, his eyes fastened behind Ramos.

"Ah, my sister's grand entry at last." Caden unsuccessfully hid his grin in the cup of ale he lifted as he shifted his gaze from Ran to the doorway.

Ran pushed past Ramos as if drawn that direction.

Ramos turned, his gaze following the young man's path, knowing before he did so that Sallie would not be alone.

Mairi's hair was loose, silken gold draped about her, as it had been last night. His pulse quickened at the memory of its feel between his fingers. She reminded him of a princess, her head held high, one hand lightly touching Andrew's arm as he escorted the women into the room, the other clasped to her heart.

And why shouldn't she look like a princess, Ramos wondered ruefully. She was, after all, the descendant of a very powerful Faerie prince.

Mairi scanned the room, searching, until her eyes captured his. She smiled and it felt as if everyone else in the room disappeared, the noise about him fading to background.

"And lovely Cousin Mairi, of course—let's not forget her," Caden added.

The young man's knowing chuckle so near his ear broke the hold Mairi had on Ramos, allowing him to turn his back to her once more. He clasped his fingers tightly around the tankard he held.

"But no Alycie," Caden sighed. "You'll excuse me?"

Ramos nodded as the young man left, but he refused to allow himself to turn and follow Caden's progress from the room. That would require his looking *her* direction, and he couldn't allow himself that luxury. Another look and he risked being drawn across the room as Ran had been.

A moment later, it was only by virtue of his intense training that Ramos prevented himself from jumping when a hand clapped on his shoulder.

"Lord Navarro." Wyn Servans bowed his head in greeting as he lowered the offending hand. "I wonder if I might have a moment of your time, sir? Privately."

What was wrong with that man, anyway?

Mairi watched in frustration as Ramos accompanied Wyn Servans out of the Great Hall without so much as a glance back. There was no doubt he'd seen her. She'd felt the jolt down to her toes when their eyes met. Then he turned away and left without acknowledging her presence in any way. It almost seemed as though he was intentionally avoiding her.

Now there was a thought that could easily bring her to her knees if she allowed herself to dwell on it.

"Bollocks!"

Sallie's whispered irritation drew Mairi's attention away from the far door and back to her immediate surroundings. She almost wished it hadn't, as the stinging sensation over her heart intensified.

"Dinna fash yerself, Sallie. Colin and I have decided to champion yer cause. You see? Even now it begins." Drew patted his sister's hand, grinning as he left them, and swaggered straight ahead.

"Great lump-headed idiots," the girl hissed, moving to Mairi's side. "Though I've none to blame but myself. I said naught a word of my plan to those two. Do you see what they're up to?"

Mairi did indeed. Colin had intercepted Ran, diverting him from his path to Sallie's side, while Drew was escorting Duke Servans to the spot where the women waited.

Unlike Ramos, the Duke appeared very much

aware of Mairi's presence, his gaze fixed on her as he approached.

"*Enchanté*," he murmured, lifting her hand to his lips, his eyes still locked on hers. "Both of you are extraordinarily lovely this evening." Reynard shifted his gaze to Sallie, capturing her hand as he had Mairi's.

"Indeed they are, yer grace," Drew agreed, taking Mairi's arm and directing her forward. "Perhaps you'd no mind escorting my sister to her seat?"

Mairi felt herself smile as Sallie tensed next to her. *How sweet.* Her cousins were doing their best to obtain for their little sister exactly what they thought she wanted. The Duke.

Sallie was getting a good lesson in being careful about what she asked for.

Once they were seated, the Duke excused himself to join Blane and the group of men surrounding him, promising to return shortly. Drew accompanied the Duke, turning to waggle his eyebrows and grin at his sister.

Her groan drew a laugh from Mairi, earning her Sallie's scowl.

"I'm sorry, Cousin, but even you must admit, it's fair amusing how hard they're trying."

Sallie fought to hide her smile but lost. "Oh, verra well. Yer right, of course. And is it no exactly what I'd expect? The lads to put full effort to a cause I've no real interest in?" She shook her head and sighed. "I suppose I'd best have a chat with my brothers on the morrow."

"About that," Mairi began. "You left unfinished yer explanation of yer new plan when we were interrupted. Perhaps now?"

"Oh, I dinna think just now," Sallie responded, her gaze fastened over Mairi's shoulder. "Good eve, Brother. Alycie."

Mairi turned to find Caden and his fiancée standing behind them.

He tipped his head in greeting, moving forward to pull out the chair next to Sallie and assisting Alycie to sit. "Would you mind Alycie's joining you? I've business to attend and I dinna see Mother or Mistress Maxwell down yet."

"No at all." Sallie smiled up at her brother, her eyes twinkling with mischief. "Welcome, *Sister*."

Alycie tensed, her eyes downcast, studying her tightly clasped hands, but she said nothing.

Caden nodded his head as if satisfied, walking away to join the knot of men across the room.

After a few moments of silence, Alycie cleared her throat and looked up. "I dinna wish us to continue to do battle, Sallie. It's no fair to my . . . to Caden." She stumbled over her words but seemed intent on finishing. "I would that we tried to be friends. For his sake, if naught else."

When Sallie didn't respond, Mairi gave her back a little nudge. She knew too well what it felt like to be on the receiving end of Sallie's wrath.

"And how do you propose we go about that, *Sister*?"

Alycie's cheeks took on a pink color, though her hands clasped together on the table were almost white from the strength of her grip. "Perhaps we could begin by yer no trying to anger me at every opportunity."

Mairi nudged her cousin's back a second time.

"Oh, verra well. I'm sorry. I'll try." Sallie turned

her head and glared at Mairi. "Though it may take me some practice," she muttered before turning back to Alycie. "And what do *you* intend to do to accomplish this change?"

"I'm going to be more accepting of what . . . of who you are." The girl took a deep breath. "And I'm set to prove it."

"Really? How?" Sallie asked suspiciously.

"By helping you with yer wee task." The girl straightened her shoulders. "I know of a place no far from here where you can find the witchwood berries you want. I'll lead you there on the morrow, if you like." The words rushed from her, as if she couldn't get rid of them fast enough.

"I'm no understanding why you would make such an offer. You hate everything about the magic. Why would you help me with this?"

"It's verra simple." The girl scanned the room nervously, her eyes darting from person to person as she reached up to finger the cross hanging around her neck. "If you find the one you seek, perhaps then you'll settle down and forget all this Faerie foolishness."

Sallie drummed her fingers thoughtfully against the table as if coming to a decision. "There is a full moon due. It would be perfect timing for the spell," she murmured. "Can we bring Mairi along with us?"

"I was going to suggest it myself," Alycie countered.

Both women turned to look expectantly at Mairi.

"Fine, I'll do whatever you want," Mairi agreed. They'd only just begun to be friends and she wanted to build on that relationship with her cousin. Besides, this was the sort of adventure the old Mairi would have jumped at. When she'd lived here before, she'd thought nothing of spending a day scampering about the countryside. And now that she didn't need to worry about Sallie any longer, perhaps it was time to try to be herself again.

She tuned out the women's conversation as they discussed the specifics of their little field trip, her mind wandering. Looking around the hall, her gaze lit on the empty doorway at the far side of the room.

The doorway Ramos had gone through with Wyn Servans.

Servans. How could she have forgotten about him? About what happened the last time she'd been with him.

Her fingers unconsciously trailed over the Faerie mark near her heart when she realized with a start that the burning sensation there was gone. Could it be because Wyn Servans was gone? No, it must not be him. She couldn't remember having felt the burn when she'd been alone with him on the terrace. Of course, with Sallie's arrival, she'd been distracted.

Just like she'd been distracted last night when she should have told Ramos about the man and what she'd seen.

No matter. She'd find him now and tell him.

"There is nothing to think about, Servans. My answer is an unequivocal no."

Ramos straightened to his full height, locked in a contest of wills with the man in front of him. He and Wyn Servans stood within feet of each other, alone on the balcony. Wyn had brought him here in search of this private conversation.

A bitter wind, damp with the promise of snow,

swept over and around them, but neither man seemed aware of it as they faced one another. Ramos recognized the tingle of magic that crept across his mind at the moment. He'd used the same too often himself not to know it.

"I'm afraid I don't understand." Surprise marked Wyn's face.

"There's nothing *to* understand. You offered for my ward's hand; I refused you. It's as simple as that."

That and the fact that your bloody compulsion won't work on me.

Wyn's perfect brow creased in a frown. "But you yourself indicated you were taking the good lady to your home in Spain for the purpose of finding her a husband. My offer would allow you to end that search right now. And I can assure you, Lord Navarro, she'll lack for nothing in my home."

Ramos smiled grimly. "Oh, I've no doubt of that, Servans." He visualized his father's palatial manor in Switzerland. He'd lacked for none of the material comforts growing up there. Emotional ones, though, that was a different story.

"Then by what reason do you withhold your permission?"

Because you're a heartless Nuadian Faerie with allegiance to the murdering monster who will one day be my father.

Perhaps the truth wasn't the best response in this particular situation.

"I have already promised Mairi's hand to another."

"I see." Wyn's eyes narrowed, his doubt of the statement clear. "Does the lady know of this arrangement you've made?"

"She does not."

Wyn shrugged his shoulders, a forced smile on his lips. "Should you change your mind, Navarro, you've but to tell me. My offer will stand." The man bowed his head as he backed to the door.

"As my decision will stand," Ramos responded, inclining his head in acknowledgment of the man's comment and his departure.

Ramos turned, leaning over the rock wall surrounding the balcony, the stones under his hands worn smooth by time and use. He stared sightlessly out into the evening gloom, his grip tightening as repressed anger whipped through his body.

Wyn had tried to use a compulsion on him! And the arrogant Fae thought to wed Mairi?

Not a chance in hell.

He'd marry her himself before he'd allow that cocksure Faerie the opportunity to put his hands on Mairi.

The thought jolted through him like electricity, though he refused to determine whether it was the idea of Servans touching Mairi or his marrying her himself that speared the raw ache in his soul.

As if marriage to him would be a good thing for Mairi. As if the lady in question would even consider it once he had her home.

He'd done enough to her already. Last night he had lost control, and though he couldn't regret it, he wouldn't allow a repeat of that mistake. He'd have to satisfy himself with that stolen moment.

Once he could determine what held Mairi in this time, he would return her to her family and then do whatever was necessary to stop his father. It was the only way to wipe the stain of evil from his soul.

That was his destiny.

He straightened as he heard the door behind him quietly close.

"I haven't changed my mind," he growled.

"Neither have I."

How could he have so seriously let his guard down? Ramos whipped around at the sound of Mairi's voice.

Even the encroaching evening gloom couldn't disguise the turquoise beauty of Ramos's eyes, open and needy. As if by magic, she floated there, suspended in the pools of his gaze, unable to remember why she'd come other than to find this. To find him.

After a moment, he blanked his expression and the spell was broken.

Thank the Fates. There was little chance she'd be able to speak of important matters if he'd continued to look at her that way. The way he'd looked at her last night, in his room.

"I thought you were someone else." He turned his back to her, a sure sign of dismissal.

"Wyn Servans?" Though Ramos remained silent, the instant tension in his stance told her she had guessed correctly. "Fortunate he's on yer mind since it's him I've come to talk about."

In the space of her next heartbeat, Ramos spun and stood in front of her, glowering down at her, his hand gripping her arm.

"What did he say to you?" His voice was quiet, but anger sparked in his eyes.

"It's no what he said, but what he did I'm here to discuss."

His hand tightened around her arm. "What's the bastard done?" he snarled.

"Ramos!" She jerked her arm from his grasp, backing up. "Calm down. I'm trying to tell you exactly that."

"Well? Go on." He crossed his arms in front of his chest and waited, like some great avenging genie come to life.

"When I came out here yesterday evening . . ." she began.

"With Sallie," he interrupted.

"Not exactly." She held up a hand to stop further interruptions. "I know what we told you, but I came out here alone. To think." She would *not* admit that she'd been thinking about him.

He remained quiet, his intense eyes boring into her.

"Before Sallie joined me, Wyn Servans showed up."

"And what did he want?"

Mairi huffed out her breath in exasperation, moving past him to pat her hand on the top of the rock wall. "He sat right here while we spoke. I was on the ground, here." She pointed to the spot where she had sat.

"And why would you sit at the man's feet, like a . . . a . . ." He sputtered to a stop, his lips tightly drawn together.

"Are you going to let me finish?"

He tilted his head in agreement, but she fancied she could hear his teeth grinding.

"We spoke for only a few minutes before Sallie interrupted us."

"What did you speak about?"

"Ramos!" He was making this so difficult she wanted to scream in her frustration. "About nothing. What I'm trying to tell you is that when Sallie came through that door, she dinna see the man, although I was sure I heard him still behind me. Then, when I stood to look at him, he was gone."

"Bloody hell!" Ramos looked furious striding across the balcony toward her. "I should have guessed they'd try something like that. No wonder he asked for your . . ." He stopped, appearing to gather his emotions and bury them again.

"You should have guessed they'd try something like what?"

The shuttered expression returned, all emotion hidden away. "Nothing for you to worry about. Why didn't you tell me this earlier?"

"I tried to. It's why I came to yer room last night, but then . . ." Mairi let the sentence fade away, watching as Ramos backed up a step, his jaw muscle tightening.

"About last night, Mairi. What happened . . . what I allowed to happen—there can be no repeat of that. Ever."

The shock of his words washed over her, leaving a numbness in its wake. "Was it . . . was I so bad? That you'd never want to . . ." She couldn't finish. Couldn't force the words past the humiliation filling her throat.

Ramos closed the distance between them, grasping both her upper arms in his large hands, pulling her toward him. "You know that's not true. You must understand, Mairi. I was sent here to protect you, to see you safely home, not to take advantage of you. What I did was wrong. I can't let it happen again."

She should have expected this response from him. Pol had all but warned her last night. Just because her soul recognized his was no guarantee of anything. She knew that.

And him, with his knight-in-shining-armor complex, of course he'd want to distance himself from any emotional involvement.

If that's what he needed, she'd let him have it. For now.

"Very well." With one last look, she steeled herself and backed away from him, putting much-needed distance between them. "If that's what you want."

"It's how it must be." He looked off into the distance for a moment then cleared his throat before continuing. "As far as Wyn Servans, you're to avoid that man at all times, do you hear me? Him and his brother."

"I'll try. But I still don't understand. How could he be there on the balcony rail one second and gone the next?"

"You're asking the wrong question. You should be more concerned with *why* he'd do something like that."

"Okay. *Why* would Wyn choose to leap to the ground?"

Ramos reached for her, taking her upper arm in his hand as he might if he were speaking to a child. "Because he'd learned all that he needed to."

"That doesn't make any sense. I'd said practically nothing to the man. And jumping almost two stories off this balcony, he could have been seriously injured."

His eyes were hard as he stared at her, but his grip loosened a bit. "Two stories is nothing for a Fae."

"A Fae? You mean those two are descended from Faeries like me?" That would mean they might have abilities she hadn't considered.

"No. Not like you, Mairi. Those two *are* Fae. Like Pol." He dropped his hand from her arm and walked toward the entryway as if to leave.

Like Pol? Her mind swirled. She looked up as he opened the door.

"Wait. How is that possible? What are they doing here?" She stopped as another thought struck her. "How do you know what they are?"

He paused, his hand on the door. After a moment, he pushed it shut and turned to meet her gaze, the sadness in his smile cutting into her heart.

"Because I am half Fae."

Eighteen

*I*t was almost too much to believe.

From under her lashes, Mairi studied Ramos, who was deep in discussion with her cousin, Caden, several seats away down the long table. Now that she knew of his Fae ancestry, she wondered at her inability to recognize it before. The remarkable beauty of his features, the sureness of his actions. All the male descendants shared those traits.

With her new knowledge it was easy to see it in others now as well.

She discreetly glanced in the other direction down the table to where the Duke and his brother sat. They were full Fae! The thought rattled her. In spite of her having learned months ago that there were others, somehow she'd still imagined Pol the only real Fae loose on the world.

There sat the physical proof she'd been wrong.

Wyn looked up and smiled at her. She quickly

turned her head, the heat she felt in her face her only acknowledgment of the man.

The Fae.

Before they returned to the feast, Ramos had told her all about Reynard's people, the Nuadians. About how they'd been cast out of the Faerie Realm. About how all they wanted was to get back in and that they needed a female descendant of the Fae to find the Portal to let them in. And about how they would stop at nothing to gain what they wanted.

At least now she understood why the Duke had come to this part of the Highlands after he'd met Ran MacPherson and heard the stories about the Faerie ancestors of the MacKiernan women. He'd hoped to use Sallie to find his way back into the Realm of Faerie.

A shudder ran the length of Mairi's body. Poor Sallie, without even the ability to see Wyn Servans in his true form, she wouldn't have stood a chance against the Duke.

Mairi chewed at her bottom lip as she turned to observe Sallie, running the scene through her mind once more of the meeting between herself and Wyn on the balcony.

Ramos had said that any amount of Fae blood would allow a descendant to see the true form of a Faerie. So Wyn now knew she carried the blood. She had seen him. But Sallie hadn't.

Odd, that.

The repeated clanking of a knife against a metal tankard drew her from her thoughts. Reynard Servans rose from his seat and lifted his drink in a toast to all those gathered.

"Lord MacKiernan, Lady MacAlister, *tous mes amis*. My brother and I wish to extend our gratitude for the warm welcome you have given us." He paused to wait for the scattered applause to end. "And I, personally, wish to thank you all for being here to witness a momentous occasion."

"What occasion might that be, yer grace?" Blane rose from his chair, lifting his own tankard toward his guest.

Reynard scanned his audience before stepping away from his seat, slowly walking the length of the great table, passing behind Blane.

"Perhaps it would have been best to approach the subject in private, Laird MacKiernan, but I am a man overcome with joy. Joy that I want to share with all my new friends."

Every eye in the room followed him as he continued to stroll the length of the table until he stood behind Sallie's chair. Stopping, he laid his hand on her shoulder and turned to face Blane.

"I am declaring my intention on this holy day. I would ask for this lady's hand in marriage."

Mairi listened to a new round of scattered applause, keeping her eyes to the table while she dropped her hands to her churning stomach. Her heart pounded so loudly in her ears she almost missed Blane's reply.

"We are most honored by yer offer, yer grace," her cousin at last responded, seating himself once again. "I will, of course, need to consult with my aunt as to her wishes for her daughter, but once—"

"There's no a need for that," Sallie interrupted, drawing everyone's attention. "All in this room are familiar with our family's heritage, Cousin, therefore I'm sure they'll understand my answering for myself."

Mairi risked a quick glance up at Reynard as he stood behind the chair next to her. The smirk he wore relayed his confidence more clearly than any words could as he took Sallie's hands to assist her in rising from her seat to face him.

"I've no doubt, yer grace, there's no a woman in this room who'd no be flattered with yer offer of marriage." Sallie pulled her hands from the Duke's and placed them on the back of her chair as if to steady herself. "I hope you'll forgive me, but I find I canna accept it."

"What?" The Duke's strangled response betrayed the calm mask he wore. He glanced toward his brother, then back to Sallie. "I was under the impression you would be receptive to my offer, *mon cher*."

"I'm sorry, yer grace." The words seemed small as they echoed in the deathly silence of the huge room. "I canna wed any save my own true love."

Reynard's expression remained unchanged except for the slight lifting of one eyebrow. "So be it," he said quietly, before lifting his head to look around the room. "I apologize for any discomfort I have caused, and I hope you all will understand if I take my leave now."

Andrew jumped from his seat. "Yer grace! I'm sure when my sister's had time to think on this . . . perhaps tomorrow after you've rested . . ." The young man stuttered to a halt as the Duke turned, his expression flat and cold.

"I don't mean to be here tomorrow, boy."

At a flick of his wrist, Reynard's men rose from their seats around the room and followed him to the exit as the hall erupted in chatter.

Sallie dropped to her seat and reached out toward Mairi. "Now I've done it," she sighed.

Mairi clasped her cousin's hand, surprised to find the girl trembling. "You did the right thing."

"Aye? Then why is all this happening?" The girl waved her free hand, encompassing the chaos around them.

Almost everyone was on their feet now, the level of noise in the room steadily rising as people milled from group to group, watching for reactions from the table on the dais.

Mairi patted the girl's shaking hand. "We'll just sit here until it's calmed a bit."

"You'll do no such thing."

She jumped at the deep sound of Ramos's voice behind her. A second later, he pulled her from her chair.

"Come on. I want you out of here now."

She held on to Sallie's hand, forcing the girl to accompany them.

"Where are we going?" She pulled back to slow him down, but he didn't stop.

"To your room. I'll feel much better when you're safely away from this lot."

He shouldered through the throng in the hallway, leading them up the stairs to the door of their room, which he then held open, allowing them to pass through.

Sallie moved silently to the edge of their bed and sat, staring wide-eyed at Ramos.

"Stay here," he ordered. "You're not to leave this room until I come back and tell you to. Do you understand?"

"I do." Mairi bit back any further reply. She wouldn't argue with Ramos in front of Sallie. Especially not with her cousin looking so frightened.

"Then try to remember it this time." He slammed the door behind him.

"Oh," she hissed from between clenched teeth. There were moments when the man completely irritated her, his behavior exactly like something she would expect from her brother.

At the sound of soft laughter behind her, she turned. Sallie's eyes sparkled as she held her hand over her mouth.

"'Then try to remember it this time,'" she mimicked, her fake baritone bringing a smile to Mairi's face in spite of her irritation. "He has quite the opinion of himself, does he no?"

"He does that," Mairi agreed. "And what about you? I thought he had you terrified."

"Pfft." The girl waved a hand dismissively in the air. "There's no a man I've met with the ability to terrify me."

"Well, you certainly had me fooled. And him, too, I'm willing to bet."

"As I wanted. It's often best to let them think they're in control. Then they leave you alone. Dinna you find it best sometimes not to let on as to all yer thinking?"

Perhaps she'd underestimated Sallie, after all.

"Come on." Sallie rose from the bed and grabbed her hand, heading toward the door.

"We canna leave the room. I promised Ramos."

Sallie made a *tsk*ing sound, shaking her head. "You dinna promise any such thing. You only agreed you understood that was what he wanted. You never said you'd do it."

No perhaps about it. She had seriously underestimated her little cousin.

"Where are we going?"

Sallie grinned. "The parapet, of course. It's the best place to watch what's happening in the courtyard. And I'm thinking there's plenty of action there now." The girl slowly opened their door and peeked out. "All clear."

Mairi followed her down the darkened hallway and up the spiral stairs. Pushing open the heavy door at the top, she paused as she stepped into the cold, damp air.

"Hurry," Sallie called, already at the wall. "Look down there. They're leaving."

Mairi joined her, trying to make out individual people in the crowded courtyard below.

"Bollocks! I dinna count on Ran going with them," Sallie grumbled. "Oh well, it willna matter."

Andrew held on to the Duke's reins, obviously pleading with him not to leave. The young man stumbled and almost fell when Reynard jerked his horse forward, leading his men to the gates without a backward glance.

"Who's that over there?"

Mairi looked in the direction her cousin pointed, to the far side of the courtyard, but saw only the swirl of a cape disappearing into the shadows as Wyn Servans strode from the area and mounted his horse.

He started toward the gates after the others but stopped, turning to stare up at the parapet.

Both girls dropped to a crouch behind the wall.

Though it was too far for her to have seen, Mairi felt sure he had smiled as he looked their direction, as if he'd known they watched him.

Beside her, Sallie shuddered. "That man may be handsome as sin, but he gives me the willies."

"Aye. He's no ordinary man," Mairi agreed, thinking of her conversation with Ramos about Wyn Servans.

"Indeed. Any man who can make himself only half visible, who'd then jump off a balcony to avoid yer seeing him, is no ordinary in the least."

"What?" Mairi turned to stare at Sallie. "I thought you said you didn't see him on the balcony last night."

The girl stood and, brushing the dirt from her dress, she shrugged. "That was one of the times I thought it wise not to let on all I saw. I dinna trust you yet, Cousin." She grinned and went to the door, pulling it open. "But perhaps I do now. We'd best get back down. We've a busy day tomorrow. I've a true love to catch."

Nineteen

Shh." Sallie held up a warning hand.

As if any of them had made a sound, Mairi thought irritably. Crouched against the outside of the castle wall under cover of dark, she almost wished someone would hear them and send them back inside.

Barely an hour had passed since Sallie's excited chatter had rudely torn her from her peaceful sleep, for the second time in as many days.

"You are the worst lay-a-bed I've ever met." The girl had laughed as she pulled the covers off Mairi and bounded across the room. "Get up and get dressed. Alycie's to meet us outside the kitchens. We have to hurry if we're to sneak out the gates when the herders go. If you continue to lie there, it'll be daylight and the guards will spot us for sure."

Now the three of them crept along beside the outer castle wall. Mairi looked up at the sky, but quickly lowered her head as the wind blew stinging mist into her face. It would still be some time before full daybreak, and the heavy clouds would obscure the sun even then.

She was cold and tired, and all of this sneaking about held less than no appeal for her. Still, she had promised to accompany her cousin and Alycie on their little field trip today. To think this used to be the sort of thing she'd thought of as fun. When she had lived here before. When she had been their age. How had she gotten so soft in her time away from here?

"Hurry!" Sallie pulled at her hand, urging her forward to the cover of the tree line.

"We've made it." Alycie peered back at the castle. "The guards dinna see us."

Sallie snorted inelegantly. "See us? They must have enjoyed themselves well at last night's feast, for they looked as if they could barely stand, let alone guard, this morning."

The girl had a point.

Mairi pulled the woolen plaid she'd wrapped about her tightly closed. The cold, driving mist managed to reach them even through the cover of the trees.

"Dinna you think it might be better to postpone this jaunt until the weather clears a bit?"

"No!" Alycie and Sallie answered in unison, both looking at one another in surprise.

"We're too close to winter's arrival. The berries won't last much longer," Alycie explained as she took the lead through the forest. "We must go this morn or there's no point in going at all."

"Besides," Sallie added quietly, dropping back to Mairi's side, "Ran's gone with the Duke. For now I'm guessing he's only at Sithean Fardach. But if the potion's to work, I'll need to have it ready before he goes off to who knows where following that man."

"Ran? Yer potion's for Ran?" At her cousin's nod, Mairi huffed out her breath and came to a stop. "Then why are we doing this? He already loves you. That's plain to anyone with half a brain."

"Well he may. But the potion is no for making him love me. It's for making him take action on that feeling. I told you before, I'm no willing to wait for him to make up his mind to do something about it. I want my true love *now*." Sallie grinned and tugged at Mairi's braid. "Come on, grumpy Mairi. Yer already out of yer warm bed. Enjoy the adventure. If nothing else, think of how irritated yer bossy guardian will be if he finds you've left the castle without his permission."

Mairi groaned. As if things weren't already confused enough with Ramos, this was just what she needed—to make him angry. He hadn't even come back last night to give her the all clear to leave her room, let alone the castle. He wouldn't just be angry. He'd be furious.

"Come on with you," Alycie called back to them. "We've a long way to go to get there and back today."

"Fine," Mairi huffed. "We'll go find yer berries and make yer stupid potion. But tomorrow yer to let me sleep."

Sallie's laugh rang out before she clamped a hand over her mouth, remembering their need for quiet. "Agreed, Cousin. Now come on. It's going to be a lovely day. I can feel it in my bones."

"I see yer taking me serious at last."

Caden lay on his back in the mud, the tip of Ramos's sword pointed at his chest.

"That I am." Ramos lifted his sword and reached out a hand to help Caden stand. He wouldn't underestimate an opponent again. It was a lesson he'd learned at the hands of this very man. "Have you had enough?"

"I dinna believe so, Spaniard. Like as no, that was naught but luck." Caden grinned as Ramos helped him to his feet.

Ramos shrugged, returning to his ready stance. He could remain focused. No problem. Mairi was safely in her room and he had nothing to worry about.

Nothing except his father and some mystery Fae running loose through the countryside, planning to wreak havoc on a level only the Fates could anticipate. Nothing except getting Mairi home safely. Nothing except having allowed himself to compromise his responsibility by taking advantage of the woman he was supposed to be protecting.

The rush of air warned him he'd let his attention wander and he raised his sword just in time to avoid a strike at his face.

"Yer drifting off again," Caden cautioned, laughter in his voice. "Thinking about my bonny cousin, are you?"

"Stand at your ready," Ramos growled, unwilling to share the line of his thoughts.

"It's no use denying it to me." Caden feinted to his left before attacking from the right, handily dodging Ramos's return thrust. "I've watched you. You wear that same look whenever she's around."

"You're crazy." Ramos followed with a lunge, his sword deflected by Caden's.

"Crazy or no, I'm no wrong. It's a gift, you might

say. I ken what's going on around me. I pay attention."
Caden avoided another thrust, twirling with his sword,
bringing it back up in a lunge of his own. "Does her
brother have any idea? That you want her for yerself?"

Ramos struck, this time putting his weight behind
his rush, throwing Caden off balance. His opponent's
feet slipped in the mud as he attempted to dodge the
sword, and once again Caden landed on his back, the
tip of Ramos's sword at his chest.

"What you speak is nonsense. I'm Mairi's Guardian,
nothing more." If he said it often enough, it would be
true. "Have you had enough now?"

Caden laughed as he took the hand Ramos offered.
"Aye, Spaniard. I believe I've had enough for this
time. My compliments for a good practice. Yer con-
centration is improving."

Good practice indeed. Ramos shook his head as
the two men headed to the little shed to clean up.
Caden was easily as good a training partner as any
he'd ever had, better even than most of the Fae he'd
learned against.

He'd just opened his mouth to tell the young man
so when the sound of Rosalyn's yells distracted him.

"Caden!" the woman called. Holding her skirts
high, she haltingly ran through the mud of the courtyard toward them, Grizel Maxwell following more
slowly behind. "Caden!"

Caden froze for only a second before leaping over
the low rail, racing to meet his mother. Ramos followed closely at his heels.

"What do you think yer doing, slopping through
this mud? Could you no wait till I came in from prac-

tice?" He grasped her arm. "Take yer time, Mother. Get yer breath."

"There's no time to take, lad. Yer sister's gone missing. I canna find her anywhere in the keep."

"And Alycie," Grizel panted as she reached them. "Alycie's gone, too."

"You've checked her chamber?" Ramos looked toward the keep. If Sallie was gone . . . His stomach clenched, his mind reaching out, sweeping the castle for any awareness of Mairi. She wasn't there.

"Of course I did. It was empty." Rosalyn grasped Caden's arm. "She's no anywhere in the keep."

Neither was Mairi. Ramos felt the empty spot in his mind where she should be.

"Bloody hell," he muttered, turning to run toward the stables.

"Dinna you fash yerself, Mother. We'll find them," Caden called, already close behind Ramos. "Drew! Get yer horse and come with us," he ordered as his brother walked out of the practice shed. "I'll explain as we go."

They quickly readied their animals and headed out through the gates.

Once outside the walls, Ramos drew his horse to a stop, scanning the horizon through the mist that fell. From the north he felt a slight tug, an awareness at the back of his conscious mind. Mairi.

"This way." He turned his mount and headed away from the road and into the forest.

The other two followed without question.

What she wouldn't give for her wonderful little car right now. Or Jesse's hulking big motorcycle. Or a horse. Or even a good pair of hiking boots.

Mairi stopped and stretched, a hand at her back. Nine years ago, she had scoured these hills and meadows barefoot and never thought a thing of it. Today her feet hurt.

"Is it much farther?" She knew she sounded whiny, but she didn't really care. They'd been hiking for hours now, always with Alycie assuring them they were getting close, as she did now.

"We're verra near. Just over this hill there's a small meadow. Once we cross that, we're into the forest where yer berries grow."

Sallie gasped as her foot slipped on the wet ground cover and Mairi grabbed at her cousin's arm, just managing to catch her as the girl lost her footing.

"Wait." Mairi steadied her cousin and leaned against a large rock. "I need to stop for a bit." She exercised regularly back home, but it certainly hadn't prepared her for traipsing uphill and down in this weather. At least the rain had stopped.

"Yer right," Sallie agreed. "I'm fair tired myself."

"Over there." Mairi pointed toward an outcropping of scraggly trees growing between some large boulders. It would provide them a little protection from the cold wind.

"We should no be wasting time," Alycie cautioned. "We've need to hurry." She looked from one to the other. "We dinna want to be caught out here at night."

"Dinna fash yerself, Alycie. We'll be back inside the walls, warm and snug, long before nightfall." Sallie dropped to the ground, huddling into the small space they'd found. "And look what I've got in my sack." As the other two joined her she pulled a cloth bag from under her plaid, revealing cheese and bread.

Mairi snuggled in next to her cousin, gratefully taking some of the food she offered. She watched silently until Alycie finished praying over the food she held.

"How is it you know of this place, Alycie? It's no as if you'd be out collecting witchwood berries yerself." The question had popped into Mairi's thoughts several times during their hike.

"Many people consider my mother a healer. For as long as I can remember, she's scoured the whole of this land for herbs and plants to make her potions. And always she dragged me along with her, regardless of what I might think about the practice."

Grizel Maxwell. That made sense.

"And obviously you've no desire to follow yer mother's footsteps and be a healer." Sallie wiped her mouth with the back of her hand.

"Obviously." The girl's eyes widened. "I believe in the power of prayer, no the potions of a backward time."

The three sat quietly munching their welcome bounty for a few minutes until Sallie broke the silence.

"I hope this whole journey is no a waste of effort."

"Why would you say that?" Mairi asked.

"Because I've never tried an enchantment before."

Mairi shrugged. "Well, for what it's worth, I dinna believe in them."

"Neither do I," Alycie added. "But we've come this far and we're no going home without yer berries."

"No, yer right, of course. It's just that this is so important to me. I'd do almost anything to make Ran declare himself and his intentions."

"Why dinna you just talk to him? Tell him how

you feel. Traipsing through the wilderness looking for berries to make some enchantment hardly seems the best way to me. You should talk to the man." Mairi popped the last bite of her cheese into her mouth, dusting the crumbs from her skirt.

"Talk to him?" Sallie shook her head in disgust and tossed the last of her roll to the ground. "Would you? I doubt it. I dinna see you as one to go bearing your soul to some man whose response you dinna trust. I'm no one to do it, either. I've my pride, you ken?"

Mairi gave her cousin a quick hug. The girl was right. Who was *she* to be giving advice? After all, she certainly hadn't run directly to Ramos to confront him with her feelings. In fact, she'd barely spoken to him, and not a single word of how she felt about him.

And why? Because, as Sallie had so accurately surmised, she couldn't bring herself to bear her soul to a man whose response she didn't trust.

Apparently pride was a fault all the MacKiernan women shared.

"Anyway"—Sallie grinned and wrinkled her reddened nose—"there's naught to do at the keep today but the cleaning from last evening's feast. An adventure to find witchwood berries for the purpose of making a real love potion sounds more to my idea of fun than that."

Alycie rose, dropping her half-eaten roll to the ground. "Come on. We've sat about for long enough. Let's be on our way."

"She drives us like sheep before the shepherd, does she no?" Sallie laughed as she pulled her wrap tightly about her head and followed after Alycie.

Trailing behind up the hill, Mairi felt a prickle against her consciousness, hardly more than a feathery, searching touch. Stopping, she scanned the area below and all that she could see from where she stood.

Nothing.

"Dinna dawdle, Mairi, we've wasted enough time. Keep up with us," Alycie called.

After one last look, Mairi hurried to catch up with the other two women.

The prickle was still there somewhere at the edge of her mind. It felt as if she could almost hear Ramos calling her name.

Silly.

She shook her head and continued to climb. That's what happened when she spent too much time thinking about the man. Either that or it was her guilty conscience at having gone on this little adventure without telling him. Of course, if she'd told him, he wouldn't have allowed her to go.

"See how close we are?" Alycie's voice rang out as they reached the crest of the hill and started down the other side.

Spread out below them was a meadow, the growth that would be a welcoming green in spring a pale brown now. A small stream cut through the middle of the meadow, trailing off into the forest on the other side.

"Thank the Fates," Sallie laughed. "Come on!" She lifted her skirts and started to run down the slick slope.

"You'd best be careful or you'll fall and hurt yerself!" Mairi called after her. As Sallie ran farther away, Mairi increased the pace of her descent as well.

The wind in her face was exhilarating. She realized with a start, she hadn't run since before she'd become obsessed with saving Sallie. Until then it had been a regular part of her weekly routine. It occurred to her now, with her breath coming in hard pants and her heart pounding, it was something she had missed.

As they drew nearer the foot of the hill, both laughing, Mairi pulled even with Sallie. She reached out and caught her cousin's hand without breaking her stride, tugging Sallie along with her.

The momentum they gained racing down the last of the slope propelled them forward. They were well out onto the level surface, sliding toward the stream, before Mairi realized the burn in her chest wasn't the result of her hurried scramble to catch up with Sallie.

Clasping her free hand to her breast, she skidded to a stop, slipping on the slick brown meadow, bringing both her and Sallie down into a tangled heap.

"Something's wrong." Mairi could hardly get the words of warning out as she gasped for breath, pulling herself up to her knees.

A quick glance back showed Alycie still descending through the scrubby brush of the slope.

"What?" Sallie laughed breathlessly, the hood of her cloak thrown back and straggles of red curls falling loose about her face. "What's that yer saying?"

"Something feels . . ." She let the words die as she looked across the stream toward the forest.

There, emerging from the dense cover of the trees were nine mounted men, heading their direction.

Mairi cast a desperate look to either side of where they sat.

Caught in the open. Nowhere to run.

"Look there." She pointed toward the approaching riders.

Sallie's eyes widened. "Oh no. May the Fae save us," she whispered.

"Whatever it is they're here for, I'm sure it's no to save us," Mairi answered, more to herself than her cousin, as Reynard Servans and his men moved steadily toward the women.

Twenty

❧

"We're close behind them now."

Ramos prodded at the crushed leaves and grass with the toe of his boot before turning to climb back up onto his mount.

"It appears they're together." Caden rose from the spot where he'd squatted, fingering a broken twig he'd picked up. "Looks like they ate here."

"And since the rain stopped, too. The bread there's damp but not wet." Ramos pulled at his reins, urging his horse toward the crest of hill. He could feel her, as he had since they'd left the castle. But he was very near her now. If he closed his eyes, he could almost see her, almost smell the sweet fragrance of her skin.

"Aye. We'll find them soon enough," Caden agreed, swinging up onto his horse's back. "And when we do, I've a good mind to make them all sorry for this."

Ramos understood the feeling completely.

"Though I'm no surprised by Sallie running off, I

expected better of Cousin Mairi." Andrew looked up at the snorting sound from Ramos. "No?"

"Your cousin is a bit more spirited than you realize."

"Mayhaps. I suppose I'll take yer word for that. But it's beyond me how either of them could get Alycie to go along. She hates Sallie."

"She does no such thing!" Caden defended.

"She does too. And yer more the fool not to see it," Andrew insisted, bringing his horse alongside his brother. "Alycie's afraid of the Fae magic. She'll never be happy at Dun Ard."

"She'll get used to it."

"Yer blind where the Maxwells are concerned, Caden. You refuse to see what's in front of you. You and Mother both."

Ramos shut out the bickering of the two brothers to concentrate on that new little spot in his mind, the spot that was filled with Mairi.

He didn't understand how this awareness had become a part of him, but he'd been raised by the Fae and knew better than to expect a logical reason for the things their magic brought about. And he had no doubt this came about because of Faerie magic. But whether it was the result of his being her Guardian or some other type of magical bond, he had no idea.

For now he wouldn't question it. He'd only be grateful that, whatever it was, it allowed him to follow her. To find her.

She was close. So close, he felt drawn to urgency. He prompted his horse to pick up the pace, needing desperately to see her with his own two eyes to relieve the baffling dread building in the pit of his stomach.

Cresting the top of the hill, he spotted her, but the

scene unfolding before him did nothing to alleviate his concern.

She and Sallie huddled on the ground near a stream at this end of the meadow while nine men on horseback approached them at a slow steady gait from the woods on the far side.

Not nine men. Seven men and two Fae.

He knew from here. He recognized his father and Wyn riding in the lead.

"Bloody hell," he growled, kicking his horse to a gallop.

"Can we make it back to the slope?" Sallie squeezed Mairi's fingers.

"Perhaps, but it would do us no good." Mairi still held her free hand to her breast, the tingle continuing to burn there. "They may walk their animals now, but if we run, they'll do the same."

Stupid, stupid, stupid.

How could she have allowed herself to do something as remarkably brainless as getting caught away from the castle like this? And by the very man she'd suspected from the beginning to be the cause of Sallie's death.

Not man, she corrected herself. Fae. As dangerous as he'd been at Dun Ard, he was far more so now. Now that he'd been publicly rejected. Now that she and Sallie were out here alone. Defenseless. She'd allowed herself the comfort of assuming she'd changed things. That Sallie was safe now. She'd been so very wrong.

"Verra well. I'm no going to make it easy for them." Sallie stood, tugging at Mairi's hand. "We'll defend ourselves."

"Right." Mairi rose and wiped her hands down her skirt to brush the wet leaves away. "Right. Okay." She could do this. After all, she'd trained with Jesse regularly. She could fight.

But not nine men.

The old familiar panic flooded her mind.

There's nothing I can do. I'm helpless. All's lost.

Mairi turned to her cousin and froze. The girl, a full head shorter than her, stood with her chin raised high, her weight shifting from one foot to the other, readying herself.

Exactly as I would have nine years ago. Exactly as she would now.

"We'll no be fighting all of them. Only one at a time," she murmured, bolstering her courage as the horsemen approaching them picked up speed.

"Perhaps we'll no have to fight them at all." Sallie nudged Mairi's arm, tilting her head back toward the slope they'd come down.

Ramos!

Mairi was so thankful to see him galloping toward her, she hardly noticed Caden and Andrew following closely behind, or Caden's leaning over to grab Alycie as his betrothed ran out into the meadow. Some other time she'd admire her cousin's strength in hauling the kicking woman onto his horse without ever allowing the animal to break its stride.

For now only one thing mattered: Ramos was here and he was coming for her.

With his body hunkered low over his horse's neck and his long hair whipping out behind him, he looked like her own dark warrior.

Within what felt like a heartbeat, his huge animal was there, bits of mud and leaves kicked up as Ramos jerked his mount to a stop.

Looking up into the unfathomable depths of his eyes, Mairi reached up for the hand he held out to her and felt herself lifted to the saddle behind him. She swung one leg across the horse, letting her skirt ride high up her legs.

"Hold tight, my sweet."

She'd already fastened herself to his back before the words were out of his mouth. Only then did she turn to see Sallie scrambling up behind her brother Andrew in much the same manner as she had.

The thundering rumble of hooves hitting the ground garnered her attention even before Ramos's shouted order.

"Let go!"

Mairi leaned away as Ramos drew his sword from the sheath he'd taken to wearing on his back as her cousins did. She had only seconds to resecure her hold before his horse lurched forward.

The clang of his sword against the weapon held by one of Servan's men reverberated through him and into her chest.

Mairi tightened her hold around Ramos, pressing her face into his back, wishing she could close her ears as well as her eyes. The sounds of men yelling and a woman's scream mingled indistinctly with the noise of swords and horses, creating a cacophony of battle.

Her eyes flew open at a hissing sound near her ear. Her plaid flapped in the breeze where it had been sliced open. Worse, the strike that had damaged her woolen had obviously passed along the side of Ramos's arm on its path to her. Blood oozed from a slit in his sleeve.

The big man she remembered from her first night at Sithean Fardach—Graham, was it?—grinned evilly as he maneuvered his horse closer and swung his sword again.

"Yer too slow, yer lordship," he taunted as Ramos jerked the reins of his horse to maintain their distance, lifting his sword, bracing to take the impact of the hit.

Graham was right. With her attached to him like some kind of a parasite, Ramos wouldn't have a chance. He was already wounded.

My fault. Just like his being stuck in this century. All my fault.

She scanned the area, trying to decide her best course of action. Caden fought off two attackers, hampered by Alycie across his horse. Andrew already lay crumpled on the ground with Sallie hunkered over him. How long before Ramos would meet the same fate?

There was really only one thing for her to do.

Mairi let go the hold she had around Ramos and gripped the back of his saddle, waiting for her opportunity. When he brought the horse to a stop, lifting his sword to block another strike of Graham's weapon, she swung her leg over the back end of the animal and slid to the ground. She bent her knees on landing, wobbling only a little before regaining her balance. Without a backward glance, she lifted her skirts and ran for all she was worth straight toward her injured cousin.

* * *

What the bloody hell? Ramos jerked his head to look behind him.

"Mairi!"

Did she fall? Was she hurt?

He'd been slow on that last return, the blade stinging against his arm as he thrust out to deflect it from Mairi.

Surely she hadn't been wounded. I'd know, wouldn't I?

Ramos attempted to turn his horse, fearing she'd be trampled—or worse.

But his opponent had other ideas. The man swung at him again, the weapon grazing Ramos's cheek in spite of his last-minute dodge.

Ramos twirled his horse, bringing him face-to-face with Graham.

The big man's grin spread as he lifted his sword again. "Perhaps I'll have the lass for myself when I've done with you."

Rather than striking out with his blade and pulling away as he'd done before, as Graham anticipated he'd do now, Ramos darted in closer and smashed the hilt of his weapon against the side of Graham's head.

Graham's eyes went blank as his arm dropped and he fell to the ground with a heavy thud.

"And perhaps not, you bloody bastard," Ramos muttered, turning his horse, searching for Mairi. Whether the man on the ground was stone dead or merely knocked cold mattered not to Ramos. He had only one concern at the moment, and he would fight his way through all the demons of hell, if necessary, to get to her.

"Mairi!"

Up meadow, to the north of him, Caden fought off

two attackers, Alycie draped unceremoniously across the saddle in front of him, her legs kicking wildly.

Caden could take care of himself. Ramos had more pressing concerns.

"Mairi!"

There she is.

A good hundred and twenty meters south of him, on the other side of the stream.

No time for relief at finding her. Instinctively he assessed the situation, not liking at all what he saw.

Andrew lay crumpled on the ground. Sallie kneeling over him. Mairi, her woolen gone, the tail of her wet skirt pulled up and tucked in her belt, facing off against two men who approached her on foot. With most of her hair loosened from its braid, falling around her shoulders, she reminded him of a fabled Amazon warrior protecting her young.

He kicked his horse, urging him in that direction, his entire being focused on the golden goddess that was his destination.

Mairi extended her arms palms up and wiggled her fingers, motioning her opponents to come on as she shifted her weight to the balls of her feet. The first man sheathed his sword and rushed her.

Ramos snapped his head around as he heard a fast-approaching horseman, raising his sword just in time to deflect the strike aimed at his head. He slashed down with his own weapon, landing a solid blow to his opponent's shoulder. Another swing with the flat of his sword and his attacker hit the ground, rolling to avoid the hooves of their horses.

Ramos jerked the reins, forcing his mount to cut back south.

By this time Mairi squatted on the ground, one long leg sweeping out in front of her in a fluid move that knocked the legs from under her attacker before he reached her. She sprang to her feet and delivered a punishing kick to his ribs that curled him into a fetal position, followed by a stomp to his leg that brought a primal scream of pain from the man.

Where did she learn to fight like that?

Mairi turned toward the second man and repeated the beckoning motion. He backed up and drew his sword.

"No!" The bellow was pulled from somewhere deep inside Ramos.

Time seemed to slow as Ramos kicked his horse to a full gallop. Down the meadow and across the water they ran until he was there, solidly between her and the man who threatened her.

He leaped from his mount, tossing the reins toward Mairi.

"Take him. Get out of here."

His sword in hand, he struck out at the man in front of him to drive him back. Back, away from Mairi.

It worked and Ramos continued to maneuver his way forward, his only goal for the moment to move the danger away from her.

Once they were far enough away, he lunged forward with deadly intent. His enemy met his thrust with a jab of his own, the sound of metal ringing out across the meadow.

This one was well trained in the art.

A small corner of his mind registered the rider approaching, passing along the other bank, the sound of water splashing as he crossed the stream.

"Ran, thank the Fae you're here to help us."

He heard Sallie call out, but the adversary he fought demanded his full attention. Besides, Ran was no threat. He was all but part of the family.

Ramos feinted to his left, pulling his opponent off balance. One final swing and it was over. A quick glance across the meadow showed him Caden had defeated one of his attackers while the other rode north.

North to where two mounted figures waited.

Waited and watched.

Ramos's field of vision narrowed, a red haze of hate and fury closing in on him as he stared at the two watchers.

Reynard and Wyn, one leaning low over his mount while the other remained arrogantly regal in his bearing. Both of them patient, observant and detached, heedless of the destruction they caused.

As always, his father instigating a battle but staying back. Far enough away to avoid the action, but close enough to gather the life essence of any Mortals who were killed. Gather their essence and incorporate it into his own, prolonging his own filth-ridden existence.

A woman's screech tore Ramos from his thoughts, pulled his attention from the figures waiting at the far end of the meadow. The red haze evaporated as the pounding of hooves approached, sending him diving to his left, just in time to avoid being trampled.

"Ramos!" Mairi screamed, her voice thick with emotion.

She needed him.

He scrambled to his feet, racing to where she knelt over Andrew.

When she turned her face to him, her expression tore at some deep corner of his being.

"Ran's taken Sallie. Drew's been . . ." Her words trailed off as she looked down at her cousin. Her fingers brushed the rusty patch of hair from the young man's pale forehead and came away coated in blood. When she looked back up at Ramos, bright tears pooled in her eyes. "Drew's badly hurt, Ramos. And I don't have any idea what to do. You have to help me. Please."

I am a worthless fool.

He should have realized his father would use Ran's friendship with the family. It took no effort on his father's part to place a human under a compulsion, and betrayal was part and parcel of Reynard's make up. Ramos had only to think of all the years his father had lied to him, of how his father had betrayed him and led him into harming others.

How could he have been so stupid? Again.

How? It was easy. He'd allowed himself to be distracted. All his life he'd known the importance of keeping his feelings closed off. And now, here in this time when it mattered most, he repeatedly lost the battle to control his emotions.

Guilt ate at him as, with one last glance at the riders retreating to the north, he dropped to his knees to examine the boy on the ground.

He would deal with his father soon. He would see to it that the evil Nuadian Fae never betrayed anyone again. But for the moment, Mairi needed him.

Everywhere. There was blood everywhere.

Mairi looked at her hands, the hands she'd stroked

over Andrew. They were both covered in blood. His blood.

Only Ramos, warm and solid, kneeling next to her, kept her from falling apart entirely.

Ramos would know what to do. He was always calm and in control. Not like her.

A horse approaching drew her eyes from her hands. Caden slid off his mount, his forearm soaked in blood, cradled against his chest. With his good arm he pulled Alycie from across his saddle, none too gently.

When her feet hit the ground, she threw herself at Caden, pummeling him with her fists.

Again using only his uninjured arm, he pushed her away and she stumbled, losing her balance and landing in the soft, wet carpet of grass.

"I hate you, Caden MacAlister. Hate you!" she screamed, her face blotched with spots of bright red.

"What's the matter with you? You nearly got us both killed back there." Caden stood over her, confusion evident in his every move. "It's as though you dinna want me to save you, woman."

"I dinna! I was to go with them. They promised me, and now you've stolen my only chance." She buried her face in her hands and sobbed.

"I dinna understand any of this," Caden whispered.

The sight of her strong, laughing cousin, his face creased in helpless concern, brought Mairi to her feet and across the distance between them.

Dropping to Alycie's side, she jerked the girl's hands from her face.

"What have you done?"

"He promised," the girl sobbed. "If I would but lead

you and Sallie to them, he promised they could root out the evil from yer family."

"Root out the . . ." Mairi dropped the girl's hands and stood, looking down at Alycie in disgust.

Tears still rolled down the girl's cheeks, leaving trails in the dirt on her face.

"You betrayed the trust of people who accepted you without question. Why? What were you to get out of this bargain?"

"My freedom!" Alycie screamed. "The Duke's brother promised they'd see me to the nunnery on Iona. He said they'd see to it I was accepted there. He promised to save me from marriage to Caden."

Next to Mairi, Caden stiffened. "Marriage to me is so distasteful you'd sacrifice my cousin? My own sister?" His face had lost all expression, frozen into a mask of unconcern.

"Aye, it is. I'd sooner die than be wed to one of the devil's own," she whispered, returning to great, heaving sobs.

Caden leaned down and, grasping Alycie's upper arms, he yanked her to her feet, pulling her face close to his. "Where have they taken Sallie?"

"I dinna ken the whole of their plan. Only what part I was to play," she whimpered. "And I'll thank you to remove yer hands from my person. I've no desire to be touched by the likes of you."

Caden jerked his hands from her arms, backing away, shaking his head. "Dinna fret yerself, lass. I'll no be touching you ever again. I release you from yer betrothal vows, Alycie Maxwell, and I'll see yer taken to Iona."

"You'll do that for me?" She reached out toward his arm but he drew away sharply.

"No. I do it out of friendship with yer brothers, out of respect for yer family. I do it because if those men harm my sister, being in a nunnery is the only thing that will save you from my wrath."

"I warned you, did I no?" Andrew's weak words brought both Caden and Mairi quickly to his side.

"Lie still, Drew." Ramos's face was without expression as he checked the crude bandages he had fashioned around the young man's forehead and his upper leg using pieces of his own shirt. He stood and walked to his horse, taking up the reins and bringing the animal back to where Mairi waited. "I'm going after Sallie."

"I canna ask you to do that." Caden looked up from where he knelt at Andrew's side. "It's my responsibility."

"No. It's mine. You need to get Drew and the women back to Dun Ard. To safety. You need to have that arm looked after."

"Then I'm going with you." Mairi ran to his side. It was only right. He shouldn't go alone. Anything could happen to him and she'd never even know. Besides, all this was her fault. She should have known better, should have kept Sallie from coming out here.

"No. Caden needs your help in getting Drew back to Dun Ard. You must do this for them, Mairi." He pulled her close, turning his back to the others and lowering his voice until only she could hear. "When you get there, go to Caden's chambers and get my bag. Inside you'll find a small leather roll tied up. It holds the syringes I brought along, injections of the antibiotic I gave you. If you use it on your cousins, they'll have every chance of recovery. Don't worry about Sallie. I'll find her. I promise."

"But . . ." Mairi didn't want to go to Dun Ard. She wanted to go with Ramos. To help him.

"No buts. Just this once, do as I tell you."

Mairi could only nod her agreement, the risk of tears too high to chance speaking.

A quick kiss to her forehead and he mounted up, galloping off across the meadow in the direction the Duke and his men had taken Sallie.

Mairi watched until he disappeared into the trees.

"Okay, Ramos," she whispered. "I'll do as you say for now."

But once Caden and Drew are safe at Dun Ard, I'm coming after you.

Twenty-one

The mist returned before they'd gone more than a mile or two. As they traveled, it changed to a cold, sleeting rain. By the time they reached Dun Ard, a heavy, wet snow fell.

Mairi rode with Andrew, holding her arms around him to prevent his falling from the horse. Her muscles ached from his weight leaning against her. Even through her cold, wet woolen plaid she could feel the heat rising from his body. Already the fever had a firm grasp on him.

A cry went up at the gates, and before they'd reached the main courtyard a crowd had gathered. Mairi barely noticed as hands reached up to pull Drew from her grasp and help her down from her horse.

She pushed away as soon as her feet hit the ground, running to Caden's chambers.

Inside and up the stairs she ran, breathless when she pushed through the door. Ramos's bag lay on a neatly made pallet by the fire.

She fell to her knees and opened it, digging through the clothing. At first she thought it was gone, but then, at the very bottom, wrapped in a pair of trousers, she found it, the little leather bag Ramos had held that first day here at Dun Ard.

Clasping it tightly to her, she ran to her aunt's chambers, sure that was where her cousins would have been taken by now.

Strong arms grabbed her as she entered the room.

Mairi pushed away, thrusting her weight to her left foot, fully intending to unleash everything she had on the attacker who kept her from helping her cousins.

Only the familiarity of his voice stopped her.

"Thank the Fae yer safe, Mairi. I dinna ken what I'd do if we lost you." Blane pulled her close in a tight embrace. "Not again," he whispered, a break in his voice.

She allowed Blane to embrace her for a moment as she caught her breath, her knees weak as the adrenaline that had flooded her system moments before left her. She pushed away, lifting a hand to her cousin's cheek.

"Thank you, Blane."

Once again she found herself fighting the tears that threatened so near the surface. Better she concentrate on the important matters at hand rather than allow herself to wallow in sentimentality.

"You've already dispatched yer men to join Ramos, aye?"

"It's no safe to do so until morning, lass. With this snow, in the dark, they'd be of no use. We'll be out on his trail at first light."

This can't be happening.

"His trail will be lost by morning, covered over by the snow."

Ramos would need help. By tomorrow no one would be able to find where the Duke had taken Sallie. But protesting would do no good. Her cousin wouldn't risk his men foolishly. And she couldn't honestly expect him to.

At a soft touch on her shoulder, Mairi turned to find her aunt, worry clouding the woman's expression.

"Do you plan to use something from yer pouch there?" Rosalyn pointed to the leather roll Mairi held.

"I do. Do you know what this is?"

Her aunt shrugged. "It's the same pouch Ramos used the day he brought you to our gates, is it no?"

Mairi nodded her agreement and Rosalyn turned to Blane.

"I would be grateful if you'd clear the room of servants. Mairi and I will deal with the lads."

As Blane ushered everyone from the room, Mairi hurried to Drew's side, pressing her hand to his forehead. If anything, he felt even warmer to her now than he had when they'd ridden into the courtyard.

Quickly she untied the roll and laid it open. There were two syringes individually sealed in paper wrappers. Reading the label, she could see they were the antibiotic Ramos had referred to. A third, slightly larger sealed syringe stood by itself in another compartment of the pouch. Examining it, she realized it must be a twin to the one Ramos had used on her, containing both an antibiotic and sedative.

Mairi tore into the first package, determined not to let her aunt see her hands shaking. She'd helped with vaccinations and shots for the horses on her brother's ranch. This couldn't be so very different. At least she hoped not.

"What is it yer doing there, Cousin?" Caden sat up, peering across the bed as Mairi prepared to administer the injection to Drew.

"Leave Mairi be." Rosalyn spoke to her eldest son without taking her eyes from Mairi's hands.

"No, Aunt. He's right to question me. This contains a medication that will help Drew's body fight the infection that causes his fever," she explained as she continued, tearing into a small sterile wipe and running it over her cousin's arm.

When she finished with Drew, she moved to the other side of the bed, examining the wound on Caden's forearm. Rosalyn had cleaned it, but there was no sense taking a chance.

"You think to stab me with one of those wee spears as well?" Caden asked.

"I do. Now bare your upper arm for me."

Her cousin shrugged out of the tattered shirt he wore. "Did I hear Blane say he'd no send anyone out after Ramos tonight?"

Her stomach roiled at the thought, but she managed to respond. "You did."

"Verra well. Finish up with me so I can be on my way. I'll go after him myself."

Rosalyn, who'd moved quietly to her side, clutched Mairi's sleeve.

"No, Caden. You need rest," Mairi replied. "To allow yerself time to begin healing."

"I'll heal later. Someone has to go before it's too late." Caden turned his head while she swiped the sterile pad over his arm, as if he didn't want to watch the process.

Someone will.

"Perhaps. But it's no going to be you, Caden MacAlister. Yer going to sleep and allow yer body the time it needs." Mairi reached into the other pocket and pulled out the larger syringe. "Now lie back, Cousin, and be very still so I can have this over with."

Caden did as she asked and didn't even flinch when she pressed the needle into his arm.

"Where did you come into possession of this strange medication?" he asked, his eyes blinking slowly.

"It came from very far away," she whispered, smiling as his lids drooped down.

"Will he sleep as you did?" Rosalyn asked while she gathered up the syringes and paper Mairi had used.

"Aye, he should. But perhaps no as long," Mairi answered, wrinkling her brow as her aunt moved to the fireplace and tossed everything into the roaring flames.

Rosalyn looked up and shrugged. "It's what Ramos did. I suppose it wouldn't do to have yer future things left about."

Mairi nodded her agreement as she tied up the leather bundle and turned to leave.

"Why have they taken my Sallie?" Rosalyn had returned to her younger son's side, draping a damp cloth over his heated forehead.

"The Duke wants her for the power of her Fae blood."

Rosalyn dipped the cloth back into a pan of water and wrung it out before returning it to her son's head. "With all the questions he asked, I feared it would be so." She swiped at her cheek, wiping away the tears that fell. "But Sallie's no so strong in the gifts. And she's such an unbridled temper. Even worse than you were at her age."

"Dinna worry, Rosalyn. Ramos will find her. We'll no allow anything to happen to her. It's why I came here." Mairi stopped as she realized she'd been able to speak of her reason for having come.

"Thank you."

Mairi left the chamber, closing the door behind her, worry and guilt clawing at her stomach as she hurried down the hall.

Why had the Faerie magic allowed her to speak of her true purpose only now?

Was it because events had already been set into motion that she would be unable to change, or, worse, was it because she was responsible for setting those events into motion?

Twenty-two

For the second time in twenty-four hours Mairi found herself sneaking away from Dun Ard.

This time it had been remarkably easier, she thought, as she kicked her horse, urging him to hurry in spite of the snow.

When she'd gone back to Caden's room to return the leather pouch to Ramos's bag, she'd helped herself to a pair of his pants and a shirt. After changing into his clothes, she'd bundled an old plaid around her, marched out to the stables, taken a horse and demanded exit at the inner gate.

The snow fell steadily, already blanketing the ground in spite of the fact that she'd taken as little time as possible to head out. She hadn't even eaten, she realized with dismay as her stomach rumbled.

No matter. Her goal now was to catch up with Ramos. Once she reached the meadow where they'd split up, she should be able to follow his tracks. The nearly full moon reflected off the snow, casting more light than she would ordinarily expect at night. That, at least, should help her find him.

She might not be a huge help, but she would be better than nothing when he reached the men who held Sallie.

There were too many of them for him to face alone.

And if something happened to him . . .

She shook her head, hunkering down closer into her horse. She wouldn't allow herself to think about that possibility. Instead she'd concentrate on finding him.

Again she urged her horse to greater speed, trying to keep the fear at bay as she rode.

The silently falling snow had obliterated all tracks.

Ramos pulled his horse to a stop and reached out to touch his fingers to the branch of the tree he passed. Twigs were broken and bent, all leaning forward as if someone had passed through them.

Someone had. Seven men, two Fae, and one unwilling woman.

He'd followed their tracks from the meadow, finding the spot where four additional riders had joined them. Their eastward progress had held, but now he could no longer count on the prints of the horses to follow.

Their tracks might be hidden, but Ramos knew there were other signs of their passing. He had only to look for them. He'd lost the trail once today. He didn't intend to let it happen again.

Fortunately the eerie glow of the moon as it danced in and out of the clouds reflected on the white landscape, providing him light to hunt his prey.

He just wished he knew this part of Scotland better. They would be headed for a likely Portal site. Standing stones would be the obvious, unless Sallie offered information about Pol's Glen. And from what he knew of Sallie, that didn't seem at all likely.

The thought of how frustrated his father must be with the headstrong young woman very nearly brought a smile to his face until he remembered how his father dealt with anyone who displeased him.

"Hang on, Sallie," he whispered. "I'll find you."

He had only to figure out where Reynard would go.

Standing stones. His mind raced. There were hundreds in Scotland, but how many were excavated now, in this time?

There was, of course, the Portal on Ian McCullough's property in southern Scotland. Ramos considered for the briefest moment seeking Ian out and asking his help. The man had been a Guardian for centuries.

Still, on horseback it would be a journey of several days, and Ramos didn't have several days. He would be lucky to have forty-eight hours. And who knew what sort of problems he'd create by meeting up with someone he knew from the future, more than seven hundred years before he should know them.

He rubbed at his forehead, squinting through the snow as it slanted to the earth. No wonder time travel was forbidden.

This was one he'd have to figure out on his own.

Too bad he didn't have a connection to Sallie similar to the one he had with Mairi. That would certainly make tracking an easier task.

At the thought of Mairi, he felt the familiar twinge

of her in that unusual corner of his mind. Almost like she was drawing closer to him.

That, of course, was impossible. Caden would have her safely back at Dun Ard by now.

Ramos shook his head and prompted his horse forward, dislodging the wet snow that had collected on them as they'd sat still.

This was no time to think about Mairi. He needed to concentrate on the task at hand, needed to stay alert, following the signs he found.

Sooner or later, something would show up to point him in the direction he needed to go.

So cold.

Mairi flexed her fingers and wiped at the heavy snow coating her eyelashes and forehead before wrapping the edges of the thin plaid over her hands again. She captured her reins within the wool, her shivering fingers cramping and burning with the contact. Once again, she urged her horse forward.

Poor creature.

Snow beat against them, hanging in frozen lumps from the animal's mane. He must be every bit as miserable as she.

Have to keep going.

She'd passed through the meadow hours ago, it seemed, and although the heavy snow obscured any tracks Ramos might have left, Mairi knew she was on the correct trail. He was somewhere up ahead.

He'd be moving slowly, hunting for whatever signs he could find of the Duke's party having passed through the area. She, on the other hand, had ridden hard knowing at least in the beginning where she headed.

Even beyond the meadow, she'd forced her mount to keep up his pace, ignoring the dangers inherent in the snow-covered terrain. Guided by nothing more than feelings, she made her way forward. It was the slight tingle in her chest that led her. The one she felt every time she was around Reynard Servans.

Some sort of Faerie danger signal, she supposed. The feeling had grown more pronounced the farther she'd gone. She simply continued to rush headlong in the direction that made the feeling stronger.

East. Is this east?

She looked up to find the moon, but it had skittered behind the clouds again. Snow pelted her face, forcing her to close her eyes.

The direction didn't matter.

Follow the feeling.

She didn't need to see where she headed. The burning tingle over her heart was all the trail she needed.

She would trust Ramos to track Servans. Sooner or later, if she maintained this pace, she would catch up with Ramos.

She kicked and her horse lurched forward, trying to give her the speed she demanded. Across this low area she would make up even more time. Surely her mount could go faster than this. Another kick and he picked up his pace, snow flying up from the flat ground as his hooves flew over it.

Unfortunately the ground wasn't as flat as the snow made it appear.

Mid-stride the horse stumbled, struggling to keep himself from falling. Mairi's cold, cramping fingers couldn't hold the reins when the animal stopped and her momentum carried her forward, over his lowered head and through the air.

When her body hit the ground, the thud sounded muffled to her ears, and she slid until something stopped her.

She opened her eyes to see the barrier she'd ended up against was a bush. She blinked, trying to focus on the twigs sticking out around her. Dark, snow-covered berries held tightly to the branches.

A witchwood, of all things.

She'd found Sallie's berries at last, though she didn't need them anymore. Oddly she couldn't remember why not.

Need to get up.

She couldn't lie here on the ground, but it was so hard to move. The snow wrapped about her like a reassuring blanket. There was some reason she shouldn't remain as she was, but for the life of her, she couldn't remember what that was, either.

So quiet. So tired.

Only the sound of her horse's heavy breathing somewhere nearby disturbed the night.

She wanted to reach out, to make sure the animal was unharmed, but she hadn't the strength to lift her hand. Couldn't make her eyes open to look at him.

Only her mind seemed to work, guilt pressing in as she thought of Ramos. Of how angry he would be when he found out she hadn't stayed at Dun Ard as he'd told her to.

"I'm sorry, Ramos," she tried to whisper, her lips too cold, too heavy to form the words.

His face was the last picture in her mind, his name

the last sound she made before the cold black closed in around her.

If Reynard's party had stopped for the night, there was still a good chance Ramos would catch them soon. If he was headed the right direction. There were no signs of their passing, the heavy, wet snow obscuring everything. And the time he'd spent taking the wrong trail earlier hadn't helped.

Ramos squatted next to his horse, running his fingers over the low branches of a large bush. The wind swept up in gusts, buffeting his body with great swirls of snow, but the heavy plaid he wore bundled around his head and shoulders, in the way Mairi had shown him, protected him from the worst of this weather.

Somehow he would find them. He would rescue Sallie, just as he'd promised Mairi he would. And then . . . Then he would deal with his father. He would find a way to keep Reynard from hurting anyone ever again.

To hell with the Fae rule. Both worlds would be safer without Reynard Servans.

Ramos had just risen to his feet when the pain hit. A spasm so intense it knocked the breath from him as he leaned against his horse to keep himself upright.

"Mairi." Her name was wrenched involuntarily from his lips.

With his eyes closed, he could see her lying in the snow. Long, thick lashes lay dark against her pale skin, her lips an unhealthy cast of blue. Limp locks of golden hair, caked with snow, fell against the side of her face.

"I'm sorry, Ramos."

Her words floated to him as if she spoke them in the air next to his ear.

The sound of her voice jolted him, snapping him out of whatever trance he'd fallen into.

He pulled himself up onto his horse and tapped deeply into that space in his mind where Mairi dwelt.

Once again, his father would have to wait.

Turning his horse back to the direction he'd come from, he leaned low and drove the animal to move as fast as it could.

He didn't know how it was possible, but Mairi was out here somewhere. And she was in trouble.

Backtracking should have been much faster, but the snow had begun to cover even the trail he had left a short time ago. Before long, the small corner of his mind that resonated with Mairi was his only means to find her. The closer he got, the more she filled that spot.

But something was very wrong.

Her presence felt different somehow. Before, when he had looked in that little corner within himself, he could see all the colors of the rainbow sparkling, dancing, cascading around the sheer white luminance that was Mairi. Now the colors were subdued, as if he looked at them through dark glasses. Or as if they were fading.

Reaching the bottom of a particularly steep slope, he pulled up on the reins to slow his mount as he came out of the forest onto a deceptively flat-looking area. From his earlier passage he knew that to be misleading. The ground here was fraught with rocks and dips, hidden now by a smooth white blanket.

He'd lost the trail here earlier today, being drawn

off to the west a bit. There he'd found a small herders' hut, likely one of those Caden had established for the local shepherds. He'd turned back shortly after that, realizing he was heading the wrong direction when all the undergrowth appeared untouched.

Peering out through the blowing snow, Ramos caught sight of a riderless horse, head bowed low to the ground. He fought down the impulse to kick his mount to a full gallop, and slowly made his way toward the lone animal.

As he drew close, he could make out a dark shape on the ground at the horse's feet. Every fiber in his being knew what—who—that bundle was.

Mairi.

It took only a moment more to reach her side.

The bush she lay against had given her some protection, though precious little. Still, the wind had blown around it, drifting the snow about her but not covering her completely.

Ramos slid his hand inside her woolen wrap and placed two fingers on her neck, refusing to believe the worst.

Her pulse beat under his touch, slow but steady. Her skin, even under the plaid, felt icy.

Hypothermia was the enemy now.

He had to get Mairi out of the cold as soon as possible, but where?

The herders' hut.

Gently Ramos gathered her up and mounted his horse, trying to jostle her as little as possible. He was keenly aware that, depending on the degree of hypothermia, any rough movement could lead to cardiac arrest. And he had no way of assessing how far her body temperature had dropped.

Laying her head against his chest, he covered her completely with his plaid as he rewrapped it around his body. He kept his mount to a slow, even pace, her horse following along behind.

Though the hut wasn't far, the journey there seemed interminably long. Ramos used the ride to reassure himself he'd reached her in time. She was, after all, of the Faerie blood. She was resilient and would heal quickly.

Like the wound to her foot.

Fast healing was normal for their kind.

And it wasn't like he was without resources of his own. After all, he'd spent one whole ski season working with the volunteer rescue patrol just after his twentieth birthday. He was trained to deal with cold-weather emergencies exactly like this.

Like hell I am.

He knew how to get on a radio and call for help. His training only covered that period of time until the helicopter arrived to airlift the victim to the hospital.

No sign of a radio here. And there certainly wouldn't be any airlift.

This rescue was up to him.

Ramos tightened his hold on his precious bundle and sighed in relief when the hut came into view.

He just prayed he was up to this.

Twenty-three

Yer a foul, slimy excuse for a man if ever I—"

Sallie's tirade ended abruptly as her head snapped back. A trickle of blood bloomed from her bottom lip, a result of the big guard's backhanded blow.

"There's no need for that, Graham." Wyn's rebuke came out sharper than he'd intended, drawing Reynard's attention.

"*Un problème, mon ami?*"

"No." Wyn's unexpected sympathy for the girl certainly wouldn't help her at all. Not for the first time, a pang of regret flashed through him. Of all the bad decisions in his mistake-laden life, his choice to back his best friend over his brother had been by far the worst.

He'd been young and foolish, convinced Reynard had everyone's best interests at heart.

And his brother? His brother had been the most arrogant, domineering creature in the Realm of Faerie, undeserved accolades and honors handed to him on a golden platter.

Or so it had seemed to Wyn at the time. Staring into the glittering eyes of the friend he'd given up so much for, he admitted that after all these centuries, he wasn't so sure anymore.

Reynard had no more compassion for a Mortal than he would for some six-legged creature he might find living under a wet log he turned with the toe of his boot. He would have one killed as easily as the other. Both without regret of any sort.

It was for this reason Wyn had chosen not to share what he'd learned about Mairi. He couldn't see placing both women at risk.

Wyn dropped his eyes respectfully, turning with a practiced shrug intended to convey complete and utter disregard for the entire situation. It was the only chance he might have to help the poor little creature.

"No problem at all, Rey." The familiar name from his youth slipped easily from his tongue, though he suspected the man to whom that name had belonged had disappeared over the centuries, if he'd ever really existed at all.

Wyn walked to the fire the men had built in the small hovel they'd commandeered and held his hands out, rubbing them together to warm them. "I care naught about the maid. It's simply that she'll be of no use to you once she's injured. If your man there closes her eyes with his blows, how will she be able to locate the Portal for us?"

Wyn kept his direct gaze averted, watching stealthily from under his lashes to see if his words had hit their mark.

Reynard stared at the girl, unconsciously brushing dirt from his sleeve.

"*Oui,*" he murmured to himself at last. "Perhaps you are correct. Leave her be."

"Beggin' yer pardon, yer grace." The guard bowed his head before continuing. "But if she spews them vile insults to yer person, am I to allow it?"

Reynard pulled a scarf from his sleeve and tossed it to the man. "Tie that about her pretty mouth if she can't keep it shut. If that merits your approval, Wyn?"

Wyn refused to meet Reynard's eyes. "Matters not to me. The less noise, the better." That seemed to satisfy his old friend.

It would have to do. He'd done everything he dared for their captive. Any more interference might result in Reynard's allowing his men to do her real damage.

Wyn snapped his fingers and the Mortal—Ran, was it?—came to his side, the dull stare of compulsion the boy's only expression.

"Prepare our bedding for the night."

At the order, Ran scuttled off to lay out bedding for both Wyn and Reynard.

With a deep mental sigh, Wyn squatted down, staring into the fire, escaping into his thoughts. He hated using compulsions. The spark of humanity that he found so interesting in Mortals completely disappeared under the force of his magic.

Besides, it took so much energy from him to maintain a good compulsion, Wyn felt drained afterward. That was why Reynard preferred to have him do it.

Interesting how Reynard had never seemed to realize that allowing Wyn to place the compulsion meant the Mortals were under Wyn's control, not Reynard's. Not that it made any difference.

Why should Reynard worry? He was secure in the

knowledge that Wyn would do whatever he wanted. What else could he do? He had nowhere to go unless he wanted to strike out on his own.

A shiver ran down Wyn's spine. If only he'd been able to capture Mairi. He could have convinced Reynard he'd merely taken a fancy to her, that he only wanted a new pet. Perhaps with her aid he would have been able to locate the Portal himself. To go home.

And then what?

Find his brother? Grovel at his older sibling's feet? Beg for mercy from the High Council?

He stood and kicked a pebble into the fire before turning away in disgust. Disgust with everything he'd ever done. Disgust with what he'd become.

There was no going home for him.

Twenty-four

Mairi floated in the warm, turquoise waters of the Indian Ocean, gentle waves lapping at her body, soothing her, rocking her.

It seemed only a short time ago she'd fought the nightmares, horrible dreams of cold and pain and shivering so hard it made her teeth ache. Dreams where the darkness closed in on her, trying to suffocate her.

Then Ramos had invaded the dream, driving away the dark and the stinging needles of pain in her hands and feet and face. She'd looked up into his eyes and had known she was safe, even without the small crooning sounds of comfort he'd made. All her pain and fear had melted away in the rejuvenating softness of his embrace. There in the depths of his blue-green gaze, she'd drifted off to her favorite dream haven, complete with glistening white sand and warm, aquamarine waves.

She reveled in the cocoon of warmth around her,

not wanting to fully awaken. But the call to reality was persistent, and little by little, perceptions of her surroundings intruded on her dream paradise. Tiny bits of information at first, all jumbled together as she fought to remain under the surface of wakefulness: the enticing smell of Ramos surrounding her, the comforting security of his arms enfolding her, the intoxicating feel of his skin next to hers.

Her eyes fluttered open as she realized the sensation of Ramos's warm skin against hers wasn't part of the dream. It was real. The darkness that engulfed her only added to her confusion.

"Ramos?" The last thing she remembered was lying in the snow after falling from her horse. Now she rested next to him, both of them tightly swaddled in what appeared to be his plaid. "I dinna remember finding you."

"You didn't. I found you."

Her heart skipped a beat at the sound of his voice. His chest, pressed against her ear, rumbled with the words. His muscles flexed under her as he reached to loosen their covering, allowing her access to the dim light of their surroundings.

"Where are we?" Though she didn't recognize what little she could see, she felt no alarm. Instinctively she knew there was nothing to fear while she was in Ramos's protective embrace.

"I believe it's one of the shelters built for shepherds. It's not much, but at least it's dry." Almost imperceptibly he tightened his hold on her. "How do you feel? Are you warm enough?"

"I'm fine."

Mairi's awareness of their skin-to-skin contact

heightened her sense of well-being. Curving the sole of her foot to his leg, she slowly stroked up his calf, pausing as she felt his body stiffen.

Better than fine.

Nestled close to the only man she would ever want, she could think of very little that might make her feel better.

"Stop that. Be still now and rest. It'll be first light soon enough."

Other than having him feel the same way, of course.

"I'm well rested." Sleep wasn't the activity on her mind at the moment. She was wide awake. Turning her head slightly, she swirled her tongue around his nipple.

His body jerked and he grabbed her upper arms, pushing her away from him.

"I said stop that. I told you before, what happened between us won't be repeated. I meant what I said."

Leaning her head back, she looked up at him. Firelight glinted off his broad, bare shoulders, long silky strands of shining black hair their only cover. That husky tremor in his voice, the jaw muscle clenching, the desire in his eyes—Mairi took it all in. Ramos may *think* he meant what he said, but she knew differently.

"Oh really? Then why am I bundled up against you, no a stitch of clothing on either one of us?" She smiled up at him, sliding her hands along his chest, enjoying the twitching response of the hard muscles under her fingers. "I'm no complaining, mind you."

"You were suffering from hypothermia. I needed to get your core temperature up if I wanted to save your life and that was the only way available. Believe me,

Mairi, that's all there is to it." The muscle at his jaw-line worked still, a telltale sign of the force of will he exerted.

Again she smiled at him, tugging her arms from his grasp and sliding them around his neck, she pulled her body up against his until their faces were level. "I'm no convinced that's yer only reason."

"It is. What I allowed to happen before was a mistake. One that I don't intend to repeat."

"Dinna you now?"

Again she curved the sole of her foot to his leg, sliding it up his calf as she shifted over his body.

"Mairi."

He growled her name in warning and she smiled down at him, slow and sure, when she heard the stress in what was supposed to be his reprimand.

"Shhh," she whispered, lowering her mouth to his, tasting him, capturing his full lower lip with her teeth, running her tongue over its surface.

He groaned, his hands back on her upper arms, but he didn't push her away this time.

She kissed her way to the side of his face, burying her nose in his neck, breathing him in, wanting to lose herself in the essence of him.

She traced the chiseled plain of his chest with her fingers, down his body, down to the ripples of muscle on his abdomen.

Lower. Down to the heated evidence of desire he couldn't disguise from her. Feathering her fingers over the stretched, velvety skin drew another groan from him.

"Mairi, we can't . . ."

The words sounded as if they'd been torn from his body against his will. She brushed them away, knowing she would have him.

He is mine.

"Oh, but we can. Dinna deny me, Ramos. No this one time. I need you. Here. Now."

She tightened her grip, slowly sliding her hand up the length of him, pausing to stroke the tip of his shaft with the pad of her thumb.

What might have been a sigh shook his chest and he enfolded her in his arms. His hands slid up behind her into her hair, cradling her head like something precious as he rolled over on top of her. His eyes burned with emotion as he looked down into her face.

"God help me, but I don't seem to have the strength to deny you anything."

He crushed his lips to hers and she opened her mouth to capture his thrusting tongue, savoring the feel of him, the taste of him.

He raised his head, kissed her eyes, her cheeks, her chin, her neck. Down he moved, outlining the tingling mark on her breast with his warm tongue, fueling the burn of her need.

His hands slid down her back, down to her waist, down to her hips as his mouth moved lower, licking a trail of fire down her center.

Her hips seemed to lift of their own accord when his tongue flicked over the core of her need. Back and forth in sharp little attacks until she could hardly catch her breath.

A sound, low and needy, hit her ears. Had that moan come from her?

She thought she might have heard Ramos chuckle before his mouth captured the hardened nub of her desire, suckling as if she were some delicacy he sampled.

But she had no time to be sure because almost immediately his finger slipped into her, probing, pushing her over the edge, beyond her ability to control. Her body clamped onto him in a series of mindnumbing pulses.

He slid up her body, peppering kisses over her breasts, her shoulders and then her face as she panted, struggling to come back into herself.

He lifted over her, a sexy, knowing, self-satisfied grin on his face.

She didn't care. He'd earned the right to wear that look.

His long silky hair curtained around them, tickling over her breasts, and suddenly she was filled with the need to earn that right herself.

She pushed against his shoulders, and he lowered himself to his back, carrying her over with him.

Straddling his body, she sat up, allowing her hair to cascade over her shoulders and dance against his skin as his had hers a moment before.

His hands skimmed up from her waist, past her ribs, stopping to knead her breasts. She let her head fall back, giving him access, enjoying the pleasure his fingers brought before pulling away.

She bent over him, tormenting the skin of his chest with her tongue as he had done to hers. Slipping in between his legs, she nibbled over his abdomen, his erection warm between her breasts as she pressed against him. The hard ridges that formed across his stomach as his muscles tensed in response to what she did delighted her, gave her a sense of power and control.

Moving down his body, she ran her hands over his steely thighs, dragging her thumbs to the inside of his legs and back up to his solid, flat stomach.

She wanted to laugh with sheer joy when his entire body jerked as she ran her tongue the length of his shaft.

"Christ, Mairi, what are you . . . ?" His voice faded into a low moan when she took the head into her mouth, swirling her tongue around the swollen tip.

"No more."

He sounded breathless as he hooked his hands under her arms and pulled her up his body, the slide of her breasts against his chest inflaming her need for him.

She hooked her legs behind his, and once again he rolled her to her back, lifting himself onto his elbows to look down at her. Slowly, slowly he lowered his head, his mouth hovering over hers, his breath feathering over her lips.

So close she could almost taste him.

He dipped his head, and as his lips met hers he entered her. She wasn't sure if the gasp she breathed in was his or hers, and she didn't really care anymore. She only knew that she wanted more of him. Deeper. Harder.

She raised her legs, locking them behind his back, lifting her hips into his next push.

"Ah, Mairi. You feel so good," he panted. "It's like I—" His words ended abruptly and he crushed his mouth to hers again, stealing her breath with his kiss.

Like you belong here.

Abandoning her mouth, he rose back up on his elbows, capturing her eyes with his own as he moved in and out, slowly, deliberately, fully, until she writhed under him, meeting him stroke for stroke.

She felt it building then, the power of release only he could bring her. She gave herself over to it, riding the crest of the sensations as her body convulsed around his, only peripherally aware of his shuddering release.

The light that shattered around them into a million colored shards had to have been her imagination.

She cuddled into him, his heart pounding rapidly under her ear, a match to her own. As it began to slow, she felt him move and tense next to her, so she shifted her weight onto one elbow and gazed down at him.

"We can't allow this to happen again, Mairi. Can't continue to allow ourselves to be caught up in the moment. You've your whole life ahead of you when you return home. You don't want to make the mistake of wasting it on someone like me."

Mairi ran her finger down the stubborn jaw, stopping at his chin to gaze into the eyes of the man she loved. She had freely chosen to forsake her family and her home to remain in this time with him, even knowing he might never accept what was meant to be between them, might never again offer her more than his protection.

Now she realized that would never be enough. And like Sallic, she wasn't patient enough to wait for her one true love to come to her. But was she strong enough to follow her own advice—the counsel she'd given Sallie just yesterday? Could she swallow her pride and simply talk to him?

"What if I think yer wrong, Ramos? What if I dinna believe what passed between us to be a mistake? What if I were to tell you I love you?"

"Don't say that!"

Ramos could barely force the strangled response from his mouth. Mairi had no idea what binding power those words could have. He had never used them. Never.

Neither would she if she knew him better. Knew what he really was. Knew the awful things he assisted his father in doing. If he were only brave enough, strong enough to tell her. But he wasn't.

He wasn't even strong enough to keep his hands off her.

"Why should I no? I love you."

She placed her soft fingers on either side of his face, holding tighter when he attempted to pull away. "I do. Dinna argue with me. Instead"—her lips curved in that slow, seductive smile that sent ripples to the core of him—"tell me about this."

Her finger traced the tattoo on his arm. The mark of a Guardian in service to the Elite Guard. He vividly remembered the day he'd been granted the right to wear the mark.

"You have earned the right to bear our symbol," Dallyn had said. "You are one of us now. Display it proudly. It is a distinction of honor in the Realm of Faerie."

Honor. He clearly had none. What would his general say if he could see him now?

He gently grasped Mairi's finger, lifting it from where she traced the design. The outline burned in the absence of the contact, as if her gentle touch had freshly etched the mark into his skin.

The burn of my own conscience.

"I bear the mark of a Fae Guardian." And because of that, he couldn't let this go any further. "Listen to me, Mairi. What you feel for me is only temporary." It would dissolve the moment she learned of his past. Of the years he had spent in service to the Nuadian Fae. Of all he had done, however unwittingly, to aid in bringing death and destruction to the World of Mortals.

"You're wrong, Ramos. We're meant to be together. I know it. Here." She placed her hand over her heart.

What had he done?

"No, Mairi. You're simply overcome by the circumstances we're in. Once I've found Sallie, we'll figure out the exact words you used that trapped you in this time and we'll send you home. You don't want things said here that you'll regret later."

She'd forget all about him once he had her safely home. He didn't doubt that for a moment. That was as it should be. She was too good for someone like him.

"The only thing I'd regret forever would be if I dinna tell you how I feel." She gently kissed his lips, her touch lighter than a breath. "Anyway, I canna go home."

It would be so easy to lose himself in her kiss. But he wouldn't. He would be stronger than that. "Don't worry. We'll figure out what's keeping you here. I will get you home." No matter what it might take. "I swear."

She glanced away, pursing her lips before responding. "I'm afraid it's too late for that."

"What?"

She was hiding something from him. He could tell by the determined glint in her eye when she looked back at him. Something she knew he wasn't going to like.

"What have you done, Mairi?"

"I already know what words I said, because I've already accomplished what the Faeries wanted of me. But I canna go home until . . ." She stopped, chewing at her bottom lip.

"Until what?" He grasped her hands, holding them together against his chest as he sat up, pulling her along with him. He spoke more roughly than he intended, but he didn't like at all where this was going.

Her words poured out in a rush. "It's no about just me. You still haven't done whatever you need to do. So"—she lifted one hand from his, traced her finger up the wound on his cheek and tucked an errant strand of hair behind his ear—"until you've fulfilled whatever bargain *you* made with the Fae, I'll be here with you. So you see, we only need to figure out what the Fae want of *you*."

"Whatever bargain? I made no . . ." He came to an abrupt halt as he remembered his request, uttered at the moment the magic was strongest.

Grant me only that I might stay until I fulfill my destiny. His destiny. He had wanted nothing more than to stop his father. Wanted so desperately to atone for all that had happened, all that he had done.

And now Mairi's future rested on his accomplishing that task.

He dropped her hands and rose to his feet, walking the short distance to the fire, where their clothes were hanging to dry. He pulled on his pants, trying to think of something to say, some reason for why Mairi had been dragged into the quagmire of his pathetic life. She deserved so much better than this. At the very least she deserved an explanation.

As he finished dressing, he spoke to her without turning. "There's nothing to figure out. I know what I have to do. It's my destiny to destroy Reynard Servans. I am, however, at a loss to understand why the Fae chose to punish you by tying your fate to mine. But don't worry. As soon as I find Sallie, I'll come back for you. Then I'll take care of my end of this *bargain* and you can go home."

Her silence didn't last long.

"You cavemen types are pretty slow-witted, are you no?"

He turned to find her standing, hands on her hips, shaking her head. She'd already slipped into the large shirt he recognized as having come from his things. It struck her midway up her shapely thighs.

He wiped at his face in an attempt to banish the thoughts the sight brought with it.

"Nobody did anything to punish me. This is all of my own choosing. My magic returned. And when it did, I refused to leave. I could have gone home, Ramos. But you had to stay, and there was no way I was leaving you here. So I chose to give up the opportunity to return until you fulfilled yer task."

The woman was completely insane. She had to be.

"That makes no sense. Why would you do that?"

She huffed out her breath, rolling her eyes as she sat down on the stool by the fire to pull on the pants she'd worn. His also, if he wasn't mistaken.

"I already told you why." She stood to tie the pants and smiled up at him. "Because I love you."

"You don't love me. You know nothing about me. If I were to tell you . . ." He couldn't deal with this now. "After I find Sallie—"

"After *we* find Sallie," she interrupted.

"No. You're staying here, where you'll be at least moderately safe." He wasn't sure he could stand another round of what he'd gone through last night. The very thought that Mairi might have died . . .

"No, I'm coming with you. Because"—she held up her hand to forestall his response—"you need me. I can lead you to them. And for the record, Ramos, I know everything I need to know about you. There's nothing you can tell me that will change how I feel."

"How can you lead me to them?" He should have thought to question earlier how she'd managed to follow *him* so well. His tracks had been completely masked by the snow, yet she had followed his path as if she'd had a trail.

"I feel *him*. Here." She placed her hand on her chest, over her heart. "The closer I get to that kidnapping Faerie piece of trash, Reynard Servans, the more my mark burns. And if you try to leave me here, I'll just follow you. Because I love you. So you might as well take me along."

She had the gall to stand there smiling as he considered his options. Her ability to track Reynard's party could make the difference in his finding them in time to save Sallie. And even if he tried to leave her here, she would follow him, he had no doubt. She'd left him with no real choice.

But about the other? This *love* she thought she had for him? The protective wall he'd built around his emotions was strong, but he wasn't sure it would survive much more of her assault. It would be so easy to allow himself to believe her words. But he couldn't permit it to continue. He had to deal with it now. Regardless of how it would hurt to see the disgust in her eyes once she knew.

"If that's what you want, I'll get the horses ready."

He shrugged as he opened the door, intending to convey a careless attitude he didn't feel. In fact, his stomach churned at the thought of what he had to do.

"But while we're sharing things 'for the record,' Mairi, you should know that 'kidnapping Faerie piece of trash' we track is my father. The man I spent my whole life trying to impress. The man whose every request I jumped to follow. All the things I told you about him, all the vile acts he was responsible for, I was a part of those, too. I'm no different from him."

The sun still hid behind a blanket of thick clouds, but the snow and rain had ceased to fall today. Somehow that in itself made Mairi feel more hopeful as she glanced over at the man riding beside her.

They had been following her 'feeling' for the last few hours, most recently turning sharply to the south. Ramos hadn't spoken more than three words since he'd walked out the door of that hut where they'd spent the night, leaving her in shock with his parting words.

Reynard Servans was his father.

And the great fool riding next to her acted as though he thought that bit of information would make a difference in the way she felt about him.

Or was it that he *wanted* it to make a difference?

She knew she took a huge risk in telling him how she felt, but she didn't regret doing it. Her only regret was that he didn't feel the same way.

Yet.

But she was the woman who'd spent her last nine years devoted to the pursuit of who she was and where she belonged. She was, if nothing else, persistent. As a result of her perseverance, she now had her answers: she was the rightful descendant of a Faerie prince and she belonged with Ramos Navarro.

And if he thought she'd give up as easily as that, well, Mr. Navarro had another think coming.

Knowing Ramos was the son of Reynard Servans did cast a whole new light on things. Certainly not on how she felt about him, but rather on what he intended to do. The repercussions of his plan to destroy Reynard—his own father—could be staggering. Besides, hadn't Pol cautioned her about doing anything drastic?

She brought her horse to a stop as she remembered her ancestor's words.

"Do we change direction again?" Ramos reined in his mount and looked back at her.

"You said you knew what you needed to do to satisfy your bargain with the Fae."

With a nudge of his legs, he brought his horse back to where she'd stopped. "I told you, you've nothing to worry over. I'll deal with things and get you home." He turned his head, staring off into the distance, his jaw muscle clenching and releasing.

"That's no what I'm asking. It's yer manner of dealing with things that concerns me."

Confusion wrinkled his brow when he focused on her again.

"You said something about destroying Reynard? You canna do that."

"It's true there's not supposed to be any way for a full-blood Fae to come to harm on the Mortal Plain. Yet I saw what happened to my father in my time. There must be a way to destroy him. I have only to find it." With a gentle kick to his horse, he started forward.

"Wait. You canna change the outcome of history. You can only alter the circumstances. Pol said . . ."

Her words trailed off to nothing as, ahead of her, Ramos brought his mount to a stop and whirled to face her, fury set in his expression as he neared.

"Don't quote Fae rules to me," he ground out. "Rules mean nothing to them. They obey only those they choose and only then when it pleases them to do so. And my father is the worst of the lot. You can't begin to imagine the horrors he's going to be responsible for. Or the things I'll do trying to win his favor. I can't allow that to happen."

For one unguarded moment, his pain showed clearly before the walls returned, once again shielding the intensity of his feelings from her. But it was too late. She'd already seen.

"Yer right. I canna imagine the horror of having such an evil father. I also canna believe you knowingly aided those such as you described the Nuadians to be.

But *you* canna destroy this man. No matter what he's yet to do. It's wrong."

"It's not about what I knew. It's what I should have known, should have seen. Let me tell you about wrong. Reynard Servans is consummate evil. He lied to me from the moment I first laid eyes on him and I never once questioned him. I admired him, did everything in my power to please him. I helped him perpetrate his foul evil." He looked away from her, shaking his head. "Destroying him before he can hurt all those people again is the only way I can atone for what I've done."

She reached out, laying her hand on his arm, drawing his attention back to her. She had to make him understand.

"Changing history could have disastrous consequences for many more people than yer father touched. You need to consider carefully what it is you really seek. Is it atonement for yer sins or is it revenge you want?"

Abruptly his eyes hardened and he jerked back from her touch, pressing his horse forward.

"I'm through talking about this. I'll do what I have to do," he called back over his shoulder.

Mairi followed after him, unwilling to allow him to face the coming crisis alone. But neither was she willing to allow him to do something the whole world would regret.

She'd think of something.

Though from the feel of it—she lifted her hand to clutch at the burn in her chest—she didn't have much longer to think.

Twenty-five

I've no idea what you want of me. I see no doors of any kind. There's naught here but stones." Sallie turned in a full circle, face colored with confusion.

Hopeless.

Exactly as Wyn had suspected it would be. This girl was of no use whatsoever. When she hadn't been able to see him in his own form, he'd known she wouldn't be able to find the Portal. He had done his best to dissuade Reynard from taking her. His best short of telling what he knew. That would have required him to share what he'd learned about Mairi.

If only . . .

He shook his head. No sense in thinking on it now. There were more pressing matters. He'd been through this scenario before and he didn't like what was yet to come.

They had arrived at this ancient place only a short time ago, setting Sallie off her mount to begin her task. She walked slowly among the large standing stones surrounding a tall earthen mound, trailing her fingers from one stone to another reverently.

Well she might. This was a place deserving of reverence, a sacred place old long before he had been born. Woods sheltered one side of the circle, while the other side opened to a flat meadow.

Reynard glared down at the girl, his patience and temper equally short. "*La petite idiote incompétente*," he hissed, dismounting and striding to her side. "The door likely *is* one of the stones. You've only to point it out and open it for me, *ma petite*, and I'll send you home."

Sallie straightened her back, her look of contempt scathing as her chin jutted out. "If you already ken it to be one of the stones, then find it yerself, you vile whoreson."

Wyn bit the inside of his lower lip, hiding the wonder that threatened to show itself.

By the Earth Mother! So much fire in such a small package.

If he had only a pittance of the girl's determination.

"Wyn!" Reynard clenched and released his hands rapidly at his sides. "I think the time has come to have this young woman's friend help us teach her the perils of defiance. Send the Mortal to my bidding."

The anticipation lighting Reynard's face sickened Wyn. It grew worse, Reynard grew worse, each time. Wyn wasn't sure he had it in him to go through this one more time.

Yet he did as he was told. With no more resistance than the pitiful Mortal held under his compulsion.

At Wyn's beckoning motion, Ran was at his side. "Reynard is as your master. Go to him."

The young man scurried to do as he'd been instructed.

Reynard reached for Sallie, capturing a long red curl in his fingers, wrapping it about his hand as she moved to pull away from him. "This is the last time I ask you nicely, *ma petite*. Show me the door."

"Or what?" she snapped. "Will you do to me as you have to Ran? Will you drive the light of life from my eyes as you have from his? I'd no help you even if I could see yer damned door!"

Reynard stared at her for a moment before speaking, his rage palpable. "I've taken a liking to this lovely lock. Draw your sword, boy, and cut it off for me. I'd have it to keep as my own."

"No!" Sallie screamed, again struggling to pull away, but Graham had joined them. Pinning her arms behind her, he held her securely.

Ran's arm shook as he sliced down with his weapon, cutting through the long curl.

Wyn felt the pull on his power as the boy fought to disobey. For that reason he remained mounted, knowing from experience it would get worse before it got better. Especially since Ran cared so much for the girl. That was why Reynard had chosen to use the young man, gaining extra pleasure from the anguish he caused to the Mortal. Pleasure, too, Wyn was beginning to suspect, from the physical pain Wyn would suffer.

Reynard dangled the severed curl in front of Sallie's face, waiting for a reaction. "Are you ready to help me now?"

The girl, her arms wrenched tightly behind her, did not waiver in her determination. "I dinna care. It's naught but hair. Shave me bald if you like, but it will make no difference. I canna see any doorways in this place."

Reynard threw the piece of hair to the ground. "Strike her. Across her insolent mouth." He turned to glare at Ran. "Strike her!" he screamed.

The drain on Wyn was enormous as the boy wrestled against the compulsion.

Tears trailed down Ran's cheeks, though he was powerless to do other than obey the order. His hand lashed out across Sallie's face, snapping her head to the side.

"If you don't do as you're told, I'll have him do it again. Harder." Reynard's eyes glittered with excitement.

Sallie lifted her head, a deep crimson print marring her cheek. But it wasn't fear in her eyes. It was fury.

Her determination humbled Wyn; her bravery awed him. If a slip of a girl like that could show so much courage in the face of Reynard's cruelty, why couldn't he find his own courage? Truly the Reynard who had been his closest friend was no more. The only thing Wyn had to fear was striking out on his own. The one thing he'd avoided for centuries—being totally alone.

"I dinna ken what you've done to Ran, you bastard, but I'll see you dead for the pain yer causing him."

Reynard's laughter echoed off the surrounding stones.

"Oh no, my little hellion, I don't think so. You haven't the power to bring harm to me."

"Unhand the woman!"

Wyn labored to lift his head to see who called out,

but the pain of Ran's struggles held him nearly immobile, bent low against his horse. With one last effort, he had a clear view of Ramos Navarro stepping into the circle, sword drawn.

"*She* may not have the power to harm you, but perhaps I do."

Think of something—before it's too late.

But nothing was coming to her.

Mairi pressed her hands tightly over the burning throb in her chest as she leaned back against the tree where Ramos had left her.

"Don't move from this spot," he'd ordered just before stepping out of the trees and into the midst of confrontation.

She turned to peek around the trunk at the group in the clearing, knowing she had to do something. Though she might not have a plan in mind, she was convinced that hiding here behind this tree was not what she'd come this far to do. And it certainly wasn't helping Ramos in any way. Or Sallie.

At the moment, her poor bedraggled little cousin stood with Ran's shaking sword at her throat, Reynard behind them, taunting. "Ah, if it isn't our future Spanish Duke. Shouldn't you be off guarding your ward? Best you toddle away from this, young 'Dukeling,' before you cause this lovely lady more distress."

"Release her," Ramos demanded simply.

Reynard shook his head in response. "I don't think so. Ran? If Navarro approaches my person, you're to run your weapon straight through that pretty little neck. It appears she's of no use to me anyway."

Mairi pulled back, pressing her forehead to the

massive tree trunk. Her heart pounded and her breath
came in short gulps of air.

Think, think, think . . .

The men who accompanied the Duke had all dismounted, except for his brother, Wyn. Within moments they would surround Ramos. Or rush him.

Not that he wasn't an excellent fighter. He was, but
not against so many.

Everything had gone so wrong.

She had no weapon of any sort. Still, if she entered
the clearing it might distract some of them. It might
give Ramos a few extra seconds to . . .

"I have to go help him." She spoke the words
aloud expecting them to build her courage, to force
her to action.

What she did *not* expect was an answer.

"How about my men and I go in yer stead?"

A woman's shrill scream echoed through the sacred
stones, breaking the spell that seemingly held everyone
in place. Men spilled into the clearing from the forest
and suddenly the circle was alive with the sounds of
battle.

Graham dropped his hold on the girl to challenge
Ramos. An ugly purple bruise covered the side of the
man's face, a reminder of his last encounter with
Mairi's guardian. . . . Wyn froze as the import of
Navarro's title sunk in. Guardian.

No wonder.

The Fates were up to their old games, dangling all
the pieces before you, waiting to see if you were intelligent enough to put them together correctly. A

glance at Reynard confirmed for him his leader still hadn't made the connection.

"Kill her," Reynard commanded the Mortal, turning his back on the carnage around him.

Enough.

Wyn could never go home, but neither could he continue on this path.

"I release you."

With his words, Ran fell to the ground and Wyn's strength returned. Straightening his back, he tugged at the reins in his hand, pointing his horse away from the battle around him.

Time to find his own way in this world.

"Caden!"

Mairi grabbed her cousin's arm as his men streamed into the clearing, battle cries on their lips.

"You scared the life from me. How could you possibly have tracked us here?"

"We dinna track you, dinna even expect you to be here. We came to this place because this is where Sallie is. You forget, Cousin, my mother is of the blood and no without her own abilities. Now, if you'll let go my arm, I'll join the battle before there's naught left for me." He waggled his eyebrows and took off running, a war cry at his lips, his sword at the ready.

Mairi darted from the shelter of the trees and made her way around the edge of the stones, avoiding the combatants as best she could. A look toward Ramos assured her he was holding his own, one man on the ground at his feet, a second already engaged.

Her goal was to reach Sallie.

But before she neared the center of the stones, where the girl was held, she heard Reynard utter the words she'd traveled seven hundred years to prevent.

"Kill her."

Reynard turned on his heel, striding toward his horse.

"No!" Mairi breathed, running headlong toward Ran and the sword he held, heedless of the battle raging around her.

This couldn't happen. Not now. Not after all they'd gone through. She had to stop it.

Two steps forward and she saw Ran fall to the ground, arms outstretched, limp as a rag doll.

By her fourth step, Sallie had retrieved Ran's sword. Swinging it up with all her might, the girl twirled once and slammed the blade into Reynard's body.

Or rather completely *through* his body.

Mairi froze as she watched the momentum of the heavy sword carry Sallie off to the side and down to the ground in a heap.

Reynard turned, fury etched into his features as he looked first to Ran and then to where his brother rode away.

Fury, but no pain.

No pain, no blood, no wound.

"Wyn!" he yelled.

Wyn raised a hand in a farewell salute without turning to look at Reynard, instead spurring his horse to a gallop.

"Onwyn Aĺ Lyre! Return to me this instant! You will not disobey me!" Reynard screamed, grabbing the reins of his own horse.

Mairi reached Sallie, falling to her knees to help her dazed cousin sit up.

The girl shook her head. "I dinna ken what just happened. I could no have missed him from that close. He should be dead or badly hurt at the least."

Mairi could only nod, still not believing what she had witnessed.

Reynard galloped away from the circle as the sounds of battle died down around them.

"No," Ramos groaned.

After all he'd gone through, Reynard was escaping.

Having dispatched his second attacker, Ramos leaned heavily on his sword, catching his breath. He had to follow. Had to stop his father. Otherwise Mairi would be stuck here forever and it would be his fault. He would have failed her. And his destiny.

Mairi!

When he'd heard her scream, he'd feared the worst. But then he'd seen her skulking around the edge of the circle, exactly as he'd told her not to do. She was, without a doubt the most obstinate, pigheaded woman he'd ever known.

Now she sat on the ground next to Sallie, who cradled Ran's head and shoulders in her lap, rocking back and forth.

He would check on them, make sure they were all right, before he went after Reynard. Miraculously Caden was here somewhere, he knew. He'd get the young man's assurance he would look after Mairi. Then Ramos could be on his way.

But first he was drawn to Mairi's side, as iron filings are drawn to a magnet. The need to touch her, to see for himself she was unharmed, was too strong to resist.

She looked up as he approached and surged to her feet, throwing her body against his, her arms around his neck, her face buried in his shoulder.

"Thank the Fates. I was terrified," she breathed into his ear.

He stiffened at her words. He should have realized she would be frightened. He'd left her alone, vulnerable to their enemies, when he'd stepped into that circle. But he'd had no choice. If he didn't deal with his father, her life would be ruined.

"I did what I had to do. Those men had no idea you were here. You would have been perfectly safe if you had stayed hidden, as I told you to."

She pulled away from him, her eyes blazing. "If I had . . ." She blustered to a stop. "It's no *my* safety I'm talking about, you great oaf, it's yers. Yer never, ever to walk into something like that again with no backup, do you hear me?"

Ramos had no idea how to answer her. She constantly surprised him, never saying or doing what he expected.

He pulled her hands from his neck, but couldn't quite make himself let go, wondering for the briefest moment what it would feel like to be the man Mairi truly fell in love with one day, allowing himself finally to acknowledge that he wished he could be that man.

But it was not to be. Not now that she knew who he was. Who his father was. He'd seen the shock on her face when he'd told her back in that little hut. And to compound matters, his failure to fulfill his destiny would trap Mairi in this time. No, his only hope was to distance himself from her, to pull away before his wounds were too deep.

"You've no reason to worry about me. I can take care of myself. For now, you'll stay with Caden while I go after my . . ." He couldn't bring himself to voice it again. "After Reynard."

"No. I canna allow you to do that." She stared up at him, remaining very still, her body close to his, her hands clasped within his.

"Pardon?" She wouldn't *allow* him to go?

Though she constantly refused to do as *she* was told, always required rescue, wandering from one disaster to another, she now arrogantly assumed she had the right to tell him what she would *allow* him to do, as she might some hired hand?

Apparently the lady had more in common with her Faerie ancestors than he'd realized.

"Careful, princess," he cautioned. "Your royal heritage is showing. You're so sure of yourself, aren't you? I know all about your kind."

Her mouth fell open as she pushed out of his arms, backing away from him. "You know nothing of me. Sure of myself? Hardly. I've spent the last nine years of my life doubting my every action, my every word. Doubting everything, right down to the reason I live. Doubting my ability to ever be sure of myself again. You've no concept of my life."

Mairi turned away, pacing, but returned to stand in front of him to jab her index finger into his chest. "I've no been sure of myself since the day my cousin's betrayal taught me I knew nothing about the world.

Until now. I *am* sure about this. You canna destroy that man. You canna put at risk the whole of history and who knows what else."

"History will thank me for it."

She poked him again, repeatedly, harder with each sentence. "No they won't, because you'll no ever have even been. If you do away with yer father centuries before yer born, you'll never exist. Destroying him now will destroy you. Have you no thought of that?"

Ramos captured her hand, holding it against his heart. "Of course I have. But it doesn't matter anymore. I have to do this, Mairi. It's my destiny to put an end to his evil. If I don't, you'll be stuck here in this time, away from your family forever. I won't be the cause of that happening to you. All that matters is getting you safely home."

"I dinna want to go home without you. I love you, dinna you realize that yet?"

"You can't!" he yelled. "You know what I am."

"I dinna care, Ramos." She clutched the fabric of his shirt, fisting it in her hands. "I'd rather spend the rest of my life in the thirteenth century with you than one moment in any other time without you. Would it be so awful for you to stay here with me?"

How could she say those things still? After he'd told her everything? There was no way she could possibly mean it.

It would be too easy to delude himself, too easy to believe the words he wanted so desperately to hear. He had to go now, before it was too late.

"I have to fulfill my destiny." Pulling her hands from his shirt, he backed a few steps away, hoping to break the hold she seemed to have on him. One deep breath to steel himself, then he turned and sprinted to the spot where he'd left his horse.

Directing his mount to the far side of the clearing, he hoped to avoid any further distraction as he picked up the trail his father had left.

One last look back was all he wanted, he told himself, before he spurred his horse to action.

She stood as he'd left her, arms limply at her sides. It appeared as if she hadn't moved at all.

His imagination was surely playing tricks on him, though, because if he didn't know better, he'd swear she was crying when she yelled something after him.

Something about his destiny.

"That's no yer destiny!" Mairi called, watching as Ramos rode away. "*I'm* yer destiny," she added in a whisper, turning to lean her forehead against one of the massive ancient stones, her legs no longer willing to hold her body up.

Her eyes had begun to blur so it took her a moment to realize what she saw on the stone. It was etched with an intricate archway, and in the center of the archway there was a carving of a snake with a slash through it.

She'd seen that symbol before, glistening in the firelight on Ramos's shoulder.

What was it he'd told her? He was a Guardian. Apparently this was part of what he was intended to guard. This stupid stone doorway.

And now he was gone. Forever.

Tears rolled down her cheeks, faster and faster.

Damn, damn, damn.

He'd made her cry. In front of everyone. She hadn't

allowed anyone that power over her in nine years.

If he came back, she'd make him pay for that.

When, not if! When!

She couldn't bear the thought he wouldn't return. The silent tears running down her cheeks morphed into all-out sobs, bringing Caden to her side, holding her up when she would have collapsed.

"There, there, Mairi. Yer going to be all right." Caden held her, petting her as he might an inconsolable child.

That's exactly how she felt. She shook her head in response to him, unable to stop crying long enough to form words. It seemed as though the dam that had held for almost a decade was splintered, and the tears would not stop.

"Come now, Cousin. Yer a strong one. You've been through much worse at the hands of a man you care for. At least this one is trying to do what he thinks is best for you, is he no?"

Caden knew who she really was?

She took a shaky breath. "You know?" she managed through the tears.

He continued to stroke her hair. "Aye. Mother had a bit of explaining to do after yer fancy medications. For now, let Ramos do as he needs to. Each man must follow his own path. Dinna fash yerself lass—we're yer family, too. You've always a home here with us."

A home with them—but without Ramos? Her breath caught and the weeping overtook her again. She didn't want to be anywhere, in any time, without Ramos.

"You dinna understand," she wailed, gulping for air between sobs. "I won't even know what happens to him." She buried her face in her cousin's big shoulder.

"Come along, lass. Pull yerself together. Let's go home." Caden wiped the tears from her cheeks clumsily with his big hands before placing a brotherly kiss on her forehead. "Mother's waiting impatiently for *all* of us to get back to Dun Ard where we belong."

Mairi nodded weakly and allowed her cousin to pull her along after him, but she knew Caden was wrong. She didn't belong at Dun Ard. She belonged with Ramos. And without him, it was exactly as she had feared for the last nine years: she didn't belong anywhere.

Twenty-six

*H*e had to be very close now.

When Ramos had found the campsite early this morning, the ashes from the fire pit had still been warm. He had known then that the time to confront his father was at hand.

After a full day of riding hard, following his father's tracks, Ramos became aware of the sounds and smells from the seaport town ahead of him.

Cromarty would be the site where he would avenge himself.

Redeem, not avenge.

Redeem himself. That was what he'd meant. Wasn't it?

Ramos shook his head in a physical attempt to throw off the doubt left behind by Mairi's earlier accusation. Her words had followed him on his journey, eating away at the back of his mind whenever he dropped his mental guard.

It *wasn't* revenge he sought. She was wrong. She had to be. It was guilt that plagued his soul, not simple, selfish hatred of the man who had betrayed him.

He couldn't afford to second-guess himself at this point. He was too near his goal.

Ramos slowed his mount, his Fae senses on full alert. He would need to be cautious, planning every move carefully. His father was close by.

He would begin his search for Reynard near the docks. Every instinct told him his father would be headed home to Switzerland and the comfort of Adira. Home to lick the wounds of his failure.

Reynard hated failing at anything. He would be angry and at his most dangerous now, requiring all the more patience and caution on Ramos's part. He was a full-blooded Fae living on the Mortal Plain. According to everything Ramos had ever been taught, there was nothing in this world that could bring harm to his father. He could only be destroyed in the Realm of Faerie. The one place he was forbidden to go.

It wasn't difficult to locate the little hole in the wall where passage on various ships departing the port could be booked. After slipping a single gold coin to the grizzled old man behind the counter, Ramos found it equally easy to verify that Reynard had indeed booked passage. Another coin and the clerk eagerly divulged the location of the inn where Reynard lodged, waiting for his ship's sailing date.

Ramos's steps slowed as he neared the entrance to the Dolphin's Head Inn. The stench of unwashed bodies and old ale assaulted his nose as he pushed open the door.

Slipping inside, he gratefully blended into the shadows, the crowd in the tavern making his entry all the more difficult to detect.

He spotted Reynard almost immediately, across the room at a table in the corner, his face a mask of unconcerned disdain as he surveyed his surroundings.

Staying to the dark edges of the room, Ramos found a small, dirty table against the wall and ordered ale. The old man who delivered the metal cup to him grinned a toothless smile before snatching up the coin Ramos tossed to the table.

Taking his first sip, he studied his father and considered how to deal with the situation. Although Mairi would be trapped in this time if he didn't fulfill his destiny, the seeds of doubt she had planted continued to grow. If he couldn't reassure himself of the purity of his motivation, he didn't think he could challenge his father. And if he *did* challenge him, he had no idea how he would defeat the man.

Even if he could find some way to destroy Reynard, Mairi's warning against violating the Faerie edict about altering history rang in his ears. Was killing Reynard worth such a risk to the future of all mankind?

Ramos finished his drink, lost in his dark dilemma, all the while watching the lone figure across the room.

It suddenly struck him that his father was always alone. From the first moment Ramos had been brought to Reynard's villa to live, he had never known the Fae to trust or confide in anyone. For so many years, he had hoped to become that confidant to Reynard. He had longed to be the one person his father would turn to for aid in his fight against the evil enemy.

Of course, that was before he found out Reynard and his people *were* the evil enemy.

Before he learned his father had lied to him, betrayed him, used him his entire life. Before he accepted that Reynard had no more care for him—his own son—than someone he considered an adversary.

Before he had been forced to admit that his father had never loved him.

Ramos looked down at his clenched, trembling hand, the empty cup he held crushed under the force of his emotion.

What had he expected? In fairness, Reynard had never feigned fatherly affection. He had never claimed to love his son.

Only one person had ever claimed to love him.

Mairi.

The one person for whom he would gladly sacrifice his life. The one person he loved in return.

Perhaps she had been closer to the truth than he realized when she accused him of wanting revenge in seeking his father. Was it also the truth when she declared her love for him? Had she meant it when she'd said she would rather spend forever in this time with him than go home without him?

He could think of only one way to find out.

Twenty-seven

~

You need to eat. You'll have no strength left to work the fool garden if you continue on this way." Sallie stood at the entrance to the partially walled area, impatiently tapping her foot.

"I'll eat after a bit. I'm no hungry just yet. Go on without me." Mairi hadn't been hungry for the last week. Food didn't matter. Nothing mattered. Ramos was gone.

"I'm telling Mother. We'll see what you have to say then." Sallie turned with a swish of fabric, almost running back to the castle.

Mairi shrugged and continued digging in the soft, wet soil, knowing her aunt would be out soon.

With Alycie gone from Dun Ard, the men had stopped work on the small chapel they'd been building for her. Rock walls had been started, but all that had been finished was a large archway at the front, with the walls on each side no more than a two-foot-high outline of the rectangle the building had been intended to be.

Mairi's first morning back at Dun Ard, Rosalyn had held her through a round of tears and then pulled her from her room and brought her out to this spot.

"You need something to occupy yer time while you wait for yer man to return," she'd said, dragging Mairi by the hand into the walled area. "I should know. I've had some experience in waiting for a man in my day."

"It's no the same. He isna returning. He willna be able to." The tears had started again, as if they'd never dry up.

Rosalyn shook her head, and lifted a hand to stop all protests. "We're no going to be thinking like that now. With the first snow melted, it's a good time to turn the earth here to prepare this patch. You can use the stones they gathered for the walls to build yer plant beds. In the spring, you can take plants from my herb garden and begin one of yer own. It'll give you focus for yer mind while you wait."

It had been easier to do as her aunt asked than to argue. And after the third day, Mairi had found that being alone out here with her hands busy did relieve her mind somewhat. She was too tired at night to do more than bathe and fall into bed.

Meals were the hardest, when everyone attempted to keep the conversation light and avoid any mention of Ramos. It had come as a shock to her at last evening's meal to notice Caden join them for the first time in a week. It was with guilt she realized her cousin must have been suffering his own loss through all of this. She hadn't given a thought to Alycie since she'd been back.

Caden had thrown himself into a new project just as she had. Apparently Rosalyn felt physical labor was a cure for all ailments of the heart.

Caden was building a new bathhouse, saying that he had no choice; either build it or run the risk of losing all their servants to broken backs caused by carrying water for Mairi's nightly baths.

She'd almost smiled at that.

She did smile now, thinking about it as she placed rocks around the last of the individual beds she planned.

The grin faded as her mind continued to race. Losing Ramos was the single most horrible thing she'd ever experienced, and the pain of that loss was compounded by her overriding burden of guilt. Guilt about what future damage she was responsible for causing by having changed history. She knew if she had it to do over again she wouldn't hesitate to save Sallie's life, but she worried constantly about the ultimate cost for what she had done.

Not knowing what that price would be, or who would have to pay it, filled her heart with dread. But that was nothing compared to her grief at having no way of knowing Ramos's fate.

When she heard the crunch of steps on the gravel behind her, she didn't bother to turn from her task. Instead she steeled herself for the lecture she would receive from her aunt for not eating again.

"I'm glad to see you've kept yourself busy, my sweet."

Shock coursed through her body at the sound of

the deep baritone voice, a voice she had thought never to hear again.

She turned slowly, afraid it was only her imagination playing tricks on her, that the voice she heard, the face she saw every night in her dreams wouldn't actually be there when she looked.

"Ramos," she breathed. Then, rising unsteadily to her feet, she yelled it. *"Ramos!"* She could think of nothing but crossing the small length of the garden and getting her hands on him before he disappeared. Her feet tangled in her skirts, pitching her forward over the pile of rocks she'd gathered, but she never touched the ground.

He was there, catching her before she could fall, pulling her close, kissing the top of her head, her cheek, her lips.

She leaned back to look up at him, the damnable tears starting again, washing down her face. "You came back to me."

"I could do nothing else," he answered as he gently brushed the tears from her cheeks with his thumbs.

"And what of yer father? Did you no find him?" Was his return only temporary?

"I followed Reynard to Cromarty. There he booked passage on a ship."

Mairi's stomach sank. Then he would go again. It was only a matter of time. "So, you lost his trail?"

"No. I reconsidered my destiny." He smiled at her, pushing the hair that had come loose from her braid back behind her ear. "He was still in Cromarty when I left, waiting at the inn for his ship's sailing date."

Suddenly she found it hard to slow her breathing. "Then why . . . ? I dinna understand."

"I came back to see if you truly meant your words.
If you'd honestly rather be with me here in this time
than in your own time without me, I think that might
not be such a bad thing."

Her heart beat so hard, she could hear the pounding inside her head. "What are you saying?"

"I'm saying"—he took her hand in his and kissed
the back of it, dirt and all, then dropped to one knee—
"I'd give all I have to spend the rest of my life with you,
Mairi, if you'll have me. I don't care where or when, I
only want to be with you. Will you marry me?"

"Screaming would be bad, right?" she asked
through renewed tears. Dropping to her knees, she
threw her arms around his neck, peppering little
kisses along his jaw, stopping only long enough to
whisper "Yes, oh yes" into his ear.

"Looks like you've got a crier on yer hands, man."

Mairi looked up through the blur of her tears to
see Caden grinning down at them, his arm around his
mother's shoulders. Sallie and Colin had joined them,
smiling as well.

"Looks like," Ramos responded, pulling Mairi
close to kiss her.

She closed her eyes and melted in the warmth of
his embrace, his kiss taking her completely away from
the muddy ground where she knelt.

Hoots and laughter sounded all around her, and
only when they'd grown muffled did she break from
the kiss to look up at her relatives.

Rosalyn laughed and clapped her hands sound-
lessly, while her children around her appeared to have
grown silent. Mairi couldn't be sure because all sound

was cut off by the shimmering green sphere that surrounded her and Ramos.

Lights sparkled, colors swirled, dancing around them and through them as the sensation of rapid movement overtook them. When the light show reached its peak, Mairi could have sworn she heard Pol's voice.

"Bargain struck. Bargain fulfilled."

Twenty-eight

"Wait, you've missed a spot." Mairi wiped a bead of white fluff from Ramos's earlobe. "How did you manage to get frosting there?"

"You're the one to be answering that question, Mrs. Navarro. As I recall, it was *you* smushing that cake all over my face." He grinned wolfishly and pulled her close. "So wouldn't you prefer to remove that bit as you did the last?"

"I think that's perhaps no the best idea right now."

After cutting their wedding cake and the ritual of smearing the cake into her groom's face—which Cate's brothers had assured her, repeatedly, was mandatory—she and Ramos had gone inside to clean up. One thing had led to another until here it was almost thirty minutes later.

Holding hands, they strolled out into the garden where their reception guests were gathered.

Ramos tugged her hand and nodded toward one little group. "Dallyn certainly seems to be enjoying himself."

The Fae General leaned toward his female counterpart, Darnee, laughing at some remark she had made. As he lifted his head, he turned and the sun etched his features in sharp profile, the light glinting off his long, golden hair.

"Oh!" Mairi gasped, lifting a hand to her chest. For an instant, she could have sworn he was someone else. But that was ridiculous.

"What? What is it?" Ramos stiffened, instantly alert.

"Nothing, really. It's just . . . I finally realized who it was he reminded me of."

"Who are you talking about?"

"Wyn Servans. Remember, I told you he reminded me of someone. When Dallyn looked up just then, for a second I thought it was Wyn."

Ramos stared at the small group, a frown creasing his brow. "I don't see it, my sweet. Come on, let's go get a piece of our cake to actually eat before it's time to open gifts." He grinned and kissed her cheek. "We certainly don't want to be late for that event."

Allowing Ramos to pull her along with him, Mairi took one last look back at the two Fae. She didn't see it now either. But for a moment there . . .

"It's about time the two of you returned. I was beginning to fear I'd have to come searching for you." Connor MacKiernan gave her a pointed look as he passed her a small plate and fork.

Mairi grinned at her older brother, who stood beside his wife, Cate, helping to serve slices of wedding cake. "Wasn't that the whole point of yer giving me away today? So that yer no longer the one to look after me?"

"So long as *he* remembers to do a proper job of it," Connor growled, tipping his head toward Mairi's new husband.

"She's home safe and sound, isn't she?" Ramos asked before biting into the cake he now held.

"Aye, well. If she'd done a better job of her homework in the first place, she'd no have had to go."

"I'm not so sure about that," Ramos disagreed. "On the surface it might appear that Mairi, not Sallie, was the daughter of the House of MacKiernan who mysteriously disappeared around the time the Duke was there. Clan stories passed from one generation to the next could well account for his being blamed for some part in her 'death.' But had Mairi not gone back . . . who knows? It could well have been Sallie."

Mairi and Ramos had gone over her research repeatedly, trying to analyze exactly that situation. They'd already put together bits and pieces of the puzzle, but there were still so many questions.

Fortunately they had found at least one answer in the course of investigating her initial work. She'd finally realized that the reason she hadn't found any trace of Sallie after the Duke's visit was that she'd been hunting for Marsali MacAlister, not Sallie MacPherson.

She smiled thinking of her impetuous little cousin. Sallie and Ran probably had descendants roaming all through those highlands, a detail she planned to follow up on.

One thing she hadn't been able to determine was what other losses the family had mourned through that season. Perhaps Ramos's disappearance or the abrupt end to Caden's betrothal was the missing answer, but whatever it was, she was determined to find out eventually. Her analysis of the scraps of evidence she'd collected would continue until she was satisfied she and Ramos hadn't done anything to substantially change history.

If anything, she had even more searching to do now. It would take quite some effort to resolve the one major loose end that had been nagging at her for the last couple of days.

Ramos set down his plate and lifted a finger to her forehead, stroking the furrow between her eyes. "What? What is it? You're doing that frown thing again. After all the time we spent going over and over those documents, you can't possibly have any concerns left about our having changed history."

It wasn't actually history bothering her this time. It was the future. But this wasn't the time to go into her new anxieties. This was their wedding day, not a time to be borrowing worries.

"Later," she murmured, pulling his hand down, kissing the fingertip that had trailed over her face.

His brilliant smile was her reward.

"Come get your cake, sweetie." Cate beckoned to her small daughter, beaming as Rosie skipped over to the table. The child still wore the lovely lilac gown she'd chosen as her flower girl's dress.

"Here you go, baby girl." Her mother handed over the paper plate bearing a large piece of cake. "It's your favorite. Chocolate." Cate wiggled her eyebrows and winked, earning a giggle from Rose.

"Da's favorite, you mean." Rosie laughed at her father's exaggerated look of innocence. All of them knew Connor could ferret out chocolate hidden anywhere in his house.

Cate smiled and held out another piece. "Do you think you could manage to take Will's plate over as well?"

Will Stroud and his parents had come to the wedding with Sarah and Ian McCullough, Ramos's best man.

"I'll carry that." Pol's large hand swept up the plate. "Lead the way, fair princess."

The two of them made their way over to where Will waited, Rosie's laughter a musical tinkling that filled the air.

"They've certainly hit it off," Mairi mused, watching her Faerie ancestor sit down under a large tree with the two children.

"Aye, they have," Connor agreed. "But I'm no sure I like it."

"It'll be okay." Cate patted her husband's arm. "Maybe it's a good thing for them both. It's about time he finally ventured out of his Glen."

"Perhaps," Connor muttered, continuing to watch the little group closely.

Mairi understood his reluctance completely. Her older brother was in full protection mode when it came to his only daughter. Not that she blamed him.

As a full Fae, Pol's individual powers might be thought to be restricted on the Mortal Plain, but Mairi had seen firsthand what he had been able to do for her.

She glanced over at her brother as he put his arm around his wife, hugging her close.

Cate stretched up to kiss his chin. "Don't worry, Connor. Look at him. He looks as much a child as they do sitting there on the ground. Besides, it looks as though his friend is getting ready to join them now, see?"

Mairi looked over to where Dallyn approached Pol. Perhaps it was only the Fae beauty of the man that had reminded her of Wyn Servans.

Then again . . . The thought fled her mind as Ramos stepped behind her, pulling her close to nibble at her ear.

"We have to leave soon, my sweet."

It was something to worry over another day. For now, she had a honeymoon flight to catch.

"Begging your pardon, your highness."

Pol looked up to see Dallyn standing over him, bowing from the waist in formal greeting as the occasion required.

Just as well. He had hoped to speak to the General at some point today. He rose from his seat on the grass where he'd been chatting with Rosie and Will.

"Dallyn Aí Lyre." He nodded an acknowledgment, addressing the great general in the ancient way, using his full name. "I want to thank you for your excellent choice of a Guardian for my Mairi Rose. She appears most pleased."

Dallyn shrugged. "It does seem to have worked out." He grinned as Darnee joined them. "All's well that stops well."

"Ends, Dallyn," she corrected with a sigh. "All's well that *ends* well."

Pol smiled down at Rosie. Though he hated to leave this most interesting discussion with the children, his current concerns took precedence. "If you will excuse us, I have some boring details to discuss with the General."

"Bye, Grandpapa."

He turned, bidding Rosie good-bye with a wave. Her happy little face made him chuckle in spite of himself. That one would be a power to reckon with one day.

"My apologies, your highness. I had no intention to draw you away from your conversation."

"No, General, I am pleased to have this opportunity to speak with you. I had hoped to meet with you privately before you returned home."

Pol glanced at Darnee and the woman's steps slowed.

"Gentlemen, if you will excuse me, I wish to pay my respects to the bride and groom before they leave."

Pol watched her retreating figure, the shadow of a smile tugging at his lips. "She's very intelligent, that one. Good thing she's on our side, is it not?" It wasn't that he didn't trust her. Only that he trusted Dallyn more.

Dallyn merely nodded his agreement. "Is there something in particular you wanted to talk to me about, your highness?"

"There is."

But where to start? How to admit that he, the infallible Hereditary High Prince of the Fae, might have made a rather unforgivable error.

Might have? There was no *might* to it. He had made errors compounding errors, all caused by his arrogant assumption that he *was* infallible.

When Mairi had confronted him in his Glen, she had rattled him to his core. The woman had stood toe to toe with him, living, breathing evidence of his fallibility. In his embarrassment, he'd freely granted her request. Without thought.

And now he needed the General's help to clean up the mess he'd made.

Pol started to explain but paused as Rosie and Will dashed past them, laughing. "On reflection, this is not the best place for our discussion. In two days I will return to my quarters in the Hall of the High Council. Perhaps, if you find yourself with some free time, you could come to me there."

"Of course, your highness. I will be there."

Pol nodded and turned away. Two days would give him time to plan. Time to decide how to ask for the help he needed. It was so important to contain this information. To minimize the damage he had caused. No one else must know of all the Mortal women who had, in the blink of an eye, with no preparation, no understanding, suddenly received the powers of the Fae. All because he had spoken the words without thought. Once again, he had allowed emotion to overtake him. Had simply reacted.

And now, instead of a number of his own descendants paying the price for his arrogant mistake, it could be the entire World of Mortals who paid.

He stopped and looked back at the General, who stared into the sky, lost in thought. "And, Dallyn?"

Dallyn's head jerked his direction.

"Three knocks will gain you entrance to my quarters. Tell no one of our meeting. And make sure you're not followed."

"Certainly, your highness."

Pol turned, crossing the lawn toward Mairi and her Guardian. It was good he'd decided to accept her invitation to come here. Good he'd finally ventured into the World of Mortals. He'd wasted more than enough time mourning in his Glen. Through the millennia he'd allowed his mind to dull, allowed himself to grow sloppy and careless.

He'd abdicated his responsibilities as the hereditary leader of his people for far too long.

In two days' time he would confront his mistakes. He only hoped it wouldn't be too late.

Epilogue

Mairi floated. Floated in the most perfect blue-green water. Floated like a leaf, her body rising and falling as the waves washed past and up onto a fine white sandy shore.

"Hey!"

She pulled herself upright, treading water, as she turned toward the beach.

"They don't make an SPF high enough to keep you from burning if you don't get out of that water right now."

Ramos stood on the beach looking like some sexy ad for men's swimwear, with his baggy beach shorts hanging low on his hips and his long shiny hair blowing in the light breeze. He pushed his sunglasses down to the end of his nose, frowning at her over the rims.

"I'm serious, Mairi. I don't want you getting sunburned. I have big plans for all that gorgeous white skin. Don't make me come out there to get you again."

She laughed, her face turning red at the memory of

what had happened last night when he'd come out into the water to "get her." She was just thankful no one else was staying on this end of the island!

"Hold on, I'm coming," she called, smiling as he picked up a large beach towel and held it out to wrap her in when she arrived.

"Enjoying your honeymoon, Mrs. Navarro?" he asked once he had her covered and snug under his arm. They strolled back to their own private palm-thatched bungalow.

"Completely." She swept back his hair and nuzzled his jawline as they walked.

Not long after they'd returned home, she'd finally admitted her fascination with his eyes and how they reminded her of the photograph she'd kept for so many years. She hadn't realized he'd paid much attention to her babbling until he'd surprised her with his gift at their reception. A honeymoon in the Maldives.

They'd flown to Malé and thirty minutes later, from the tiny window of the seaplane, she'd looked down on a coral island fringed with white sand set in a turquoise sea. It could have been the very spot from her photograph.

She laughed out loud, joyful in the knowledge she'd finally found her courage, her path, her place in life.

"Come on," he encouraged her, breaking into a run. "Get dressed so we can go up to the main house for dinner. I'm starved."

Things couldn't be any better, she'd never been happier. And yet . . .

One small worry wouldn't let her be.

Ramos waited for her at the door, his sunglasses pushed up on his forehead.

"I know that look. So what tiny little detail is still rattling around in that overdeveloped brain of yours, my sweet?"

"I'm sure it's nothing." She shook her head, unable to completely eliminate the nagging thought that sat at the back of her mind like a tiny splinter festering just under the skin.

As she started past him, he grabbed her forearm and swung her body up next to his, kissing her senseless, ending by sucking on her bottom lip, allowing it to slowly slide between his teeth as he pulled away.

"Why don't you tell me what's been on your mind since before the wedding so we can both decide it's nothing and put it to rest." His eyes met hers as his fingers worked at the towel he'd cocooned her into earlier.

"I'm sure it's silly, but after what you said about words having so much power?" She waited while he nodded. "I just keep thinking about that day in Pol's Glen, when I asked him to restore my rightful Fae gifts to me and to all those like me."

Ramos continued to nod as he traced the rose shape over her heart with one finger. "And?"

"Well, I know what happened to me," she responded a bit breathlessly as his finger set the mark to tingling pleasantly. "But what about all those others? All the ones who have no idea what they are? If I ended up with this mark on my chest, and the power to travel through time, I can't help but wonder what might have happened to them. What fears they might have."

"What damage they might cause? It's a valid concern, my sweet," he acknowledged, and smiled. "But for now, I'm too hungry to worry about it. Still, I'll offer you a deal. While we're here, you put all that out of your mind and simply enjoy yourself, and when we return home, we'll set about finding those others." He swept an arm under her legs and lifted her, bringing their faces close together. "Bargain?" he whispered, just before kissing down the side of her neck.

"Bargain struck," she murmured, letting her head drop back as his tongue traced over the mark on her breast.

"Bargain fulfilled," he countered, carrying her into the bungalow and kicking the door shut behind them.

Discover the darker side of passion with these bestselling paranormal romances from Pocket Books!

Kresley Cole
Wicked Deed on a Winter's Night
Immortal enemies…forbidden temptation.

Alexis Morgan
Redeemed in Darkness
She vowed to protect her world from the enemy—
until her enemy turned her world upside down.

Katie MacAlister
Ain't Myth-Behaving
He's a God. A legend. A man of mythic proportions…
And he'll make you long to myth-behave.

Melissa Mayhue
Highland Guardian
For mortals caught in Faeire schemes,
passion can be dangerous…

Enough desire for a lifetime... and beyond.

Gena Showalter
Savor Me Slowly
Her mind is programmed to kill—
but her heart tells her otherwise.

Sharie Kohler
Marked by Moonlight
When a good girl goes werewolf, attraction can be lethal.

**Susan Sizemore, Maggie Shayne,
Lori Handeland, and Caridad Piñeiro**
Moon Fever
Passions suddenly turn primal in this unforgettable
collection by four of today's hottest writers.

**Allison Brennan, Roxanne St. Claire,
and Karin Tabke**
What You Can't See
Three dark and dangerous tales from rising stars
in paranormal romance!

Delve into a timeless passion...
Pick up a bestselling historical romance from Pocket Books!

Karen Hawkins
To Catch a Highlander
In this game of hearts, love is the only prize.

Johanna Lindsey
The Devil Who Tamed Her
He loves a challenge...and she is an irresistible one.

Jane Feather
To Wed a Wicked Prince
This prince has more than marriage on his mind...

Sabrina Jeffries
Let Sleeping Rogues Lie
Enroll in the School for Heiresses, and discover that desire has its own rules...and temptations its own rewards.

Meredith Duran
The Duke of Shadows
Born an outcast. Raised to nobility. Only one dangerous passion can unlock his heart.

Ana Leigh
One Night With a Sweet-Talking Man
He talked his way into her heart.
Can he do the same with her bed?

Available wherever books are sold or at www.simonsayslove.com.